ALSO BY THOMAS SANCHEZ

Mile Zero

Zoot-Suit Murders

Rabbit Boss

Day of the Bees

Day of
the Bees

a novel

THOMAS SANCHEZ

Alfred A. Knopf   NEW YORK   2000

This Is a Borzoi Book
Published by Alfred A. Knopf

Copyright © 2000 by Thomas Sanchez

All rights reserved under International and Pan-American Copyright Conventions. Published in the United States by Alfred A. Knopf, a division of Random House, Inc., New York, and simultaneously in Canada by Random House of Canada Limited, Toronto. Distributed by Random House, Inc., New York.

www.aaknopf.com

Knopf, Borzoi Books, and the colophon are registered trademarks of Random House, Inc.

Library of Congress Cataloging-in-Publication Data
Sanchez, Thomas.
    Day of the bees / by Thomas Sanchez. — 1st ed.
        p.   cm.
    ISBN 0–375–40162–8 (alk. paper)
    1. France—History—German occupation, 1940–1945 Fiction.
2. World War, 1939–1945—France Fiction.   I. Title.
PS3569.A469D39   2000
813'.54—dc21   99–31385
                                                    CIP

Manufactured in the United States of America
First Edition

For the three Muses
and
A. Green

CONTENTS

Contents

PART ONE

❧

Discovery

FRANCISCO ZERMANO IS a great painter, one of the most innovative artists of all time. Among the volumes written about his vast body of work, and I have contributed two modest books myself, there is never a hint that he achieved anything less than defining our sense of the modern. Zermano's vision prefigured the future, conjured its shape and purpose, translated it to the human. From the singular moment of a baby's first cry to the monolithic skyscraping cities created between two world wars, Zermano captured it all; yet mysteries regarding his private life remain. Most of these mysteries can be explained or rationalized by theories of art, of psychology, even theology. One mystery has defied all interpretation, shimmered as a prize beyond the reach of scholars and biographers—that of Zermano's relationship with Louise Collard. After all these years the truth can now be revealed. The story is something of an adventure, one in which I myself played a role, for it was I who made the discovery that changed everything.

I discovered the truth quite by accident. Had it not been for a serendipitous bump in the road this story would have been lost forever, as half a century has passed since the brief time Zermano and Louise spent together. Zermano, now in his old age, has retreated from the public. Experts the world over have searched high and low for what he left behind, the fact and artifact of his epoch. On the other hand, Louise's life, after she disappeared from the spotlight surrounding Zermano, was deemed nothing more than an intriguing footnote. For was she not merely his mistress? How wrong the world has been, how extraordinary the real truth is.

The world thought Zermano had long ago finished with his beautiful cast-off Louise, the muse whose flesh and spirit once fired his inspiration. Historians recorded that Zermano threw Louise from the heights of her womanly powers to be devoured by the wolves of time. Historians know nothing. What can now be revealed is a private universe where mortals existed at their most vulnerable. But it wasn't Zermano who showed me the truth, and even though I had walked in Zermano's shoes while pursuing my research of his life, I too was unaware. It was Louise in the end who left the legacy. Louise led the way.

I was drawn to Louise through Zermano's paintings of her. She radiated a lunar force, yet her pose always remained natural. Those who studied Zermano's life or claimed to have associated with him could never fathom why he walked away from such a woman. All other women, wives and lovers, were mere appetite to Zermano; Louise was the feast. This was confirmed recently by a scholar at another university, who proved through the use of infrared photography that the compositions of Zermano's later paintings all began with the figure of one woman. The figure was then transformed, either to the abstract or rudimentarily figurative, never betraying the identity of the original source. Zermano had been so masterful in his ruse, so exquisitely duplicitous in his execution, that no one but he knew of this figure, the passionate memory from which all else flowed. The number of paintings shown by infrared light to have been composed this way now number two hundred, including the monumental canvas painted in Paris in 1941 depicting the horror of modern war, *Archangel Gabriel Flames Down the Sky.*

Until now Louise has been perceived in a purely romantic light, a tragic woman broken by the love of a great man. She was considered to be one of those women who, when at a crossroads in life, meets the right man at the wrong time and in her heart's confusion turns away. Such women, common knowledge holds, discover their mistake years later when they awaken in a hollow marriage, step from a bed of broken promises, and think back to what might have been had they not turned away from the right man. Such conventional wisdom has no basis in fact here. Louise's story has more in common with that of an eccentric English bride now famous in modern folklore.

The English bride waited one sunny day at the chapel with family and friends for the expected arrival of her husband-to-be. She waited for hours, refusing to believe the truth. She waited until the sun had gone down and her family and friends departed, knowing the groom would never come. The bride returned to her parents' home, but did not go inside the house. She went into the garden behind, and in her bridal gown she built a shelter from branches and twigs, sleeping that night on fresh-cut boughs. She never set foot in her parents' house again. As the years passed her parents died and she inherited the house, but the garden shelter had become her home, furnished with torn car seats and buttressed by colorful old umbrellas lashed together. The bride waited in that garden for thirty-five years, until the groom of death took her away with him to spend eternity. There is something of Louise in that woman, for Louise too chose to live in the garden of her spirit, cultivating her aloneness and discovering herself. What grew in Louise's garden is every bit as astonishing and enduring as the paintings by Zermano hanging in the world's great museums.

Had it not been for my chance discovery, the truth of Louise's garden might never have bloomed. Scholars and biographers have always believed that Zermano took Louise to Provence during the calamitous events at the beginning of World War II. It was thought, and never disproved until now, that after their last week together Zermano drove Louise from Nice and left her in Ville Rouge. It came as a surprise to learn upon her death that Louise had lived out her life unrecognized in the medieval hilltop village of Reigne, far across the valley from Ville Rouge. The media went into a frenzy, luridly recounting Zermano's period with Louise, depicting her as history's most famous reclusive muse. Zermano's paintings of her were used to illustrate the sensational story. Wherever one turned, visions of Louise rose like angelic ghosts from television screens, magazine covers, and newspaper front pages. It became clear that more than one incongruity needed to be resolved, so I flew to France.

I rented a car in Nice and journeyed through the countryside that Zermano and Louise loved so much. I could not help but wonder what it must have been like the night they made that very trip fifty years earlier. What happened between them that last summer? Why did Zermano abandon her? Was it raining the night they made their final drive? Did the mistral sweep the sky clear of clouds to expose stars above the landscape of Provence?

I drove to Ville Rouge through hills that for a thousand years had been quarried for their ochre rock. Ville Rouge clung to the highest hill, above a cut-away cliff with exposed veins of yellow and orange earth melding into vivid red. This was the red Zermano used so prominently in his palette, a color that carried its own legend. Ville Rouge is written about in French schoolbooks. A powerful nobleman once ruled there from a castle overlooking the valley below. One day a troubadour appeared at the castle and was invited to stay and sing for the nobleman's court. The troubadour performed to the delight of all and eventually became the favorite of the nobleman's wife. When the nobleman discovered this he confronted the velvet-voiced troubadour. The troubadour denied any wrongdoing but the nobleman brandished his sword. The troubadour, with nothing to defend himself with but a song, began to sing. The nobleman ran the troubadour's throat through with his blade. That night after dinner, seated at the head of the banquet table, the nobleman inquired if the finely cooked morsel served to his wife had pleased her. She replied it was the sweetest morsel ever to pass her lips. The laughing nobleman informed her she had just tasted the heart of her beloved troubadour. The wife gagged and vomited, declaring she would never eat again. Indeed she did not. At dawn she hurled herself from the high cliff down to the valley below. Her blood spread across the fields, soaking the soil, staining it crimson for all time.

Thus Ville Rouge is legendary in its own right, and now even more so since we know Zermano left Louise there, then later returned and tried to find her. It is the only recorded time in the mature life of this prolific painter that he did not paint. We do know that he spent many days at the café in front of the Roman fountain on the city square, hoping to see Louise pass by, all the while drinking the local pastis, which added to the storm already blowing in his head. We do know that shortly thereafter he entered a prodigious period of painting, which in terms of quality and variety remains the centerpiece of his life's work.

Beyond Ville Rouge on the road to the village of Reigne, the landscape is still dominated by vineyards and orchards. From the manicured rows of vines and trees rise the imposing edifices of old stone farmhouses, now restored by those enamored of rustic architecture. When Zermano and Louise arrived here it was a forgotten land. The hilltops were dotted with nearly deserted villages, decaying stone mausoleums visited mostly by the wind and the ghosts of the turbulent Wars of Religion that raged through the countryside in the sixteenth century. During the Second World War a different population took up residence. The villages became strongholds for Resistance fighters, sprang into action with combat and intrigue, with terror and execution, with neighbor warring against neighbor. This too would play its part in the lives of Louise and Zermano—but I am getting ahead of myself.

Of all the medieval villages flung across the crests of the Provençal countryside, Reigne is the most inspirational. It is a wreath of stone buildings crowning a mountain's brow. Lower mountains of purple and green wrap their arms around the bottom of the village, evoking nature's embrace. Reigne is architecture dictated from the window of a warrior's soul, a fortified place designed for death, and when the final fall comes it will be a fall into maternal arms. How exquisite of Louise to choose this place.

Driving up the road to Reigne I saw Château-Colline in the distant summer haze, another place that I was soon to discover held a buried mystery for Zermano and Louise. Even though Château-Colline is one of Provence's most photographed sights, attracting tour buses from across Europe, it still has not surrendered its delinquent beauty. Its towers of scabrous stone lean in defiance of gravity against the horizon. The castle was once home to an illustrious writer, a predator whose outlawed pleasures made his tortured pen flow. The blood of victims was his ink. This man, the "divine Marquis," hoodwinked history by reinventing his own. Château-Colline stands as a perversion in this otherwise bucolic scene, its empty shell looming on the landscape, its secrets still haunting those who come too close. Certainly Louise and Zermano came under its spell.

When finally I drove into Reigne through the stone columns of the old Roman gate at the village entrance, I was amazed by the numbers of cars lining the narrow streets. These were not the cars of humble villagers, but shiny limousines from Paris, Zurich, London, and Madrid. Men in silk suits and women in stylish dresses crowded the village, for this was the day of the important auction. A venerable New York art gallery was to liquidate paintings and drawings by Zermano found in Louise's small cottage. All the art had Louise as its subject. The New York gallery had sent a catalog of the works to prestigious institutions and collectors around the world. Depending on one's point of view, the catalog documented a treasure of lost art, a country's pride, a tax collector's dream, or prizes for a wealthy few. My university had received a copy of this expensively printed item, entitled *Louise Collard: The Muse Exposed*. Since the university owns two rare early drawings by Zermano we were placed on the list of potential bidders at today's affair. Of course the university was without funds to sit in on such a high-stakes international poker game, and it certainly had no intention of sending me to the auction to display its shallow pockets. I had come to Reigne on my own.

I did not plan to attend the auction. I wished the art could remain where it had been for a half-century, in Louise's humble home. She could have become very rich had she chosen to sell. She sold not one item, not the smallest scrap of paper that might have borne the charcoal image of her in youth, drawn by Zermano's swift hand as he gazed at her sleeping, or after making love by the fire, or after taking the first sip of wine before a dinner she prepared. Even in a black-and-white drawing Louise's cheeks burned with promise. I couldn't tolerate seeing what was hers in life denied her in death. I wanted to miss the auction, even though as a scholar it meant I was somewhat derelict in my obligations. What I did not want to miss was the opportunity to gain entrance to her home, to see with my own eyes where Louise had lived for so many years with her secrets.

I parked my car and walked in the direction the elegantly dressed crowd was coming from, for they could only be returning from the auction at Louise's. I passed the village café, which was doing a business never thought possible in calmer times. It was thronged with international media and art moguls, all there because of Reigne's newly discovered famous daughter. When Louise arrived there fifty years earlier it had been a lost place, with no jet airport at the nearby Côte d'Azur, no freeway slicing through the countryside, no bullet train shooting between Europe's capitals in mere hours. Reigne was remote then, not only in setting but in its perceptions of the outside world. To Reigne there was no world beyond the surrounding vineyards and orchards, beyond the high forest ripe with truffles and wildflowers. Reigne's concerns extended no further than its main market center across the valley, Ville Rouge. The fabled lights of Paris were as distant as the sun. Reigne would not have known a Francisco Zermano painting from a bowl of peaches, and given the choice would prefer the peaches. The village knew the best vintage years of its vineyards but did not know Louise's real name. Reigne was unaware of the fame that surrounded Louise when she lived with Zermano. In Reigne, Louise had been a simple daughter of the countryside, and the village was a tolerant parent.

Now Reigne was a proud parent, made famous overnight in the

media's glare. Its postmaster, doctor, greengrocer, mayor, farmers, and vintners—all gave interviews on Louise's life, every one an instant authority. Yes, some said, they knew her well, were best of friends, what a gregarious and fun-loving woman she was. No, chorused others, she never left her house except for essentials, never talked to women, only to men, and then in the barest of conversation. She was closed off, aloof, frightened, skittish, paranoid. Nonsense, shouted the baker, she was my lover, tender as a rabbit in a hutch. All lies, declared the butcher, she was no man's lover, and she was never tame, I can testify to that!

I passed the village church with its romantic wedding-cake architecture and turned up the street leading to Louise's house. I was struck with vertigo, for the street quickly became no more than a stony path along the top of a crumbling medieval rampart, giving way on one side in a thousand-foot drop to the valley below. Birds circled in the sky over the valley. Behind them the peak of Mont Ventoux soared from a distant chain of mountains, its barren windswept peak a mute reminder of a world beyond reach. My vertigo was not brought on by the heady reality of gazing at such splendor from such a lofty perch, but by the fact that I was coming so close to Louise, to where she actually lived. If only I knew what lay ahead I might have turned back. I felt Louise was calling me. She knew someone like me would appear, the curious one who would probe, who would find what she herself in life could not bear to reveal.

Facing the stone wall of her house with its sunny flowers creeping from long vines, with its pale blue wooden door, I couldn't turn back. What I didn't know I didn't know. I pushed open the door and stepped in. The first thing I felt on my skin was the cool freshness of the interior after the heat of the outdoors. I did not have the sensation that someone had grown old and tired here. Instead there was the silent tick of life being lived, of continuity. The walls held a vibrant ochre tint in their smoothed plaster surfaces. The rooms were not large, but their proportions made one aware of the greater world through the open shutters of the tall windows, where everything in the distance could be observed: Château-Colline, Ville Rouge, Mont Ventoux. Exploring room to room gave one a sensation of being in midair, tumbling across a landscape of time.

"May I be of assistance?"

The solicitous voice came from everywhere and nowhere. I looked around and saw no one.

"I'm afraid the auction is concluded, not an item of art left. Case closed."

I found the voice. It was coming in through the open window of Louise's bedroom. I was standing next to the high-backed cherry-wood bed where Louise had slept until she was discovered one morning, asleep forever. The voice came from outside on the stone terrace, from a man sitting in a wicker chair deftly working a calculator. I went out to the terrace. The man, dressed in a fashionably tailored suit, rose and offered his hand in greeting.

"I'm Ralph Norrison of New York. Our gallery represents Zermano worldwide. Since all of the works of Mademoiselle Collard were created by Zermano, he has the rights to them. As no one came forward to challenge those rights we have disposed of the art at the children's request—with a generous tax consideration for the various governments involved, I might add."

I hadn't asked him to add anything. He appeared defensive as I introduced myself and shook his hand. I quickly assured him I wasn't a tax collector, nor had I come to attend the auction. Since I was a scholar my interest was purely of an academic nature; I only wanted to have a look at Louise's home. He seemed relieved I wasn't a tax agent dispensed to savage his windfall profit. He sank back in the wicker chair, addressing me in an expansive manner, as if to underscore that what he had to say was of such significance it was destined to become a footnote to the grand life of Francisco Zermano.

"Your name sounds familiar. I think I read an article of yours in some obscure journal. What was it? If I recall correctly it was a theory about Zermano's middle period, how it could be interpreted through his paintings of Louise. Not a very unique idea, most of you academic boys have chewed all the meat off that old bone. Which is not to say that Louise is totally without significance. I don't know why he disposed of her in such a violent fashion, a real opera-stopper. Then to top it off she shows up dead in this nowhere village. Nobody here knew who she was, although they all like to lie about it. That is part of the opera, because we'll never really know what happened. We never got the second and third acts. No one left to tell the story. The curtain closed."

The last thing I had traveled here for was to hear a mangled critique of my theories. I quickly nudged the conversation onto neutral ground. I inquired as to Louise's personal items. Clothing? Jewelry? Was there anything left behind that could offer insight into her life?

"Some gold Art Deco jewelry was the only thing of value. We are having it appraised in Paris. Obviously it was given to her by Zermano. She kept it in an old paint box under her bed. I suppose she brought the box with her when she came to Reigne, since it once contained Zermano's oils. It was something personal to remember him by. Sad what disappointed lovers will cling to—an old scarf, an empty checkbook, a keychain, the strangest things. I suppose love dies but hope does not."

I wondered about the art work. How did Louise manage to come by it?

"There's not much of a mystery there. Before the war Zermano was already one of the dominant painters in Europe. He was not above living up to his own expectations of himself. The life he led on the Riviera with Louise was nothing short of storybook: the soirées, the movie stars and royalty coming for a look at the incandescent couple in the pink villa on the promontory overlooking the sea. Zermano had a Stutz Bearcat, a rarity even then, a luxury automobile the size of a hotel room. There's a story he got it by trading a painting to a collector for it. Another story is that he won it in Monte Carlo at the Casino. Who knows? It's probably rusting away now in a rich Arab's sandy backyard. You can stuff a good deal of art into a Stutz Bearcat, you could get a small museum into it. The legend is that Zermano loaded Louise into the Bearcat with the paintings and drawings, drove to Ville Rouge, and dumped her off with the goods. For some reason he wanted her, and the art he made with her, out of his life."

I reminded him what an odd notion that was. The critical consensus held that after the war Louise inspired some of Zermano's greatest masterpieces. The paintings and drawings done of her from memory were uncannily similar to those he created when they lived together. Which underscores my thesis that Louise was not only his model in life, she was his very model *of* life.

"That's self-evident, it can be seen in the works sold here today. But Zermano is a mimic as well as a true alchemist. If you look at his last Spanish period you observe just what a great mimic he can be. He painted at least twenty versions of Velázquez's *Las Meninas*, trying to improve upon it I suppose. And certainly he is not above mimicking himself. I'm afraid all great artists stand guilty of that if they live long enough. Some are guilty of it even if they don't live long at all."

This merchant's handling of Zermano's artistic reputation was preposterous, but not out of character for his breed. He was a member of the irredeemable class that believes, when it divines genius in a work of art, that only through it alone can that genius be disseminated to a dull and unsuspecting public. This spectacle on the wicker chair—waving his cigarette authoritatively, poking it into the day's eye, not noticing the loving care with which Louise had set the potted flowers around the terrace—was the kind Zermano tormented all his life by abruptly abandoning his painting style once it had been pounced on and pronounced "genius" by those in the know. Had this man dared speak about Louise before Zermano as he now spoke to me, Zermano would have taken his head between two strong hands and squeezed it down to the size of a copper penny. This creature was part of a species that speaks bravely against the great, when the great are safely six feet under or incapable of defending themselves. So he kept on talking.

"I think Louise's impact on Zermano's aesthetic has been exaggerated, mostly by pedants who themselves have fallen in love with her. She was a seductress, that much is clear. If she could seduce Zermano away from his work, she could seduce Jesus down from the cross. I think that's why he dumped her. After a time he couldn't paint with her around. She was jealous of his art and competed with it. It's a challenge with a woman like that. When she finds a true artist it becomes imperative to seduce him from his art, to make him prove she is the higher aspiration. Since Louise possessed with her body an art more ancient than all others, she eventually led Zermano to a personal standstill in the fury of their passion. It's a wonder he ever painted again. Most people think he slowed down because of the war. No, it was Louise who took the brush from his hand and brought him to his knees."

I had never heard anything so absurd. I held my tongue. There was something I wanted from this loquacious bully. I was wondering, had Louise left any writings behind?

"What kind of writings?"

I was thinking along the lines of diaries. Letters perhaps?

"Nothing. Not a thing. I don't think she was very clever in that way, you know?"

No, I didn't know. But certainly there must be something left behind. How odd for someone to live more than fifty years in one house and not leave the merest scribble.

"Not so odd, people do it all the time. Not everybody can be Proust. Wait. There is one thing."

One?

"A diary actually."

Really?

"But you can't call it a diary."

I don't understand.

"It's a little black book, but all the pages are blank."

So there's nothing?

"Except the one thing."

What thing?

"When I found the diary I turned every page to see if she had hidden a Zermano drawing there as a precaution against thieves who might one day show up and strip everything off the walls."

Did she?

"No such luck."

What was the one thing then?

"A newspaper clipping."

Of what?

"Nothing of particular interest. About someone dying during the war, a suicide or something in Ville Rouge."

You don't recall who it was?

"No, but I have the clipping."

Where?

"Right where I found it. It's still in the diary. Shall we have a look?"

Yes!

I followed my host to the living room. A stone fireplace arched across the back wall, giving the feeling one was wrapped in a cave. I envisioned Louise sitting there in the well-worn leather chair, next to a crackling fire, flames dancing on ochre walls around her, not alone with her memories, not alone at all.

"It's a pity she didn't keep a diary." My host took down a small black book from the fireplace mantel, thumbing idly through its blank pages. "I'm sure if she had it would have been quite a salacious slice. Louise's power wasn't simply that men desired her. Men wanted to make her pregnant. That's the difference between sex and destiny. She was a different breed of cat altogether."

Irreverent fool.

"Quite unusual she didn't have any children, considering the appetite she provoked in men. Don't you think?"

No, I don't think.

"Ah, here it is, the little nothing." He fished up a faded scrap of newspaper and held it before me.

May I read it?

"Not much to read." He started right in reading it himself, translating aloud. "'The badly decomposed body of Monsieur Richard Royer was discovered in the early hours of this morning at the bottom of an ochre pit beneath the south-facing cliffs of Ville Rouge. Royer is survived by his wife of seventeen years. He spent his entire career with the Postal Authority. Police are investigating whether or not the death was accidental.'"

"That's all?"

"What did you expect? I told you it was nothing, just the death of some guy in World War Two. Read it for yourself if you think I've left anything out."

I took the clipping. He hadn't left anything out. I flipped through the pages of the diary. He was right, they were blank.

"So you see, she left nothing."

So I saw, and how sad it was. I had come hoping to find something of her; the smallest revelation would have made my journey worthwhile. Now there were no paintings on the walls, no mementos. Everything seemed monastic, stripped bare, leaving a void as vast as that between the village of Reigne and Mont Ventoux in the distance. She was gone from here, and with her had gone her spirit. Perhaps that's as it should be; perhaps what is most intimate should never be revealed.

"I'm going to lock up now. I'm taking the express train back to Paris tonight."

Yes, certainly. I must be on my way as well. Thank you for your time.

"That's all right. I may not seem it, but I am touched you really care about her. When you said you were a scholar I took you for one of those academic headhunters out to make his reputation. With everyone else it's only been him, that's all they want—Zermano. No one was ever much interested in her for her own sake. It's only natural I suppose, the life of the artist is creation, the creation of woman is life."

What an amazing thing to suppose.

"Sorry you didn't get here earlier. Louise's collection was breathtaking. It will never be seen in one place again."

His words came to me as I started to leave the room, passing by a highly polished antique bread-table. On its top was a basket constructed of twisted branches forming a deep bowl beneath a curved handle, as if designed by an overly ambitious bird. Sunlight from the window fell across the basket, striking the bright balls of yarn mounded within. It was a beautiful still life, the kind Zermano would have painted—if he had painted still lifes.

"It was Louise's basket. She was always knitting. Knitted those heavy fisherman's sweaters one sees around Marseille in wintertime. The yarn is very special to this area, from the sheep on the high slopes of Mont Ventoux. It must have been difficult for her to knit because her hands were deformed."

You mean her hands were arthritic from old age?

"No. They were like two stumps, as if she had been injured in some strange way. It had to have been after she parted from Zermano, because we don't see the deformity in any of the paintings he made of her at the time."

What do you mean by a strange injury?

"Very odd. When the autopsy was done the coroner said it looked as if she had been crucified."

You can't be serious.

"Crucified by the hands, not the feet. It isn't as if we have a case of a female Christ here."

This was startling information, almost too much to take in. I picked up one of the bright balls in the basket, an orange one, a burst of sun between my fingers. Here was something tangible of hers, something tender. Maybe I was touching the most personal of her things. She must have spent hours, thousands of hours, sitting in the leather chair before the fireplace, knitting, the days and nights passing by. Did her hands hurt? What was she thinking? Was she thinking her life could have turned out differently? Maybe she wasn't thinking anything at all. Maybe she was trying to forget.

"You can have that basket if you like."

I hadn't thought about taking it.

"The basket's not on the inventoried list of valuables."

I would like it. I would like it very much.

"In that case take all of them."

All of them?

"In the cellar. There are three more old-fashioned baskets just like this one."

I've come this far, no need to go home empty-handed. I'll take them.

"Let's make it quick then. I have to catch that train."

I followed him down dimly lit steps into a cellar that had been cut into stone long ago. A musty scent filled the air, not unlike the unmistakable odor one encounters in the wine cellars of ancient châteaux. My host shone a flashlight on a wall of wooden shelves weighted by dusty jars sealed with wax. The jars contained the preserved fruits of Provence: plum marmalades, cherry jams, blackberry spreads.

"Louise was an industrious one, despite her injuries. Look at these." He reached up and pulled down jars from a high shelf, every jar filled with a different kind of honey; honey of lavender, honey of wild forests, jar after jar, each labeled with a handwritten piece of paper pasted around glass.

"Have you ever seen so much honey? She certainly had a sweet tooth. I suppose it's what happens to every woman without a man."

Why suppose that?

"Ah, there they are. The baskets."

The flashlight beam went to the top shelf. Sure enough, there were three baskets in a neat row, all exactly like the one upstairs. I climbed up on the shelves and handed the baskets down to my host, who managed to almost drop them in the dim light. I brought them up the slippery stairs.

With all the baskets piled in my arms I stood in Louise's living room. I thanked my host. He wasn't bad. He had given me something of Louise's, although I had no idea what to do with four baskets. He allowed me to walk outside onto the terrace for a final look.

"You know what I think?"

As I gazed across the valley to Mont Ventoux I had no idea what my host thought.

"I think it was a game between them."

A game between Louise and Zermano?

"I think in the end the game played them."

I think you are a foolish fellow. I think you never understood one thing about them. No one did.

I left Reigne and drove back to Nice.

My plane to America was not scheduled to leave Nice until the following morning so I remained overnight. I could not resist staying in the same hotel where Zermano and Louise spent their last week together. The hotel was on a twisting alley, halfway up the hill to where a fortress once stood. Nothing seemed to have changed in the back streets of Nice. There was still a swaggering air of dilapidation, sun-colored walls closing in on each other. Behind shuttered windows secrets lingered in bedrooms, while inside cafés long-silent shouts of accusation and denial still clung to the air. Everywhere disoriented tourists walked reverentially, careful not to disturb the town's private reveries.

My small hotel room seemed crowded with an oversized bed and decorative armoire. Perhaps it was the same room where Zermano and Louise had stayed. Humidity breathed through the window's open shutters; outside, the palms along the curve of the bay swayed in salty air. It was a summer evening on the French Riviera, the perfect time to take a walk. I joined the disoriented tourists in the narrow streets. Because of the day's events and the long drive from Reigne, I was feeling light-headed myself. The emotion of having been inside Louise's actual home, of making contact with her, left me with a strange sense of daring. On a whim I took one of her baskets along on the walk. It was like having her with me. I followed the snaking street in front of the hotel, up past the excavated Roman ruins, where a steep staircase led to the top of the hill. Below me all of Nice spread out around the Baie des Anges, basking in a burnished light reflected from the sea's surface. Across the town's red-tile rooftops time was caught in a memory of sunsets past, blending into each other. My mind was overrun, without enough space to contain everything, going blank like the pages of Louise's diary, shimmering white.

I waited at the summit until darkness fell before descending the circuitous route to the hotel. I lost my way, wandering for more than an hour. I stopped where a man-made waterfall cascaded from rocks above and sat with welcome relief on a bench. Lovers, hand in hand, glided by me in the dusk. What an odd sight I made, a man alone on the French Riviera on a summer night with a twig basket balanced on his knees. It even seemed odd to me.

Peering into the well of the basket I noticed something I hadn't seen before. I could make out the shape of a once bright metal hinge, now dulled to a muted color the same as the wood surrounding it. I remembered my aunt who, when on holiday at our home, seemed always to be knitting. She was a lawyer who found her relaxation in the simple rhythm of gliding needles. She had a special place at the bottom of her basket where she kept needles and scissors safely hidden from adventurous children. There was a hinged trap door that she could lift to expose a hollow space under the basket's false bottom.

I pried at the trap door of Louise's basket. My fingernails scraped against wood. The door was tenacious, probably not having been opened for decades. The old hinge creaked. The door sprang up. I stared in disbelief. Bundled neatly and bound by blue ribbons were letters, arranged carefully, filling the entire bottom of the basket. I lifted one of the packets and untied its ribbon, freeing the letters. I could barely make out the handwriting on the envelopes in the dim light. There was a pale moon over the pine trees on the slope above me. The handwriting shimmered into focus. I knew it well. I knew it because I had read many journals written in that hand, journals I had researched for my books and articles—the journals of Francisco Zermano.

I looked quickly through the rest of the letters. Disappointingly, none were from Louise. But of course there were no letters from Louise, she would have mailed hers to Zermano, they wouldn't be in the basket. What had he done with her letters? No letters from her have ever been mentioned in his journals or made available for publication. Perhaps he burned them. In any event they were lost to history, so what was hidden in the basket was a true treasure. Louise had kept it safe, entrusting it to no one.

I made my way in the dark to the hotel, guarding Louise's treasure. She could have sold Zermano's letters for a king's ransom. Instead they remained locked in her heart, tucked cleverly into the bottom of a simple knitting basket. As I came closer to the lights of the hotel I realized there were more baskets, three more. What if she had filled them all with letters? I ran as quickly as I have ever run in my life.

In the hotel room I grabbed one of the remaining baskets and pried its trap door open. A rain of letters tumbled out, scattering across the bed. I couldn't believe what was happening. I was the first to touch these letters since Louise. If there were guests in the next room they must have thought my room was occupied by a newly-wed couple, for as I upended each basket I shouted with pleasure, each shout louder than the last, until all of the baskets were emptied, their contents covering the bed.

I pulled one of the envelopes out from the pile. Looking at the address I was surprised. The letter was not in Zermano's hand. The still bright white envelope was addressed to Zermano and bore Louise's exquisite handwriting. I quickly examined each letter in the pile. Here were Louise's letters that had never been mailed, the letters Zermano never saw.

Day of the Bees

I sat down on the edge of the bed. I had become part of Louise's plan, led to her cellar, to the baskets set among the preserved fruits of Provence, waiting decades for the right person to harvest them.

I now submit these letters for examination. Since Louise did not date hers, the precise times when they were written are unknown. She may have responded immediately to Zermano's letters, or composed her answers years later. The utmost care has been taken to marry Louise's thoughts and responses to Zermano's letters. Sometimes this presented difficulties, as Louise was not only responding to Zermano, but also presenting her emotions within the context of dangerous wartime realities.

It is impossible to ascertain if Louise received all of Zermano's letters. Some might have been seized by government censors, others may have been lost in transit as war spread across Europe. Louise herself may have destroyed the more intensely intimate ones, although what remains is intimate enough. The political contents of some could have condemned Louise to death had they been discovered at the time. In an attempt to fit all the pieces of the puzzle together I have held nothing back.

Professor of Art History
Department of Art
University of California

PART TWO

Journey to Reigne

Villa Trône-sur-Mer
Côte d'Azur

Louise. I look at my hands. Are these the hands of a creator or a strangler? What is the difference now that my life is cut off from yours? What am I in the end without you? A chest-pounder, a grandstander, a carnival magician. It is more rare in this universe to find a true love than to make a great piece of art. Why won't you write? You promised in the hotel in Nice that you would write. This was our agreement. You can't walk away from it. I must find the truth. How can you tear the face off such recent memory?

I have gone to Ville Rouge at noon every Friday. We were to meet in front of the Roman Fountain, that was part of the agreement. You are never there. I inquire if anyone has seen you. No one has. Not the butcher, the baker, not even Monsieur Royer at the post office. The room above the café, where you were to stay until you found a safe home—they say you left there immediately. It's as if you were never in Ville Rouge, that I dreamed it, driving with you there just two weeks ago. But I can't stay in Ville Rouge to find you, things are too dangerous for that.

The exhibition of my paintings in London has been canceled. Things everywhere are falling into confusion. It is all I can do to keep working, trying to paint my way out of this crazy corner the world has painted me into. I must continue to paint through this confusion of borders falling and countries crumbling. Who could have foreseen this? I suppose I did and that is why I made a plan to spare you from it all. Trust me, I said. You said you would, and now you have broken the trust, disappeared.

I don't want to close Villa Trône, it's like closing our life together, but I might be forced to leave and go back to Paris. It seems my absence in Paris is taken by some as cowardice, abandoning a sinking ship. I prefer to return to Spain, but that is impossible. Things in Spain are even more confused than here and it would put me too far away from you. I must go on painting to find form, then I can bend the rules in order to escape this terrible present. The problem now is that there are no rules, only chaos. Our personal chaos is so slight in the storm that surrounds us. But what seems slight to others is a mortal wound to me.

I send this letter to you care of the post office in Ville Rouge. I have no idea if you will get it. My sweet Louise, you said we would be together for eternity, and now you won't write. Do I have to wait until the next lifetime for you to answer me? Who am I speaking to? A ghost of love? My worst fear is that something unspeakable has already happened to you.

I try to console myself with a vision of you that day in the cherry orchard, light showering through leaves over your head, the smile on your face. The sun of that summer splits a path of hope through this darkness that separates us. I lay my brush down at the end of each day, remembering our last drive to Ville Rouge. Don't let me think that I will never see you again. Hold on my dearest woman, wherever you are.

FRANCISCO

Village of Reigne

Darling Francisco,

I have nothing to hide now except myself. Our agreement? It wasn't our agreement, it was *your* plan. You seem to think that who you are would put me at risk. Where else should a woman stand in time of risk but next to the one she loves? Could you not see in my eyes the sadness of parting from you? No. You were crazy with protecting me, sending me far from harm's way. If bombs are to fall why shouldn't I be a target as well? Why should I be saved? What life is left after separation from the one you love? No matter how I pleaded you could not hear my side. Your Spanish temper raged. You got your way but you didn't get me.

When you came looking for me in Ville Rouge I was there. I saw you hobbling on your cane, your knees still not healed from what happened last summer. I wanted to run to you, to tell you what I now know. But if I had confessed the truth you would have been more emphatic at keeping me hidden. You said you knew of cruelty

(27)

in men that I could never understand, that no woman could understand. Tell me, is there a greater cruelty in the world than a mother losing her child? What makes you think women know less of pain than men? When the trigger is pulled the bullet is blind to its target. Your nature is to protect those you love, but in this instance it is your own tragedy. You should have let me make the choice.

It was all about choice from the very beginning. . . . I remember everything as if it were yesterday.

I don't think any woman was ever seduced by a man the way I was seduced by you. I had gone to a gallery opening in Paris. The gallery was not displaying your work, but the paintings of another artist. People thought you might be there because the artist being shown was one of your disciples. So people came, a large crowd. I had not come for you. I happened to be with a man of the antiquarian trade whom you knew quite well. I thought I could never be attracted to a man like you. I did not want what you had, I did not want who you were in public. I could not help but recognize you; even in Paris you stood out. Accomplished as you were, you still looked unfinished, restless, hungry. Yet you were already more than famous, more than rich. What good was any of it to me, a woman who had no interest unless there was love? But as a young girl I had learned Aunt Mimi's lesson of the belt. Without that lesson I would have missed the essential in you. Without that lesson I never would have gone the first time to Cathedral Sainte-Chapelle on that rainy Sunday morning.

In the crowded art gallery the antiquarian pushed me forward, offering me to you as his calling card. You paid no attention to me, which is always the first thing a woman notices, a man pretending not to notice, a tired trick. A man would never ignore another man who was standing right before him, under his nose. But let it be a woman a man is interested in and suddenly there is a disinterested glaze over the eyes, the spot on the ceiling becomes more fascinating than she. I thought you were smarter than that. You were just as small as the rest. In the crush of admirers and fawning critics you offhandedly thanked me for coming. It was then I noticed your nose. Some men have noses like that if they are boxers but were lucky enough to have deflected the major blows aimed at their face, avoiding a broken nose yet displaying the imprint of many blows. Your nose looked as if God had put a hand on it, holding you back at birth because you were running too fast at life, rushing into it, pushing against all hesitancy. I noticed the flat line of your nose, and then the crowd encircled you.

When you awakened me early the next morning I was not surprised. I had been called by married men before. I had never gone to any of them. You were not telephoning me for a normal meeting, one that could be carried out virtuously in the eye of the public. You did not say, for example: Let's meet for tea in the Luxembourg Gardens. You did not say: Let's meet in the square with the fountain of Neptune. Nor did you offer me anything improper by saying: Let's meet at the small hotel at number five off the Carrefour Odéon. You simply said: Go to nine o'clock mass this morning in the upper sanctuary of Cathedral Sainte-Chapelle, where they keep a holy vial of the Virgin Mary's milk. Hurtling through the static of the phone line your words came into me, slicing a new wound.

After your phone call the rain beat on the roof above my head. There was a gray tinge outside my window. I arose to dress for you. I thought only black should be worn against my pale skin, but somehow that was wrong. I should go as a bride. Under my dress would be garters and stockings, cinching legs and thighs. I slipped these on but their silken lightness was uncomfortable. This was not the bride you wanted, too ephemeral. I took everything off, standing with my bare feet on the cold floor. What were you expecting? What was it you knew would be waiting for you, exactly as it was meant to be?

Listening to the cathedral bells tolling in the distance I opened my bottom dresser drawer, pulling out piles of clothes. I found what I had not worn for years, folded and white—a schoolgirl's cotton underpants. They fit high on the waist, low on the thighs, the taut fabric smooth against me. Over this I wore a sensible dress buttoned to the neck. With a hat on my head and rubbers over my shoes, I made my way beneath an umbrella to the cathedral.

On rain-slick streets I was coming to you. I would never be the same again. The people I passed were unaware of what was under my coat. What was hidden was what you wanted. You were going to make me yours, offer me no exit. In cold air the breath rose from my lips, a misty ghost kissing this virgin for the last time.

I crossed the bridge over the Seine as rain slashed at the river. Ahead loomed the cathedral. The twelve stone apostles guarding from atop its towering spire gazed down upon me. I climbed the cathedral steps and pushed open the bronze doors, stepping out of the wet into a vaulted hush. My eyes blurred, trying to adjust to the dim light. The singsong Latin chant of a priest echoed through the shadows. I was late. The mass had already begun. I failed your first command: *Go to nine o'clock mass.* It was to be our mass, our celebration. I had ruined it by taking too much time deciding what to wear. My eyes sought you out in the rows of pews leading to the distant altar. All I saw were the backs of worshippers kneeling in prayer, steam rising from their damp clothes. Along the walls candles illuminated the stares of plaster saints. Where were you? Gone? The priest at the altar swung his censer of smoking incense, blue smoke filled the air. How could I have walked so easily into your trap? The animal in you knew instinctively how to hunt my kind, the sophisticated Parisian woman. You planned to take me back to when I was just a dreaming girl, before the woman awoke, before there were any other men, even a father, back to original sin. You were offering me the heaven before the hell.

The worshippers in the pews shunned me with their curved backs. I pushed on the heavy door to get away, but the wind on the outside pushed back. I pushed harder. The wind was strong as a man, trapping me. *The vial.* You had said to meet you in the upper sanctuary where the holy vial of the Virgin's milk is kept. I turned, my eyes searched through the forest of stone pillars. In a distant corner a staircase spiraled into the heights.

I ascended the staircase. Stained-glass windows surrounded me, illuminating vivid scenes from the Old and New Testaments: the parting of the Red Sea, Noah's animals boarding the ark, dead men walking, sermons and miracles, baptism and ultimate crucifixion. The illuminated world swirled, my head spun. The floor rumbled from the moan of a wind organ below. I stumbled forward, pushed by the organ's escalating notes. I came face to face with the Virgin Mary, her graceful life-sized statue standing guard at the entrance to a marble grotto. She held her baby Jesus toward me in the cradle of her arm. A sweetly dank odor seeped from the grotto. What was it? The centuries-old musk of misspent passion from fervent pilgrims? The dusty feathers of fallen angels? The scent pulled me in.

Deep in the grotto candles flickered before an altar supporting a golden bowl behind protective glass. I knelt at the altar. The moan of the organ beneath me stopped. The Latin chant of the priest floated up. I felt your eyes on me, peeling the clothes off my back. I turned. You were not there. I could not see you but I heard your heartbeat. I looked to the Virgin for guidance. Her sad crease of a smile beckoned. Within the golden bowl was a crystal vial, filled with her milk, eternally fresh from a breast never suckled by an infant God. The cruelest hoax.

Was your telephone call to me a hoax, a summons into which I had misread desire? I was dressed in mourning but I had all the expectations of a bride. Foolish woman. Foolish virgin that never was. I was determined you would not have me with your silence. I hurried down the spiral staircase. The mass was over. I joined the parishioners headed toward the door, searching their pious faces. Their eyes avoided mine, guarding their own sorrows. At the door I dipped my fingers into the basin of holy water before departing God's house. Another hand quickly covered mine, plunging my hand underwater, pinning it to the bottom of the basin. I struggled to turn around but a powerful body blocked me from behind. I felt the breath of words imprinting the back of my neck: "Go home."

I rushed along the wet streets toward my apartment. I heard no footsteps behind me. I did not turn to see if you were following. When I crossed the bridge over the river a faint shadow, my own, flickered on the water's surface. I slowed down and drew myself erect, walking coolly the rest of the way to my apartment. I climbed the steps and opened the door. No one was there. I pulled the black dress over my head and threw it into the corner. I lay down on the bed, listening for your footsteps.

I know you are standing at the bottom of my staircase. Rain splashes from your slicker onto the steps as you climb them. Your footsteps are at the top of the stairs, the doorknob turns in your hand as you enter. You take off your slicker and it crumples into a dark pool around you. You are a stranger, which is why I am able to give myself so completely. If I knew you only halfway there would not be this moment, for there would have been reasons and excuses to turn back. After all, you were a man falling from a marriage and I was ascending to womanhood. There was nothing symbolic here, only you sliding a pearl-handled straight razor from your pocket and flicking out its shiny blade.

You stripped your shirt off, turning your back to me as you bent over the wash basin. You lathered your face with soap and water and began shaving. In the reflection of the mirror above the basin your eyes glided over me lying on the bed. Your glance penetrated me. All things were mathematical shapes to you, nothing more than abstract furniture, furniture taken and stacked up on one side of your mind. Then the other side of your mind smashed the furniture, redistributing its pieces, denying memory and mathematical equations, inventing a new disorder free of gravity. You didn't see *me* at all. You were making a painting of me in the circumstance. The strokes of your razor cleared away the lather, exposing a newborn face. The blade against your bearded stubble sounded like a paintbrush against canvas. I did not move, took no breath, not a bone in my rib cage shifted. I wanted you to hear my words. I wanted you to hear them shouted into violent silence: *A broken heart is like a cut flower, the longer you keep it in memory's water, the longer it will suffer.* But no words escaped my lips. There was only the cut through silence, the downward stroke of a razor on flesh.

You finished shaving and wiped the razor blade clean against your pants. You set the razor on the sink, its blade shining against white porcelain. You came to me. You unhooked the leather suspenders strapped over your bare shoulders and your pants fell to the floor. I saw how urgent you were. Swiftly, with the suspenders, you tied me by the wrists and ankles to the bedposts. Your hand reached between my thighs, ripping away the thin material covering me there, exposing me to your fingers, which knotted into the curls of my hair as you shouted: "I am going to shave it!"

Your words struck me as unspeakably funny. As if I wanted to be your little girl! I could not control my laughter, it burst from me. I didn't care about your Spanish pride, I didn't care about the heat of your urgency. I just wanted you to understand that I knew every move you were going to make before you made it. Now we could get on with the real game. You looked at me quizzically. The furniture so carefully rearranged in your mind scattered again. You were caught in my laughter. The belittled peasant inside you could rise up and strike me—or the proud Iberian gentleman could drag his deflated ego out the door. Instead, your chest burst with laughter, a gift from the angels showering upon me, music in my ears. Your hands slid over my skin, my nipples quickened. How beautiful you were when you laughed. My thighs opened, my sea glistened in the sun of your smiling gaze. I stared into the sun, a bird passed, my heart in its beak. Your laughing lips covered mine, your kiss exploding in my mouth. I felt the skin of your shaved face on my cheek. "My darling," I said. "The only way to keep me tied to you is to set me free."

You pushed up suddenly from the bed and went to the sink, grabbing the straight razor. The blade flashed in your hand as you came back and towered over me. You slashed at the leather straps binding me to the bedposts. Your laughter roared in the room. I was released. I fell to my knees and pressed my face close to you with a moan. Your skin had the faint musty scent of the holy water in the cathedral basin, a heady swampy mix stirred by many fingers. What felt like splashes of rain from above were your tears falling into my hair.

We both knew that love is where one fears to go most, where no articulation of self exists nor architecture looms to define the fleshy halls wandered, all gives way beneath a finger's imprint, collapsing from the heart's faintest murmur, reappearing at the merest breath. It is the purest real estate, the perspiration across Cupid's lip, the butter melting on an angel's tongue, the soul's atmosphere.

My famous man, Francisco Zermano, between laughter and tears there is only life. The muse gave you her gift but you did not obey her rules.

YOUR LOUISE

Villa Trône-sur-Mer
Côte d'Azur

Louise, I am under a deadline to leave here so I am busy packing everything. Who knows if this place will still be standing after all this is over. I have sent my man Roderigo to Ville Rouge to find you. He is there every day at the café in front of the Roman fountain. He has instructions not to leave until he has contacted you.

The situation in Paris grows worse by the day. Our home there will be destroyed if I don't return. You remain the center of my thoughts. I won't rest until I know you are secure. How much money do you have? How long can you last? I left so much of my art with you. What good is the art to me without you? It was made for you. Sell it all, take the money while there is still some small market left. Tell me you have done that so I know you are safe, so that I know you aren't being compromised.

Can it be that only one month has passed since last I saw your face, kissed your lips, held your body? The longest month of my life.

Day of the Bees

I did not know there were so many hours in a day, hundreds, so many minutes in an hour, thousands, each second stretching to eternity. I know you did not want to leave me, you made that clear in Nice, but you must trust me. In the remoteness of Provence you are probably not aware of what is happening each day, how completely the world is coming undone. Are you still in Provence? How can I know anything for certain?

All I can do is feast on memory. My mind goes back to the summer, we are traveling away from the humidity of the seacoast, the vineyards open before us, orchards shimmer in the heat. The road is bumpy with stones laid down centuries before by the Romans in their chariot-driven conquest. We drive deep into a landscape lush with suspicion, where the inhabitants monitor the passage of each trespasser into their paradise. Our passion was open; we did not hide it. If I could have seen what was coming I would have stopped it. If I had seen him in time I would have strangled him with my bare hands. I saw only you, sun-radiant. I was blinded. I couldn't see him until it was too late, but I recognized him. You always receive the best in a man, but man is a deceiver with his face of generosity, his mask of caring, he craves only what is beneath your dress, between your thighs while you are young and supple, after he has what he wants his sword shrivels to a worm, he crawls from the craven hole he has bored into the perfect apple, only the magpies are left screeching in the sky overhead, waiting their turn to descend and peck at the ruined fruit.

Right now I hate men. I hate myself. I hate this confusion raging around me. The magpies of war are descending. I am alone without you, each day a funeral.

FRANCISCO

Village of Reigne

Oh Francisco how you break me. How I want to take you to my breast, stroke your face. What you think you should have done as a man still haunts you. Couldn't you see love's consequence? I remember that day we drove from the coast. On both sides of the road fields of sunflowers turned their faces to us as we passed. I had no cares, only desires. Behind the steering wheel you watched for dangerous curves ahead as we laughed. It felt like a day without end, that long summer afternoon, the eternity one would choose if one could only choose. I wanted to share with you the memories of my youth, far from the fashionable clutter of the Côte d'Azur.

I could not have been happier, sitting at your side in the Bearcat, in which you took so much pride because you got it away from the cagey art collector, Elouard. I can still picture that afternoon at Trône, Elouard and his wife tiptoeing through your studio, speaking in whispers, their nostrils twitching at the scent of paint and linseed oil. All of Elouard's money could not buy him the talent to paint one inch of one of twenty paintings stacked along the studio walls. He was like the wealthy everywhere who, since they cannot buy talent for themselves, attempt to buy the artist—or at least the moment of his creation, his work of art. Elouard stammered that he wanted to purchase a painting, but he was sorry he had forgotten his check-book. Standing there without money put him in an uncomfortable position in front of his wife and me, and most of all you, whom he thought he could buy no matter how famous you were. You studied him, aware of his torment. You were so cheerful when you tossed him the bait, "How about if we trade for a painting?"

Elouard was delighted, certain he had turned the game in his favor. Now he had you in the land where he was king, in the realm of barter and steal, strike and win. He winked at his wife, who was covered in gold: earrings, bracelets, a watch; gold chains weighing down her neck.

I did not wear jewelry until I met you. You insisted on my wearing gold because you said it made my red hair burn brighter, it drew the apricot glow from my skin. I knew you were going to strip Elouard's wife of her gold. I knew from the gleam in your eye you were going to strip her and later, after they had gone, you were going to remove my dress and decorate me with her gold, lay my body across the bed and tie my legs open with gold chains wrapped around my ankles.

You started easy with Elouard. "I don't like to sell directly from my studio. It can get me in trouble with my gallery dealers in New York and London, and in even deeper trouble with the tax man in Paris. I spoke too soon."

"Too soon?" Elouard wanted the ball back in his court. This was supposed to be his game. "Not soon enough! Had I known you would allow me the honor of purchasing a new Zermano, I would have arrived prepared for the occasion. As it is," he looked at his wife conspiratorially, "I am at a disadvantage."

You looked at his wife too. All that bright gold was too much on her. You had an expensive idea of how we were going to spend the rest of the afternoon.

Elouard caught you eyeing his wife's gold. "That's it," he proposed craftily. "We'll trade the Stutz Bearcat we drove here in. We'll trade the auto for that big blue painting in the corner!"

"The Bearcat for the *big* painting?"

"I'm not trying to pull a fast one. I understand what your art commands at auction. The Bearcat might not be enough."

"It isn't."

"A big blue Zermano is one of a kind, priceless. There is always another Bearcat to be had. Why don't I—"

"What?"

"Throw in all my wife's jewelry to even the deal?"

"Done."

So you had your car. But where to go on our first trip in the Bearcat? I said I wanted to take you to the lost country of my childhood, to dance in Ville Rouge in front of the Roman fountain at the Bastille Day celebration. I wanted to make you part of my memory.

I kiss you softly,
Louise

Villa Trône-sur-Mer
Côte d'Azur

I rip the sky, I bray at the moon, a man is a stupid creature without the love of his woman, a worm crawling across cowardly ground. I know this sounds bombastic but I can only express myself in the clumsiest of ways. I am not a writer, I am a painter stripped of his weapons. I can only touch you, or hope to touch you, with these words. How I wish I were a writer, to have my words sing in your ear, embrace you with crafted care. Now I must arm myself with metaphors, but no matter how I try to state my emotions for you they seem trite. I have written page after page, insignificant missiles that miss their mark. I have balled up many letters in my fist and tossed them into the fire. Finally I am forced to put something to paper that can be sent to you. I dress up my thoughts in bright clothes hoping to portray my battered heart, which drifts night after night in dreams of you. I am making love to a ghost. But our love is not ghostly, it has flesh and meaning, it breathes. In the day I feel your hands slipping around me as I paint, your fingers locking over my eyes, your lips on the back of my neck. I set down my paintbrush and turn, your red hair falling over me as we tumble to the floor. You are a cloud opening to a world where no man has journeyed, you bring me in. I am dreaming. I want reality.

There are certain things that happen in life and a man travels back to them. I keep coming back to that afternoon in the cherry orchard. Am I writing of this to explain what happened? Do we really need an explanation? We were not yet husband and wife then, but we were getting close. We were snakes shedding skin, writhing from one passion to another. Our eyes were on each other in the Bearcat as we drove through your lost country, not noticing the dangerous curves. Your skirt slid up on the leather seat, the whites of your thighs flashed. Your hand went between my legs, as if you were steering the car there. We almost didn't notice when the tire blew. A bang in the heat. The front of the Bearcat dropped with a thud. Steel dug into asphalt, trailing sparks across the road. I tried to regain control, to hold back the car as it went up on its side. I held on to you as the car rolled. You were always afraid one of us would die without the other, you couldn't bear that. You preferred that we die together, even in a crash on the roadway, with the flowers of our flesh pressed between closing steel.

Where are you? I paint your face with my fingers.

FRANCISCO

Villa Trône-sur-Mer
Côte d'Azur

Dearest woman, there is still no news of you from Roderigo in Ville Rouge. I have kept him there for weeks on the constant lookout for you, but I cannot leave him there forever. He wants to return to Spain because of what is happening with Franco. Go to him and tell him you are safe. Send me a kiss wrapped in the Italian scarf I bought you on our last visit to Nice. When I gave you the scarf you said you would cherish it forever, its amber silk was imprinted with your favorite fruits of summer. You wrapped it around bare shoulders, it clung to the outline of your breasts as you turned before me. In your French way you had taken something simple and created a luxurious garment. In your French way you elevated the commonplace; you swirled around in a blur, then stopped, out of breath, your arms outstretched, offering fragile wrists. I unwrapped the scarf, revealing your body. In my Spanish way I made something practical, tying the silk scarf into a knot around your wrists. You shuddered, bound. We both remembered that hot summer day in the cherry orchard.

I should have known someone was following us on our way to the cherry orchard. But I was aware only of you until the Bearcat slammed to the pavement, throwing us nearly through the windshield before dragging to a sparking stop. The engine shuddered, we held each other in disbelief. The sound of our breathing slowly came back to us, threading us into the present, two people lucky to be alive. Your laughter filled the car, your fingers still gripping my arm. I turned and realized you were laughing with relief, tears glistening on your cheeks. You were still laughing as we climbed from the Bearcat.

The right front of the car was collapsed, its tire blown to shreds. We were stranded. If there was no spare tire in the trunk it was going to be a long walk to find help. You stood on the black asphalt in your white summer dress, your body profiled against the sunlight. You watched as I cautiously jacked the front end of the Bearcat up from the pavement. The massive hulk of the automobile groaned, its weight suspended on a slender steel perch. I carefully slipped off the gnarled tire and skinned my hands blood-red as I maneuvered a new tire onto the hub. Sweat ran from my forehead, blurring my vision. I felt your bare legs next to me, the hem of your dress coming up as you wiped my eyes with the soft material. I could see well enough to muscle the tire into place. You knelt next to me, your hands on the jack handle, preparing to crank. If you cranked too fast the automobile would jump its perch and crush us both. I watched you through stinging eyes, your lower lip trembled. You didn't care if the Bearcat buried us under its weight as long as we were together. You leaned in to me as you turned the iron handle with certainty. The car creaked and rocked, sinking with a sigh against the pavement as your tongue slipped into my mouth. Your own sigh sank deep into me. My grease-blackened hands caressed you through the thin dress. I pushed the dress high over your hips.

My eyes stung from salty perspiration, blurring your shape. You disappeared.

I searched for you in the cherry orchard at the side of the road. Your laughter slipped around tree trunks, rippled through leaves. I couldn't see you. I was a blind bear plunging toward honey. Branches struck my face, the stony ground snapped under my feet. I did not hear you approach from behind, your hands covering my eyes, your body coiling around mine, your bare knees bending into sharp stones. Sunlight flamed your red hair as your fingers undid my belt. You knew what you were doing. I didn't recognize my own voice as your insistent lips pulled a roar of pleasure from my throat, startling the birds in branches around us. I lifted you up by your shoulders. You were unaware that your knees had been stabbed by sharp pebbles, pricks of blood trickled down your legs. I slipped the white dress off your body. Your lips, redder than all the surrounding red cherries, found my mouth. Your moan rocked us both. I backed you against a tree trunk. Your hands automatically snaked high overhead into sturdy branches, the blue veins of your wrists throbbing. I turned you to me and wrapped my belt around your wrists and yanked. Your body arched up. You did not see the cherries framing your flushed face, brushing against your cheeks as I looped the end of the belt over a high branch and secured it. You did not see sunlight through leaves slicing across the swell of your breasts as my face fell between them. The taste of your nipple filled my mouth as I rose up between your legs. The moan from your lips hardened to a presence in the orchard, a fierce presence we were swallowed into, where glass broke, a baby cried, a man was running. I saw him. The man was actually there, staring at you tied to a thick branch by my belt. I saw him over your naked shoulder. He studied the rhythmic curve of your body receiving me, your flesh exposed. He was perfectly still beneath the shelter of trees. He was unashamed and patient, an animal waiting for what had crossed its path. I caught his eyes with mine. The animal in me recognized what the other was waiting for, what it anticipated. You were the prey. It expected to make a meal of this tied and moaning female. The son of a bitch was waiting to fuck you.

Can you ever forgive me?

FRANCISCO

Villa Trône-sur-Mer
Côte d'Azur

Still no word of you. Each morning when I awake my arm goes around your waist to pull the warmth of you next to me. There is only empty space and silence. You are nowhere to be found.

With great sorrow I must bring Roderigo back from Ville Rouge. His loyalty runs deep, but I cannot in good conscience employ him further in this task. The situation in Spain has worsened. Roderigo has a chance to return there through the Pyrenees before the border closes completely. It is a dangerous plan but one that must be acted on.

I am closing Villa Trône, boarding it up and returning to Paris. Roderigo will help me secure everything, then he is gone. He fears he will never see his family again. I fear I will never see you again. My spirit is breaking without you.

FRANCISCO

Village of Reigne

Francisco, my rough man with gentle hands, how I long for your touch in these long days. It pains me to hear your pain, but I have reason to be strong now, I must stay steady on the course. My life grows despite our lives growing apart. I can't return. I thank God our love exists, hovering above, a grace of memories to sustain me.

My heart aches for Roderigo and his family. I remember when we visited them in Andalucia, the stone cottage by the sea, the children, the goats, the olive trees. I wonder how much that land has changed. I pray no harm has come to Roderigo's wife and children. It is better he has left Ville Rouge. I am certain he told you there are many soldiers here now. The country is not safe, the days and nights are a danger and a curse to all.

It is so sad to hear you must leave Villa Trône. Not only is our love there, but your studio, the space and light with you at its center, with your creation growing from it. You were dripping with so many ideas, always stroking brushes to paint, paint to canvas. I felt pregnant with you, something was forever on its way to being born. What a lucky woman I was. Every day ripe with ideas. Every day in a new way you folded yourself into my body as I opened to you. Every day the excitement of not knowing who you were at any moment, not knowing where we were going, what we were to become. Each time you were a new you creating another us. How I craved your brushing me, stroking me, trusting my yielding to you until I had you completely, right where I wanted you, originating new life on the canvas. I was your woman.

Now in this fearful time normalcy begins to fade, the past seems strange with its everydayness. Perhaps this is why I too cling to our memories, reading your letters over and over, seeing the same events through different eyes. If this war had not come between us something else might have. You always desired to make my body more than it was meant to be. You continually attempted to go beyond the mere possession of flesh. You did not see that in the end only the female bears fruit. What is created by the hands of man can never be anything more than man.

The first pleasure boys handle is between their legs. They have time for that as long as it gratifies them, then their hands go on to making or unmaking other things. It is later, when boys become men, they pursue the knowledge of handling women in order to gain greater pleasure. Such pleasure for a man only resides in the moment; for a woman it begins in that moment. My great-aunt Mimi taught me this.

Mimi taught me many things during the time I lived with her as a girl. She taught me how to be handled by men so that I could handle them. She had the education given most girls of small villages in the heart of France. The most that was expected of her was to count the eggs and measure the flour. But Mimi knew from the beginning that between men and women, one and one make three. So devoted was Mimi to her man, Alphonse, she left her village to marry him. She loved Alphonse's drooping mustache, his hooded eyes gazing at her, his worker's hands holding her in a steady way that never changed from their first night. Alphonse was lock master of an isolated country canal. I was sent to live with them during the last war—to live with her actually, for Alphonse was drafted into the army.

Right after I arrived at their little house next to the rushing water, Alphonse went off looking very handsome in his uniform ironed stiff by Mimi. She told me he left to fight the good fight in a far and distant forest. Since I was from a large Provençal family I could be spared and put to best use by being with Mimi while she was alone, to keep her company and her spirits up. Perhaps I was only really meant to keep Mimi warm during winter.

The house was two simple rooms and the toilet was in a shed behind, a cold run in the snow if a girl had to go. During the day Mimi braided my hair by the light of the few coals she could afford to keep glowing in the brazier. In bed her numb toes rubbed against my warm body, like a grasshopper scraping its skinny wings in the sun. At all hours of the night we were awakened when the bell from the canal rang. Out into the darkness Mimi went with her lantern swinging, lighting her way to raise and lower the water level in the locks, allowing loaded barges to pass through. With her husband gone she had inherited his work. There were soldiers on the barges gliding by, their rifles at guard, cigarettes glowing, respectfully saluting Mimi spotlighted by her lantern.

I saw all of this from my window. I was too afraid of the soldiers to venture out. Mimi said I should leave the house and learn. She said, what if an enemy came and shot her dead? Then it would be left for me to know the ways of the canal water, its flows and levels, its inky life in steel locks. She said if something happened to her I would become the new Joan of Arc, responsible for the military supply barges headed to war. "Saint Louise of the Locks," Mimi laughed often at me in bed, pulling me to her, her body shaking mirthfully through her thin gown, her grasshopper legs rubbing for warmth as I sank between the valley of her breasts, far from the sight of soldiers rising and falling on dark water as they passed in the night.

There were no men around the canal during the day. Only boys strutted along the canal path, reveling because there were no real men to put them in their place, to peck them into the orderly behavior they surely needed. The real men had gone off to soldier; everyone knew they might not come back. If they did, most likely they would be leaning on a crutch, or wearing a bandage over their eyes, or be like Alphonse.

The day Aunt Mimi and I saw Alphonse coming along the canal path, returning from the far forest, we knew something was not right. But it remained unsaid. Mimi ran to Alphonse, squeezing the hand that once had handled her in a steady way. The other hand was gone, his arm blown away at the socket. An empty sleeve flapped at Alphonse's side. Something else had been blown away that Alphonse could never replace. He sat out the rest of his life in the little house while Mimi maneuvered the canal locks. The paychecks still came in Alphonse's name.

I did not remain in the little house after Alphonse returned. I did stay long enough to see what was missing in him turn up in Aunt Mimi. She gained a certain command of life. She knew the man who returned to her would never be capable of giving her a child. He became that child for her. What happened in the muddy trenches of the far forest had removed his bravado and replaced it with a child's fragility. It made no difference to Mimi. She counted herself lucky. At least her husband had come home.

Francisco, how fearful I am. This madness of nations can take not only your body from me but your spirit as well. I couldn't survive the loss of both. I would be broken to know you were lost to the world. As long as you are alive and kept from harm I feel safe, knowing your hands are free to create, knowing your memory can touch mine. I am here, wherever the here is, loving you always.

LOUISE OF THE LOCKS

Villa Trône-sur-Mer
Côte d'Azur

I write quickly, the last letter from Villa Trône. There is no longer electricity here. One of the main power lines from Cannes was sabotaged. We can't get any information about when power will be restored—we can't get information about anything at all. Everything is in darkness tonight so I write by candlelight. At dawn I will leave on the train for Paris, if trains still run to Paris. The Bearcat cannot be driven north; petrol is scarce and the roads are unsafe. So I have asked Roderigo to take it to the farm of the collector, Elouard, and bury it beneath the hay in the cow barn. I have left instructions that if anything should happen to me you are to be given the key to the Bearcat. I want you then to go to the barn and look in the Bearcat. In its trunk you will find something I have left for you, something you must know in the event of my death.

I keep writing these letters in hope you will answer. Do you receive them? Everyone constantly asks about you. When I am vague with my answer they smile knowingly, certain that I have sent you out of the country. It is best they think that, for it spares them the loss of yet another loved one. But I suffer the loss. I am tortured by the damnedest memories, heartened by the sweetness of others, such as the day we saw the naked children laughing under the clock tower on Château-Colline. I don't know what it is about us that caught fire so quickly and continues to burn right through my soul. It's as if love's flames can't get enough oxygen in this world, they have to burn memory too. Each remembered moment is another log thrown on the fire. I keep pricking memory to keep the fire going. That is why losing you so quickly made me like a man who walks out into freezing weather without gloves, distracted by his thoughts. The man puts his warm hand on an iron pipe, remembering too late he is without protection. His flesh is caught to the iron as he pulls his hand away, ripping the skin, leaving his own imprint in the cold.

I go cold even though I am within the hot memory of you in the cherry orchard. I look over your bare shoulder, sunlight drifting down through the leaves. I look into the eyes of the man watching. He is oblivious to me. He is transfixed by your wrists tied with my belt to the limb of a tree, the naked rhythm of your body swaying beneath. As I come out of you the slickness of your skin sucks back on me, your head rolls involuntarily, your teeth bite into my lips. Your eyes flicker apart. You hear the sound of birds. You are aware of your exposure. You feel the intense stare of the other man fingering down your back, along your stiffening spine, the curve of your buttocks. You follow my gaze going over your shoulder and see what I see—the man in uniform, an officer in the army of the new emperor who has occupied our land. Your toes curl into sharp pebbly ground. The Officer shifts his stance, legs spread apart. His eyes lock on to yours.

Insects hum in the weeds as I move toward the Officer. He doesn't regard me as a threat; he doesn't regard me at all. His military uniform is crisply pressed, the handle of his revolver gleams from a black holster strapped at his waist. I am shirtless and shoeless, with a beautiful woman tied to a tree whom I can protect only with my bare hands. Bare hands are not enough against bullets. The Officer doesn't take his eyes from you as I walk past him. He smells the scent of your sex on me. I keep walking. I hear his boots scraping across the pebbly earth as he moves toward you. I reach the edge of the road, stepping through the last row of trees onto pavement. Next to the Bearcat is the tire iron we used to jack up the car. The iron weight is comforting in my hand as I lift it. Now I have something to protect you with. I turn back toward the orchard. The sound of my own voice precedes me. The sound is not a scream or a plea, but a hurtling challenge as the Officer steps before you.

The Officer ignores my challenge. He is fixated on the deep-breathing heave of your breasts. His eyes trace down the contours of your belly, contemplating the glistening dampness in the dark V between your thighs. He sees the thin pricks of blood dripping from your knees, left from when you knelt before me. Did he watch that too? I am coming as quickly as I can, running to you. His eyes follow the smoothness beneath your upstretched arms to where your wrists are tightly bound by the leather belt. He leans down and pulls a knife from a sheath in his boot. His face is close to your face. His breath mingles with your breath. He places the knife blade to the pulse of your throat. A rush of anger erupts from my chest. He turns, seeing me coming at him. He knows that before the tire iron I hold in my hand cracks his skull he can pull the knife across your throat. Then what is won? Only his death after yours. The ticking pulse in your throat against his sharp blade binds us all. We know the price of pleasure. Without warning your swollen lips open, firing a kiss of spit into his face. The Officer recoils, stunned. You have gone past the animal in him and disarmed his male pride. He shoves the knife back into its sheath. Before I can reach him he is gone.

*   *   *

Louise, the candle by which I write this letter has burned down to a pool of wax, the wick is flickering, my mind is wavering. I am concerned if our atelier in Paris is safe. Are my paintings still there? Have they become like so many other things, leaves blown away in the storm? The candlelight is gone. I write in darkness. I embrace you across time, across land, across the sea of memory. Your Columbus of the night sails on,

FRANCISCO

Village of Reigne

My Francisco,

There was a time not so long ago when I needed your love as protection, but you abandoned me. You drove me to Ville Rouge on the one tank of petrol you were able to find. We made the drive from Nice at night. Because there was a blackout curfew we could not use the Bearcat's headlights. Even under a full moon it was a dangerous drive. Glancing over at me you saw my sadness but did not know its true origin. You were blind in the end. Even so, I could not bear to be parted from you. As we drove I sucked in oxygen, drinking it like a drunkard, knowing it was the last air we would breathe together. Overhead the night sky was swept clear of clouds by the mistral. Stars fell over darkened hills. A fox darted across the road before us, disappearing quickly into the shadows of a vineyard. In the moonlight an ancient village was silhouetted, its stone ramparts wrapped around the peak of a distant mountain. As we sped past the village it looked deserted, a lost and secret place. It is where I am now, with secrets beating in my heart. From the heights of this village I can look down onto the road we traveled together that last night on the way to Ville Rouge.

I write this letter in a stone cottage dusted by clouds high in the village of Reigne. Desire still runs in my veins for you. Tears run down my cheeks. You do not know the price I pay. You do not know that without your letters I might give up. I fear you might meet the horrible fate so many are meeting now, both the innocent and the not so innocent. Your letters hold back the fear. Even though I do not mail you my answers I am secretly overjoyed that you continue to write. Your love refuses to surrender to my silence.

I have had to make a compromise with a certain postal official in Ville Rouge in order to obtain your letters. Ville Rouge was too dangerous for me to stay in. I knew when you did not find me there you would search for me, ask everyone in the area if they had seen me. I knew you would send Roderigo, the one you trust most, to keep up the search. If I stayed in Ville Rouge I would be discovered and you would be alerted. So I went to Reigne, the nearly deserted village we once glimpsed from the road below. It can only be reached by a treacherous mountain path. When one finally arrives in Reigne there is nothing of consequence. There is no future, only a past forgotten by the present.

Monsieur Royer, the postal official in Ville Rouge, is an odious man. I had no choice but to turn to him. Even he does not know my true whereabouts—Reigne, my secret in stone. I knew you would go to the post office in Ville Rouge asking if I had collected your letters and where I might be found. I needed someone in the post office to intercept those letters and hold them for me, someone to tell you they had been called for by a person with no address. I wanted you to know I was receiving your letters so you wouldn't stop writing. I need you to write to me but not to find me.

Royer is a monster dressed in the boring cloak of normalcy. He has itchy fingers and a nose always twitching to find a morsel overlooked. He has a large appetite and an ambitious wife, all of which must be accommodated on his tiny paycheck in this most austere of times. He mistakes my fear of being discovered as timidity, and believes I am a woman in distress who won't protest his fingers lingering on her shoulder while he chivalrously guides her out the door of the post office. His fingers itch to feel more, his dull eyes pop open as if he is about to be served a delicious meal. He watches me walk away from the post office clutching your letters. Sometimes he follows me through the twisting streets. He keeps a careful distance behind me, avoiding curious passersby and suspicious soldiers. He doesn't want to be caught following me any more than he wants you to discover me. He wants me all to himself, he wants my secret to be his secret. He knows who you are, he knows your fame. He sees the name and return address on your letters to me and believes he is going to taste the best meal of his life. He follows me with nostrils flaring, like those men who surrounded me that Day of the Bees, when you fell to your knees before me, nearly crippled. What those men did to you terrified me more than the Officer holding the knife to my throat in the cherry orchard. Perhaps if I had not intervened, and you had smashed the Officer with the tire iron, then what happened later with the bees would never have occurred and we would not now be separated.

I wonder why so much violence surrounds us. Does it surround all lovers, is it lurking in the shadows? Do people in love attract violent thoughts from a world that cannot love? I wonder about this while you are fresh in my thoughts. Why do I feel a subdued anger when I see two lovers kissing, caressing in the street, oblivious to all except each other? Why is my heart seized by the jealous thought of nullifying their happiness as mine has been nullified? I feel the weight of jealousy in my hands. I let it go. It is a stone dropping on a butterfly, crushing the lovers. What a shameless way to think. I should defend the lovers, I am of their tribe. I should protect their short kisses from withering in life's harsh realities. I should run to them, throw my arms around them, bind them together, but I do not. The real reason people cry at weddings is because they are ashamed of their jealousy.

Royer wants to follow me home. He wants to discover me in my bedroom. He wants me undressed. He wants to exact a price for sharing my secret. I always manage to lose him in our game of cat and mouse after leaving the post office, but we both know that someday I will be caught. One way or another I shall have to pay the price of guarding you, keeping you to myself through your letters. Royer knows the longer this continues, the more he stands to gain.

When I close my eyes to sleep I know I will not have the chance to cry at my own wedding.

LOUISE

Atelier Quai St.-Michel
Paris

What a train ride to Paris! A trip normally done in one day took three. We were constantly being sidetracked to allow other trains to pass. The military trains were painted in some army engineer's idea of camouflage. This war was started by a house painter, it seems his clumsy mark touches everything. My identification papers were checked over and over, but no one looked me in the eye. No one ever looks anyone in the eye, it's as if everyone is in a trance. I think this is because people believe that if the situation suddenly turned murderous, then nothing personal would be lost. Actually, it already has been lost.

So much of what we love in Paris is gone. Yet what pains me most is that you are gone. I've turned into a ghost myself, haunting the streets and bridges we once walked. An ominous fog hangs over the city even on its brightest day. I cannot distinguish if the world has gone to hell on its own, or if life without you is the hell I have been condemned to. I cannot even tell if there is a war on, because my life has been turned off. The one saving grace is that our atelier has escaped substantial harm and I am now living in it, sleeping on a mattress on the floor among the paintings. They seem to date from another time, painted by another person, their origins obscured. Because they were made when you were with me I trace their surfaces, hoping to feel the inspiration that brought them into being.

It has been so hard to paint, so hard to sleep, night sirens in the streets, dreaming of you. In the morning my hands shake. I look through the dusty windows of the atelier. The waters of the Seine slice beneath the bridge below me. Across the river, perched on the tower of Cathedral Sainte-Chapelle, the twelve stone apostles stand guard against the madness in the streets below. On the peak of the steeple above the apostles the Angel Gabriel blows his golden horn. Gabriel's marble wings are not intended for flight. His job is one of witness and warning. I take Gabriel's warning seriously. His graceful trumpet bends to the shape of a bow, an arrow is released from the bow, flying through my heart. The arrow continues its flight and falls at your feet. When you stoop to retrieve it the arrow flutters, turning into a dove. You hold the dove in your hands, not knowing whether to release it and return to me what I have lost. You bring the feathered body to your lips, look into its eyes and see me here in my humility, my empty hands shaking, unable to create. What right have I to swim in such self-pity? Outside my window, in the concrete fields of the city, men are contemplating the final destruction. What right have I to moan about my emotional debasement? What right other than the right of the betrayed? Like revolution, love betrays itself first. If only I had known the nature of that betrayal before it was too late!

I stare at my shaking hands, these hands of a strangler or a creator, which must be harder than any stone they chisel, more fragile than any heart they break, softer than the curves of any flesh they caress. These hands of a man gone mad, tearing at yellow, tearing at the sun. Behind it is your face, your eyes seeing into my eyes in the eyes of the dove. I am painting again. The dip of brush in oils, strokes across canvas. I am tearing at blue, the sky rips. I am melding gold, the moon spills. I am fusing hues, rainbows flame. I am shaping the object, projecting the essence, moving through form, sailing through sky. White clouds are billowing. I see you there among the women of Europe, sheltering against each other's naked bodies, guarding hearts from men suited for war. I paint a path to you through bombs opening graceful as flowers, through graves birthing babies with musical mouths, through voices tumbling bright as cherished toys in the wind. Across the waters of the Seine the Angel Gabriel watches me try to accomplish my journey in an eight-by-twelve-foot canvas, which in the end will be nothing like my original vision. The Angel blows his horn into the eye of a dimming Paris sky. Art from chaos? Chaos from art? Absurd! Gabriel blows the truth. How naked a fool is when clothed only in his ideas.

Louise, I trust you will read this and forgive me, the betrayer on his knees. I would take your feet in my hands and wash them with my tears if that would bring you back to me. Now I know why Christ wept, washing the feet of Mary Magdalene. Her feet were two fish swimming away in his sea of tears, the passion and love he could never have. He held her feet but not her heart. I do not want to make that mistake. I want you to see me exposed. I hide behind nothing. What's the use in a useless light? I am no Christ meant for suffering. I am your Columbus. I'll take any new world you will give me.

FRANCISCO

Village of Reigne

My darling Columbus, how you make me homesick for you, how you break my heart with your honest talk. I admire you for not fearing to be the fool. The fool in love is a courageous captain, he sails a sea without a shore. So you are my Columbus, always.

You say so much of what we loved is gone from Paris. What is lost are only the simplest things. If only I could tell! you what has been found here, how quickly you would come to me. But you could not see it in my eyes that night driving from Nice.

In your letters you dwell on certain events that now seem to have happened long ago. These events have the distant murmur of history. I know how troublesome things are now, just by the amount of time it takes for a letter to reach Ville Rouge from Paris. It is a wonder there is mail service at all. I am searching for something important to my survival in your letters. What a fierce taskmaster memory proves to be! I am not living for yesterday, I am trying to make peace with the present. With my sudden departure and cruel silence I hope to kill your love for me. But my actions are contrary to what is in my heart.

It becomes more and more difficult for me to get your letters. Soldiers are everywhere. The journey from my home to Ville Rouge is treacherous, and when I do arrive there is always the twitchy Royer to deal with. A war of distrust is also being waged. Who is on one side, who on the other? Who collaborates? Who resists? Does anyone really know? I seek my solitary comforts. I have your letters. I have your paintings surrounding me. At night the mistral beats against the door of my cottage. Some nights I go to the door thinking it is you knocking. Even though I fear it, I want it to be true. But when I open the door and peer into the darkness, you are not there. Each morning when I wake I wonder, will there be a letter for me today? The bridge to Ville Rouge has been blown up. Suspicion hangs in the air, everyone is under surveillance, secret judgments are being passed. I have learned it does not take two people to make a war. One can be at war with oneself in one's own heart.

Last week something unnerving took place, an encounter that involved the Bee Keeper. I know you don't want to hear anything about him, but since he saved us both that day in the mountains I thought you should hear this. As usual I had gone to Ville Rouge to see if there were letters from you. Royer was behind his desk in the post office. When he saw me he sniffed the air to determine if this was the day the table would be set for him, the meal served. It was not difficult for him to see the state of anticipation I was in. He ceremoniously presented a packet of your letters. My hands trembled. Touching the envelopes I was touching you again, even though it was just paper—for inside were your thoughts. I was holding your thoughts. Royer ballooned up in front of me, puffy and eager, a pushy boy needing to be pushed away. He licked the corners of his lips, his body moved closer to mine. "Mademoiselle was expecting these intimate little notes?"

I did not answer. I never open your letters in front of him; that would be sacrilege. I quickly slipped the letters into my purse.

"Perhaps Mademoiselle should read her correspondence now,

before waiting to go home. There could be good news inside she could share with Monsieur Royer. Good news from Paris."

"Thank you." I served my words to him sunny as two eggs on a platter. I had to flatter him; he has the power to cut me off from you.

"Mademoiselle might consider an apéritif at the café before returning home? She could relax and read these intimacies at her leisure while giving Monsieur Royer the pleasure of her company. I myself am a married man and offer this invitation in all sincerity. As a public servant I am ready to assist. These are rude times. A mademoiselle must be careful with whom she is seen. A mademoiselle must not appear to be one who cannot be trusted by public authorities. She must not give the impression she is one who conspires."

"Conspires?"

"Conspires against what is correct."

"And what is correct?"

Royer looked through the window at the soldiers with rifles guarding the City Hall across the street. "That is what is correct."

"I must be leaving."

"I can offer you a ride? As a postal official I am entitled to petrol for my auto. How else would the mail arrive? How else would you obtain your letters, your precious Paris letters?"

"How else?"

"If Mademoiselle accepts my offer of a ride she is being very correct. It is unwise to be on the roads alone with so much danger lurking about."

"Thank you for your concern, but I have many tasks to attend to before returning home. I wouldn't want to waste the time of such an important public official on a woman's trivial errands."

"On the contrary, I would be honored to accompany you. I am incapable of being bored in the presence of such an enchantress. Perhaps we might drive to a private place in the country and read your little intimacies together?"

The sudden expression on my face was enough to cause Royer to shut his twitchy little mouth. He understood that if he ever opened one of your letters he would close me off to him forever. Not that I was open to him, except in his own mind, which is where I wanted to keep it.

When I left the post office Royer followed. This was not unusual. I always used different tricks to lose him. Once I sought out a boulangerie with a long line of people waiting for their ration of bread. When I arrived at the front of the line I pretended I had forgotten my ration book, then returned to the back of the line. Royer was forced to race home to his wife, or risk his lechery being exposed in a bakery. Sometimes Royer was easy to lose, sometimes not. He was always crafty and persistent.

After leaving the post office Royer followed me through the streets. I sought refuge in Madame Happy's shop, which sold only baby clothes. I was certain Royer would not follow me in. He would appear out of place and risk gossip as to why he was there. But in he came, the little bell above the door tinkling as he entered. Madame Happy turned her attention from me and announced his name with great familiarity.

"Ahhh, Monsieur Roooyeer! I haven't had the pleasure in years. What wonderful news do you bring? Does this visit mean you and Madame Royer are *very* happy together?"

Royer pretended not to see me hiding behind Madame Happy's formidable figure.

"Yes, Madame Royer and I are happy. No health problems. Although Madame Royer does have a little touch of the—"

"But the two of you are still like lovebirds?"

"Lovebirds twittering in the treetops."

"That's why I am in business! I dress the little fledglings of happiness. Even in these uncertain times happiness can fly through your window when least expected. One must not forget that. Without happiness there is no Madame Happy's baby shop. I owe it all to you, Monsieur. Your happiness is Madame Happy's success."

"Thank you, Madame. I'm only a simple postal official, but postal officials have dreams of happiness too." Royer poked his head around her, attempting to sneak a look at me.

"Ahhh, poetically stated. When may I be expecting the little bundle of happiness?"

"Little bundle? Oh yes, I mean, oh no. Madame Royer is not the reason I am here."

Madame Happy was affronted, huffing herself up to a mountain of probity. "If you are not here for Madame Royer, then what earthly reason would bring you through my door? This is a very specialized shop!"

"Certainly most special."

"Then why are you here?" Madame Happy sensed a scandal ruinous to her good reputation. She wanted no part of it.

Royer backed toward the door, caught in his own trap. His mouth opened, gasping for a plausible way out. "My niece in Nice!"

"Your niece in Nice?"

"She is so happy. Her husband is so happy. Madame Royer is so happy. That is why I am here, to tell you how happy everyone is."

"In that case," Madame Happy aimed her nose down the mountain of her considerable self, targeting the sweating prey at the door, "you have entered the land of happiness. Might I show the honorable monsieur the latest fashion in christening gowns? I have chiffons fit for an angel, pinks and blues, ruffles and bows, all silk-lined from cap to booties."

"Exactly what I came to see! You are a mind reader." Royer bowed his head and stretched his hands out, as if expecting the clamp of handcuffs.

"I am interested only in happiness." The handcuffs clicked shut.

Royer rolled his eyes as Madame opened drawers and boxes, proudly displaying her arsenal of dainty baptismal garments. I slipped past them to the door, its bell tinkling behind as I made my escape. My own happiness was in my purse, your packet of letters.

When I was safely beyond Ville Rouge I still did not open your letters, fearing someone would apprehend me, discover my true identity and read the words you had written. I never took your letters from my purse until I was secure within the stone walls of my cottage. Even when halfway up the road back to Reigne, past the vineyards, the orchards, the last farmer's house, when it seemed safe to open the letters, I did not. I waited, afraid the sun itself could read over my shoulder, stealing my secret. Which is why I was startled to hear a commotion on the normally deserted road. I thought the shouting had to do with me, that the soldiers tensely pointing their rifles were part of a trap set by Royer to expose my identity. Soldiers stood along both sides of the road leading up into the hills. One of them approached, motioning me to stop with his pistol.

It was the Officer from the cherry orchard. He showed no sign that he knew me, or that he remembered that Day of the Bees, when you were clubbed in the knees and brought to the ground before me. The Officer's face stiffened as he ordered me to open my purse. I obeyed. He watched, irritated. He grabbed the purse and flipped it over. Your letters spilled into the dirt. The Officer pushed at them carefully with the tip of his boot, as if they were explosives set to go off at any moment. He turned back to me. "Do you have anything on your person?"

I held my purse open to him like a beggar, showing that it was empty.

"I see that it's empty. Do you think I'm a fool? Maybe you are hiding something under your dress?"

The other soldiers were watching. I spoke in a low voice to the Officer. "Why don't you have a look? You already did once. Do you want all the others to know just what kind of a look you've had? Do you want me to shout it out to them?"

The stiff expression on the Officer's face did not change. He swiftly bent down and gathered up the letters, then stuffed them into my purse. "Last night an electrical transformer coming from Ville Rouge was sabotaged. If you see anything unusual I want you to report it directly to me at the town hall. Do you understand that?"

"I understand."

He did not let go of my purse. "Have you seen anything out of the ordinary today?"

"Only the dog at the last farmhouse."

"What about it?"

"It didn't bark as I passed."

"Get out of here."

I pulled my purse away from him. Had he only known the fear that seized my heart when he held your letters, and how ashamed I was for feeling that. I think people would rather be discovered carrying explosives than love letters. Love letters can seem so trite. The nakedness of desire interests only those in love; to those outside the love it is insignificant. I wanted at that moment not to be a woman in love. I wanted to be the fugitive in the hills, the one who had blown up the electrical line coming from Ville Rouge. I turned to leave but the Officer grabbed my arm. He heard something. I heard it too: dogs barking, the whine of a motorbike coming around a bend in the road. The Officer raised his pistol.

The motorbike stopped before us, surrounded by panting dogs. Straddling the motorbike seat was the Bee Keeper. Roped behind him to the wide fender were three wooden hives wrapped in empty flour sacks. From inside the hives came a sound that never dies out of my days, never leaves my dreams: a dark humming of bright bodies. I felt the buzz of bees against my skin. A shiver ran through me.

You and I first met the Bee Keeper on a market day. The streets of Ville Rouge were crowded with people pushing among the stalls displaying olives, melons, cheeses, rabbits, truffles, and herbs—the bounty of Provence spread out in the sun. Amid the noisy crush of people stood the Bee Keeper, aloof in his simple pride. His sharp face with piercing eyes surveyed the surge of shoppers surrounding his table of glass jars sealed with wax tops. The jars were filled with creamy honey. Each jar had pasted to it a scrap of paper bearing the Bee Keeper's scrawl: *Honey of Lavender, Honey of the Roses of Abbé Sénanque, Honey of Mont Ventoux, Honey of Wild Rosemary.* You bought me every variety the Bee Keeper offered, enough, you said, for a thousand mornings of our being together. You had a theory about the solitary Bee Keeper. When a man gathers his own honey and has no wife, he spreads the sweet stuff on bread and shares it with his dogs. A man with dogs doesn't have to share with another person.

The Bee Keeper's dogs circled me and the Officer in the road. The Officer pointed his pistol at the dogs, commanding the Bee Keeper to call them off, but the Bee Keeper only smiled as the dogs licked my ankles. The Officer shouted at him to present his identification. The Bee Keeper didn't make a move. The Officer stepped up and pressed his pistol to the Bee Keeper's temple, demanding to know what was in the three wrapped boxes roped to the motorbike's rear fender. The intense gaze of the Bee Keeper's eyes was fixed on me—large, bulging bee eyes. I noticed his misshapen hands on the handlebars of the motorbike, hands familiar with the flutter of light-winged bodies on the skin, at peace with a multitude of stinging insults.

Under the Bee Keeper's gaze I felt the same way I had as a girl playing outside Aunt Mimi's house next to the canal, when I first became aware of another game being played. From the woods behind the canal a group of boys emerged. Their eyes lingered on my naked back as I bent, drawing my dream house in the dirt with a stick. I turned to the boys, my throat tight. No noise came from anywhere. I waited for the sound of my own voice, my own breath. Silence. I waited for Aunt Mimi to come running, to rescue me. The eyes of the boys moved over my skin. I was at an age when a girl doesn't yet think of covering up in the summer sun; my rounding body was changing too fast for shame or joy. Only in the eyes of those boys did I see for the first time what age I was, what sex I was. My female eyes locked into male eyes. I knew instinctively that if I ran I would be hunted. I did not turn as Aunt Mimi approached from behind me. Her hands came down firmly on my trembling bare shoulders. I could not see but I knew her eyes were on the boys. Between them and us a distance was shortening, across the hard earth with its burnt summer grass an idea was growing. My hand went up to

Mimi's waist. She always wore Uncle Alphonse's wide leather belt over her long dress. I undid the buckle and slipped the belt off, wrapping it around my bare chest, cinching the leather over my stiff nipples. Mocking male laughter burst in my ears. It was the first of many times I would hear that sound. A sound that said, I'm not looking at you, what makes you think you are worth looking at? A sound that said, what makes you think I need you, what makes you think you are special? A sound that said, next time you won't be hearing this laughter, you'll be hearing something else, and it won't be funny. As the boys laughed and disappeared back into the woods Aunt Mimi's words came down to me:

"Never be ashamed of how God made you, Louise. Someday you must go where the men go. You must not be afraid, for they are the fearful ones. If you open yourself to them as a woman, then you will lead. That is the power of a woman, but only if the woman knows who she is, only if she knows where she is going."

The soldiers guarding the road laughed as the Bee Keeper's dogs pressed their noses to the hem of my dress, their tongues lapping at my bare legs. I walked past the soldiers to the Bee Keeper on his motorbike. Aunt Mimi's words were in my ears. *Only if the woman knows where she is going.* The soldiers fell silent.

I placed my hands on the shoulders of the Bee Keeper. His clear gaze turned to me. I felt the vibration of bright humming bodies in the hives stacked on the fender behind him.

"He cannot speak." I spoke these words for him.

The Officer pressed the tip of his pistol deeper into the Bee Keeper's temple. "I want him to open these boxes!"

"There are only bees inside."

"So then he can open them!"

"No, he can't."

"Why not?"

"Because he is transporting a queen."

"Let's see her."

"If he exposes her, you will be attacked by the colony."

"Shit!"

"It's best you let him pass, especially if you like honey on your toast."

The Officer angrily turned his pistol on me. "Why should I give a damn about honey?"

The bright buzzing sound of golden bodies was in my blood, as it had been on the Day of the Bees, when the Officer pressed his sex into me. This time the Officer was holding a pistol. This time he had another way to kill me.

The Officer waved his pistol. "You tell that son of a bitch to keep his queen at home where she belongs."

"He is taking her home."

"Then he should get out of here and not waste my time. He's only dumb, not crippled."

I lifted my hands from the Bee Keeper's shoulders. "Yes, he is only a dumb keeper of bees."

I watched the Bee Keeper turn his motorbike around and clatter away down the twist of road away from Reigne, his barking dogs chasing behind.

The Officer slipped his pistol back into its holster and allowed me to pass, giving me a sarcastic salute. I continued my journey with your letters in my purse. I walked the stony road to Reigne laid down centuries before by Roman conquerors. Aunt Mimi's words came to me along the road, just as they had when I walked the rain-slick streets of Paris to meet you that very first time at dawn in Cathedral Sainte-Chapelle.

Only if the woman knows where she is going, my love.

PART THREE

Day of the Bees

Village of Reigne

My Most Darling Francisco,

I sit in front of my morning fire and attempt to write. It is a letter
from a talking bird. Feathers and flight and bursts of song. A song
that begins to repeat itself, sung over and over. Our song. Words of
love always sound so mundane to others, but they strike a perfect
note to the ear of the beloved—the beat of their own music, a blood
pulse stronger than any symphony.

Do you want to know what I dreamt last night? I dreamt of a fire,
just like the one in the fireplace before me now. But in the dream I
am inside the fire, I am the flames illuminating a view outward, my
invisible flesh radiates a comforting heat. I am the only witness to a
miraculous moment. I do not exaggerate; the quality of the dream is
so rich it smells of the hot spice of your skin. So it must be real.
Someone I cannot see plays a folk song on an accordion. The dancing
notes come from far away, quick and agile, snake-wrapping around

the melody, our melody. It undulates through the scene I am about to relate. Remember, listen to the music: without it you cannot see my dream.

A mournful fiddle joins the accordion. All at once from inside the fire I see a dark silhouette—your back, bent in thought. Behind you the wide windows are open to the night. From the dark pitches a sparkling of light, white on blackness—a moth. Ordinary, except the moth's wings are woven of satin tulle. The winged creature is the size of a green apple, a ripe green apple like those found dangling from a lone tree in front of a deserted farmhouse.

I follow the slow movement of the creature. It seems to float as its delicate bowed wings flit rhythmically. You do not notice its approach. Lost in your own world, you peer at an empty canvas on a tall easel before you. I know the hovering apparition is benevolent. It is goodness. Its trajectory lies in your direction. It moves from the dark exterior toward the light of your studio, following a course across the room; and as it does, its color changes from green to that of aged linen, to an increasingly brighter cream on the absolute edge of incandescence. Then its wings burst into the petals of a voluptuous gardenia. I can smell the scent of its pure flower.

You come into my frame of vision, a brown shadow standing before the fire in deepening thought. Your fingers hold your paintbrush, ready to conjure your inward vision. Your brush moves up, preparing to stroke from air a shape, the shape of an emotion. Behind you, over your shoulder, the moth slows its pace until it hangs suspended in air. Perhaps the light that drew it has blinded its delicate sight, or it respects your intense concentration. It barely moves, hovering above your shoulder, then comes to rest upon your fingers curled around the paintbrush. It does not stir for some time. You remain unaware of its weight on your skin as its velvet wings begin to pulse. You turn abruptly toward the easel. The brush dips into the oils, then slashes color across the canvas. It happens so suddenly I almost lose sight of the moth, then see it darting toward me. I shout for it to stop but it doesn't—it flies straight into my flames.

In the hiss of an instant it is extinguished. No one would know it ever existed, except for the faint essence of . . . not gardenia . . . but bee pollen, its golden hue clinging to dust motes floating in your studio.

This was my dream. Then I awoke and thought, "Yes, *she* will be attracted to the quality of light. Magical and bewitching light."

LOUISE

Village of Reigne

Darling Man,

    I am going to confess to you in this letter. Confession is the wrong word—it will be a revelation, a clarity between us, the truth about the Day of the Bees from this woman's point of view. Since I had the dream of the moth consumed in flames I realized that only my own fire can illuminate the truth, and not the winged muse perched on your shoulder, whispering into your ear.

    How I wish I could tell you of my daily life here in more detail, give you all the intimate, tiny moments that go to make up my days without you. How I once craved to have you share those moments. Was I too harsh, demanding everything from you? Demanding that you give yourself up to me as I had to you? You told me some do not seek to be artists, they seek to be the art. So what was my sin? The art of life? The art of loving you? The art of losing myself to you? Was the ultimate sin the fact that I have regained myself? Now that is an art!

I never knew if I put myself in the hands of a monster, because love is a monster, or if I put the monster of myself in the hands of a man. Women think this way: that if they had only been a bit saner, older, wiser, more calculating, then the monster within could have been contained, what was craved could become instead something created. Do not think you are the only one who awakens with shaking hands, fearing what those hands are capable of. Don't be misled. It's just that I have other ways, other motives. A calm woman is not a disarmed woman. See how I talk, carry on, a circle without a center. I am without you now—for that I can forgive neither you nor myself. Time is moving fast and I am haunted by the cries and laughter of unborn children. I accept nothing less than this passionate mystery, all else is false. I am willing to stand alone. My roots weren't strong enough before; now they are. New things crowd my days, things worth living for. I hear that accordion in the moth dream. That sound I know: I've heard it before in the non-dreaming world. It reverberates in my bones.

There was an accordion player on a bandstand beneath a full moon. I see him swaying heavily from side to side as he squeezes out his tune. Behind him a band made up of local farmers backs up his every note with cheerful, off-key playing. The small plaza is filled with dancers swirling around us. We have already forgotten that afternoon in the cherry orchard. We have forgotten it is the Bastille Day celebration in Ville Rouge. It is midnight, it is hot, we are in each other's arms. That is all that matters, holding tight, as if to prevent our very spirits from flying away in sweet delirium. Was I ever so happy? In such a moment happiness seems a bright string unraveling into eternity's darkness. Even when you miss a dance step and slip, taking a bad fall—lying on the cobblestones beneath me, you are not hurt. I dance over you, our rhythm carries on, my skirts billow out around my waist, my legs are bare; you gaze up in wonder. Was I ever so happy? And if I had eyes to see others, I would have noticed how many men envied what you had—a woman unguarded, open to all love's promise. How many men approached me asking for a dance that was denied? How many men tried to break our spell?

How many watched silently from the crowded café tables surrounding the plaza? Was I ever so happy? Was I ever so oblivious? Lovers who have eyes only for each other are blind to the world, and the world is unforgiving to those who lose sight of it.

We lost sight, my darling. That earlier afternoon in the cherry orchard, with my hands tied and my head in a cloud of blossoms, the game shifted. I *wanted* to be tied, yearned to be bound, ached to be chained by you—and I was. I lost sight of those who had sensed our vulnerability, watching us all night in Ville Rouge into the early dawn. The crowd cleared from the plaza, the little band packed up and left. We continued our dance around the Roman fountain, its splashing water all the music we needed. The sound of the water merged with the first chirp of birds calling from the bell tower of the church. It was our dawn. We were the first and only ones on a newly born earth. Such is the conceit of lovers, and we were no different.

We were ahead of the rising sun as you drove from Ville Rouge into the mountains. There was no way to stop the rhythm still undulating in our blood. You pulled over to the side of the road, next to the ruins of an abandoned abbey. The Bearcat motor hummed, then you turned the engine off and another humming surrounded us: the morning's rising heat had awakened the cicadas in the tall sycamore trees lining the road. The insect humming became more insistent, a scratching sound rubbing open the eye of the sun to a fierce glow. We left the Bearcat and drifted into the stone shadows of what had once been the abbey's inner cloister. It was here I became your Salome, dancing sacrilegiously in the temple. You slumped back against a broken stone pillar, sliding to the ground with exhilaration, exhausted from the night but ready to be my audience. You watched my every move. Where those moves came from I'll never know, fluid and precise, not so much to entice as to express the most humble of all origins, the selflessness of an innate sensuality given over to another. So I served myself on a platter to you, food for the soul, and I both the chef and the feast. I glimpsed you through the swirl of my transparent skirts twirling above your head. Now we weren't surrounded by people as we had been in the plaza when I danced over you after you slipped on the stones. You did what you could not do in the plaza: your hands slid up my bare legs and traced my thighs. I was naked for you. All that glistened at the center of me was reflected in your eyes. You opened your pants and I lowered myself upon you. The rasps of the cicadas' cacophony licked the air around us. I felt you coming to me with a shudder. My breath exclaimed into your mouth as our lips met in a violent kiss. I clung to you as if I could suck that kiss into my very being, as if the very exclamation of my moan was beginning a new life, as if a shadow fell across my soul that wasn't my own, wasn't yours, and took its own form, unexpected and insistent. *Only if a woman knows where she is going, my love.* I knew in that instant where I had gone with you. There was no turning back. A woman knows when she is ready to be made pregnant.

YOUR LOUISE

Village of Reigne

Darling Francisco,

Forgive me for stopping my last letter where I did. I never told you before that I was pregnant, nor did I tell you the moment when it might have happened. I suppose when I stopped writing last night I was exhausted from the toll of reliving so much happiness, as we were exhausted that morning in the abbey when the sun rose above the ruins. You were still seated on the ground with your back against the stone column; I was on your lap, facing you, my legs spread open. As the sun warmed us I could feel you move inside me again. I opened my eyes, you were still asleep and yet you moved inside of me. Do you know how it is for a woman when a man does that? It is a reassurance that even in his dreams his wandering will take him straight to her. That even in his dreams she will receive him. And all I had to do was shift the weight of my hips and you would come running harder to me. I shifted my hips. My laughter, at how easy and miraculous this was, awakened you. Your eyes opening became the sun for me, the light burning all shadows of doubt from my life. You said you never had been awakened like this before, with such laughter. I wanted to hear more. You said the sound of my happiness was the purest you ever heard, a laughter that flowed like honey from the horn of an angel.

If only my own laughter could have drowned out the other! A mocking laughter came through the stone columns. We turned to find the source of the sound, but saw no one. The laughter grew louder. We hurried back to the Bearcat. Footsteps sounded behind us in the abbey, the scuffling of stones disturbed by many feet. When we got back into the car you started the engine. As we quickly rolled up the windows we saw the empty abbey. But above the rumble of the engine the laughter still echoed, accusatory and ugly. We drove away, the fields blurring as the Bearcat's heavy bulk swerved around corners of the twisting mountain road. You kept looking into the rear view mirror, trying to angle it for a view of the road behind. The morning sun glared off the glass, slashing a cold white light into your eyes. You pushed the mirror away in frustration, driving faster into the mountains. I placed my hand on your knee and squeezed, not out of fear, but to reassure you that we were in this together. My body had your love and that was comforting. Perhaps what we heard in the abbey was not laughter, but the echo of distant crows cackling in the dawn light. As supple as my body was, yours was growing more rigid, the animal in your blood rising instinctively.

"See if anyone is following us," you said.

I swung around. Through the dusty back window the road unraveled and disappeared around a curve. I assured you, "There's no one."

"Keep watching!"

Your foot pressed harder on the accelerator as I kept watch out the back window. Then I saw them. At first I thought they were only black specks in the rapidly disappearing road behind. Specks? Or maybe black crows? But . . . crows on a road? The specks grew larger, closing the gap.

"Yes," I murmured under my breath, fearful that someone could overhear my words. "Something is back there. Something is following us."

"Bastards!" You gripped the rear view mirror again to try and get a view.

We both could see them now. The specks took form, as if we were being pursued by speeding winged insects with slick heads and bulbous eyes. The sun glinted off them as they gained on us.

"They must have been watching all night in Ville Rouge! They must have followed us to the abbey! Why the hell wasn't I aware?"

"Aware?"

The insects sped closer. Now I could see—the wings coming from their bodies were actually their elbows, bent out at the sides of their motorbikes. Their slick heads were leather helmets. The bulbous eyes were large glass goggles strapped to their faces. The whine of their engines screamed with menace as they closed in on us. You rolled down your window and stuck your arm out, waving them to go around us, but they did not. They sped right up to the back bumper of the Bearcat. Your arm out the window clenched into a raised fist. Your foot pressed down on the accelerator. A smell of burning rubber cut the air. We could go no faster. The insects swerved out on either side of us, pulling along-side on their motorbikes, their eyes masked by goggles, their snarling laughter as loud as the whining engines. The laughter was the same we had heard in the abbey. Fists pounded the outside of the Bearcat. Something thudded against my side window, cracking the glass. Then quickly the insects peeled away, darting ahead, their bikes leaning into the curve of the highway as they sped out of sight.

I didn't realize until after they disappeared that my hand on your knee had become a claw, my fingernails digging into your flesh through your trousers. I raised my hand and gently brushed the sweat from your forehead. What was this menace you still saw so clearly on the empty road ahead, as if a howling storm darkened the summer sky? A loud pop sounded in our ears, and then another: the rapid pop-pop-pop of the engine backfiring. We both looked quickly at the gas gauge—the indicator arrow pointed to empty. The engine sputtered into silence. The whir of the tires on pavement was the only sound. The Bearcat rolled to a stop. We looked at each other in the sudden stillness. We smiled, relieved there hadn't been another blowout, relieved the insects were gone. We had each other. What else mattered?

You continued smiling and said, "Maybe I never should have traded that big blue painting to Elouard for this Bearcat."

"And what about the gold chains of Elouard's wife you also got when you traded the painting? If you hadn't had those I never would have been chained to your bed."

My eyes told you I didn't mean that. I didn't need gold to be tied down with. All I needed was your loving glance, your kind thoughts while you treated me roughly as only the true lover can.

We climbed out of the Bearcat, wanting each other again. For lovers, between desire and the end of the world, there is only desire. There is only the eternal instant of *now*.

The distant shrill of cicadas filled the air, the sun-hot metal of the Bearcat pressed against my flesh as you pulled my dress down over my shoulders and pinned me across the long sweep of the fender. I closed my eyes. The shrilling of cicadas grew more insistent. The acrid scent of exhaust came to my nostrils. My eyes were closed to the outside world so that I could feel only you. The cicadas whined in a metallic whir. I opened my eyes as you opened yours. We were surrounded. We were not hearing cicadas, but the whine of menacing insects—men on motorbikes surrounding us, circling the Bearcat, their stubby bike tires kicking up dust and pebbles.

What happened to us next, Francisco? How do two people remember the same event? As your Spanish poet once said: *In the land of the blind, the one-eyed man is king.* Lovers live in the land of the blind, blind to the outside world. They see only each other, the contours of each others' souls. They each have one eye; in their domain they are supreme rulers. But their two eyes together only allow them to see better in *one* direction, they have a perverted clarity. Surrounding them the big picture of the universe swirls. They are oblivious.

What you saw that Day of the Bees with your one eye you will spend the rest of your life reliving. And I wonder if that was not the price of our happiness—everything that came after only served to illuminate how high we had climbed and how low we had fallen. Lovers do not descend of their own accord. It seems to be a law that when lovers go so high they are too close to God. And God will topple them back to earth if they are beyond the reach of a jealous world. Is this what happened to us on what should have been the happiest day of our lives?

What I saw that Day of the Bees has such clarity! It replays constantly in my mind, like a loop of motion picture film continually spooling through a projector. If I write down what I saw, if I relive with you what my own heart felt, if I tell it to you with my own lips, then perhaps you will not feel the remorse of a man. A helpless man.

My one eye recorded everything that should have been forgotten but wasn't: the two of us stranded at the top of the world with the insects circling on their motorbikes in a cloud of spewing exhaust. The insects stopped their bikes and climbed off without removing their leather helmets and goggles. They cut their engines and laughed—the same laughter we had heard in the abbey, the same cynical sound that I had ignored the night before in Ville Rouge when I turned away every other man who wanted to dance with me.

As the insects laughed I saw you moving toward the trunk of the Bearcat where the tire iron was. The leader of the insects laughed all the louder. He reached into the saddlebag strapped to his motorbike and took out his own tire iron. The crisp uniform he wore, the pants tucked into jackboots, the gun holstered on his hip—he was the Officer from the cherry orchard.

"Is this what you are looking for?" He smacked the tire iron into the open palm of his hand.

You didn't answer, nearing the car trunk where your own iron was.

"Is this what you want?" The Officer raised the tire iron. "Then let me give it to you." He moved swiftly, his iron slicing through the air, smashing into your knee.

Your startled groan filled my ears as I moved to help you. But the other men held me back. You slumped against the Bearcat in pain.

The Officer raised his tire iron to crack your skull, then stopped. He had a thought. "Maybe you want to watch us?"

The anguish in your voice answered. "Watch! I want to goddamn kill you!" You lunged at him, grabbing for his throat. Your smashed knee gave way and you stumbled to the ground. The Officer yanked you up by the shirt and slammed you against the Bearcat. I could see the blood seeping through the knee of your trousers. The Officer shoved the tire iron into your throat; you gasped for breath. With his free hand, the Officer undid your belt buckle and ripped the belt free from your pants. He stepped back, swinging the belt in one hand, the tire iron in the other.

"You can watch—or you can die," he sneered.

"You'll have to kill me!" You came at him again as he swung his tire iron into your other knee, and I could hear the crack of your bone as if all the bones in my body were being crushed. You staggered to the ground, struggling to stay erect, refusing to bow your head.

"Now it's your turn to watch!" The Officer shouted the words in your face. "We watched all last night and this morning!" He spun around and came toward me, his men holding me by each arm. I could not see his eyes through his dark-tinted goggles, but I spat at him.

He laughed. "This time I was ready for you." He wiped the splattered spit off his goggles and grabbed me by the throat. He ripped away my dress with his other hand.

He stepped quickly behind me and tied my arms with your belt. He dug his chin into my bare shoulder.

"This is how you like it. You aren't afraid of men, are you? This is your lucky day. You can have us all."

The Officer unzipped his pants. You struggled on broken knees to reach me. He moved roughly at me from behind. The heat of his sex was a sharp pain pushing down along the crevice of my buttocks, searching for an opening.

I whipped my head around, bit his cheek, and a piece of his flesh ripped off in my teeth. His blood spurted onto me. His hands clamped onto my head, holding me in a powerful grip. His finger-nails dug into my temples. Then I heard a snap like a rabbit's neck being wrung. I was unaware that it was my own neck twisting violently just before I passed out.

When truly unspeakable things happen, some people lose all memory of the event. Other people remember every detail. And still others relive the event over and over until each act of memory re-invents the actual; it is perpetually occurring for the first time, all its horrors unfolding in the fresh terror of not knowing what will hap-pen next. I am always living in this last way.

What happened to me when my neck was nearly broken and I passed out? If I could remember, would I want to? And when mem-ory, or fear, flashes through my mind, each time it is different: the Officer inside me, then his men. Or was it only the Officer again and again? Or was it the men all at once? I have had time to reflect on this, even though I haven't wanted to. I have discovered something unnerving—that a woman in sexual ecstasy with her man forgets all detail; when it's over she wants to return and explore this abyss that still makes her tremble. The same thing can happen when she is raped, but for a different reason. Where joy once deleted memory, horror now destroys it. In two acts in her life can a woman lose all consciousness: in the act of lovemaking, and in rape, its cruel parody.

I heard your shouted curses in the far distance. I struggled to focus. I saw, through a veil of tears, you kneeling on useless knees. Only your voice had power, but it was overwhelmed by surrounding laughter. I stifled my own cries, swallowing all the comfort and pity I wanted to convey to you. I wasn't going to let the laughing men take that from me—the sorrow I felt for your humiliation. As for myself, I didn't care any more. There was nothing left inside me that wasn't already torn.

Dogs barked. Was I hallucinating? Did I hear them? Wasn't it my own breath heaving in rasping gulps of air? The laughter of the men stopped. I held my breath. The barking of the dogs came closer. For the first time I was able to focus on the men around me, fumbling for their pants, pulling them on, buttoning them up. They saw something in the distance that made them afraid. Something coming through the furrowed rows of the lavender field alongside the road. Something that did not stop. The Officer pulled his gun out of its holster and aimed it.

"Call off your dogs!"

I tried to see beyond the men. My bruised eyes were too weak for the bright daylight. Everything blurred into one, the rows of blooming lavender meeting the lavender sky. Lavender infinity with dogs barking from it, the Officer's voice shouting into it.

"I said stop your goddamn dogs!"

The loud bang of the gun went off right next to my ear. Maybe the Officer shot me, I didn't know. I wouldn't have felt it. Maybe I was already dead. Then I heard the whimper of a dog as it fell. Its death whine faded into lavender infinity.

"If you don't stop I'll shoot!"

Another shot fired.

"That's the only warning you'll get!"

Now I could see something in the lavender light taking shape. A man walking. The silhouette of his straw hat shadowed against the sun. Beneath the brim of the hat glowed his eyes. I recognized those eyes, odd and oval, polished smooth as stones, white as mirrored eggshells, reflecting the blue of sky and lavender, a startling clarity that saw all, or the nothing of all. It was the Bee Keeper from whom we had once bought honey. The Bee Keeper kept walking.

"Oh . . . I get it. You want some of this too." The Officer reached down and yanked me up from the ground. He held me straight, for my legs would not support me.

"I can't blame you for wanting some of this. It's what we all want." The Officer pointed to you on your smashed knees. "Why should only one man have it when there's enough for us all?"

The Officer's men laughed. The Bee Keeper stopped in front of me. His eyes were expressionless, as if he did not see my dirty, blood-smeared body trembling before him, as if he did not see you, groaning with humiliation. The Bee Keeper just stood there, unmoving. Not only his eyes but his whole being seemed made of stone. The Officer pushed me toward him.

"Go on!" The Officer put the gun to the Bee Keeper's head. "It's your turn!"

The Bee Keeper said nothing. He began to unwrap something from a straw basket he was carrying.

"What the hell's in there?" The Officer waved his gun at the basket. "I'm telling you, if I don't like it I'm pulling the trigger on you!"

The Bee Keeper unfolded the cloth wrapped around a large lump in the basket. He held the lump in his hand, letting the basket fall. I could see that what he held was a honeycomb.

"This isn't no goddamn picnic!" the Officer shoved the gun up to the Bee Keeper's temple.

The Bee Keeper snapped the honeycomb in two. Honey oozed onto his fingers. He suddenly reached out and took me by the shoulders, then stroked down over my breasts and held me between my legs.

"That's more like it!" the Officer shouted.

The Bee Keeper's eyes held me more than his hands between my legs. I could feel the honey running from his fingers, dripping down my thighs. I could hear you plead with him.

"Don't do it, man! I'm begging you! Don't be a part of it!"

I couldn't speak because the Bee Keeper's eyes compelled me to silence. They turned from lavender blue to the stone blue of a hard winter sky, like the eyes of a blind man, which do not see, but feel—a penetrating gaze peering into my heart. What were his eyes saying to me? What was he searching for?

"Hurry up!" the Officer growled. "We haven't got all day! Do it to her!"

The Bee Keeper did not move. There was only stillness. The long silence of hope. Hope is the most violent of emotions. Where was this hope coming from? It came from the Bee Keeper's eyes. Now I knew what they were saying, what he was looking for. He was looking for his queen.

I listened to my own silence. It was a new language I had to master if I was going to speak with him. To survive I needed to hear him. He was searching in my heart for his queen, the mother of the honey dripping from my body. His silent words pierced through me and roved across the distant lavender fields.

We are speaking the same language now. He is looking in the lavender bushes for the boxed wooden beehives sheltered beneath ancient oak trees. He is calling his queen. The hum begins within wooden confines. I feel it in my belly even though it is happening far from me. Thousands of wings stir. Bright bee bodies emerge from the hives, spiraling into the hazy air above the fragrant rows of lavender. The hum becomes a roar. They are coming across the field toward us. The Officer and his men hear it too. They look around, bewildered. Bees continue to pour from the hives, as if the earth has opened in a volcanic crack and golden steam ascends higher and higher, clouding the sky, swirling in a glittering halo above me. The Officer is confused, his men frightened. The Bee Keeper does not take his eyes off me. I hear him calming my fears and asking his queen to call her bees down.

The Officer pulls his gun away from the Bee Keeper's head. "What the hell is happening? What are you doing?" He and his men back away, their bravado turning to confusion as they look anxiously above at a sky darkening with bees.

The Bee Keeper's eyes penetrate deeper into me. I embrace his thought. I feel his queen pulsing in the heart of her hive. The Bee Keeper is the husband of the queen. Each bee above us is a bit of their union, a bright atom forging their communication. I must trust this husband as the bees hover above me.

One bee lands on my quivering lip. I feel its slight body tingle along my flesh as it crawls, wedging itself into the corner of my mouth. I am perfectly still. There is a flittering rush of wings as a second bee settles on my cheek. Another bee comes to rest on my bare shoulder, another on my back. Others land on my fingers, my nose, my eyelashes. More and more descend from the sky. Their wings brush me intimately as kisses as they crawl over my skin. Their bodies exude a dusty scent of pollen, the sweet smell of lavender, the pungent crush of wild thyme and rosemary.

I stare into the stone blue eyes of the Bee Keeper. I am not blind; I am silent. I hear what the blind man sees. Honey and death. Honey and venom. Pollen and sperm. Wings brushing kisses. Conception and misconception. Hope dressed in all its iridescent irony. The excited buzz is overwhelming. The bees above unravel like a cloud from the sky and spiral around my body. I close my eyes as they land on me by the thousands, bright atoms called upon by their queen to clothe my nakedness in a living cloak of gold.

I hear the Officer shout in panic. "Let's get the hell out of here!"

There are footsteps of men running, motorbikes starting, the whine of engines dying away in the distance.

I am left inside a dominating hum, a steady strum pulling me away in its current as the golden cloak unravels back into the sky. The bees spool heavenward. I am with them. I am leaving you Francisco. I see you below me on smashed knees. Already a new life is growing in me. But who is its father? My lover or my enemy?

Village of Reigne

My Dearest Love,

I am desperate to hear from you. I have received no letters. Perhaps the postal official Royer is holding them? Each time I make the journey to Ville Rouge I pray that Royer will have a packet from you—weeks and months of letters arriving all at once, a great gift. I worry that what I told you in my last letter, about the Day of the Bees, has caused you not to write. I do not blame you. I understand your Spanish pride so well. How difficult it must be for you to share this torment of a child conceived in joy and pain. Then I realize I haven't mailed my last letter to you. But did I really need to mail it? Wasn't the message already conveyed with every glance I gave you in our last days before you left me in Ville Rouge? Maybe I will never mail that letter. Maybe I will wait until this war is over so that I can hand it to you myself. But what if this war never ends? What if we are only at the beginning, standing on the first dune of an endless desert? This thought is too cruel to contemplate.

Day of the Bees

I am here alone within my stone walls. How long have I been here? The wind drums around me outside. Is it the wind? Or is it a giant moth turning into a butterfly with a woman's body, beating her translucent wings against my door? She thinks you are here with me, standing at your easel before the fireplace. The problem with the muse is that the sucking of inspiration drains her. She becomes used, the butterfly turns gray. All I wanted was to hold you as a married woman in this temporal world. You denied me that in a time of crisis. If only you had eyes to see! I told you in the beginning, if you would come to me I would give you everything I had as a woman. If I were only a mistress-muse I would be lost to you. What do I care if I am immortalized in your art? I wanted to be your wife. It is a crime against nature to squander love. Time is the jury. Now time ticks inside of me. It is a ticking of a different nature. Is it a bomb or is it beauty? All the sucking of inspiration from the muse hollows her heart, the butterfly turns into a worm. Does she have the will to begin again? Does she have the strength to live for a child that so divides her heart? God will surely strike me dead for such thoughts. But then God will probably not even hear me. God turns a deaf ear to self-pity.

How many days have passed since I began writing you this letter? How many weeks have slipped by as I try to catch my random thoughts on paper? How many trips to Ville Rouge have I made with the hope of having word from you? How many encounters with Monsieur Royer? Royer with his pudgy fingers pawing the air around me, convinced I am about to set the table for him and serve the meal. Royer in his stiff-brimmed cap, his tight-fitting uniform with its medal of officious rank pinned prominently to the jacket lapel. Every other minute he strikes a heroic stance, as if posing for the bronze statue he is certain will be erected to him in the town square, memorializing his sacrifice to public service. He struts and puffs. Sometimes you would think him a Vichy officer, or a German officer, or a militia officer, or an officer of Pétain's police. It seems everyone is an officer of one sort or another in this countryside that is now frozen to an eerie standstill at the center of a world that boils with war.

Strange news comes to us every day, but not in the newspapers. In the newspapers there is only celebration of local agricultural feats: who has raised the biggest goat, how much jam was preserved by this or that farmer's wife, how lousy the grape harvest was, how many tons of potatoes were grown this season compared to last. There is no news of what is actually occurring here—of the people in rags who travel the back roads with their few belongings, plunging into the bushes at the slightest sound of someone approaching; of the troop trains moving constantly; of the airplanes droning in the sky throughout the night. Nor is there real news of what is happening in darkened Paris, in frozen Russia, in burning London. No, this news is never found in print or on the radio. This news is carried on the lips of the people. A snatch here, from the baker when one gets bread. A trifle there, when one is at the greengrocer. Or in the butcher shop, where there is no meat but only a snippet of gossip, a slight innuendo, a scrap of a secret. Nowhere is a whole truth spoken, never is an entire sentence finished. Just the beginnings of things are hinted at; even then the speaker looks at you while pretending not to look at you, watching you trying to make sense of the tidbit just heard. The speaker wants to see your reaction. Are you happy about it? Are you sad? Are you indifferent? The speaker wants to know what side you are on without divulging his or her own. There is a show of patriotism, but it is paranoid patriotism. So the paranoia becomes reality, and in a way this becomes our strange defeat, for lies, innuendo, and facts merge together—unanswerable, unprovable. Are the foxes crazy? Is it true the troop trains don't all have soldiers in them, but men, women, and children being shipped east? And to what? Is icy Russia freezing armies in their shoes? Is London burning from a blitz of rockets? Is the farmer's pig pregnant? Are all the squirrels rabid? Can you trust your husband or is he an informer, and for whom? So we all are culpable in this conspiracy. In war rumor becomes fact, and fact is the sum of many minds trying to rationalize their compromise. What price survival? Can anyone truly condemn another unless he or she too has had a pistol placed to the head? Does one choose to live by emptying one's conscience slowly, drip by drip, each excruciating day?

I have so much time to think of these matters. Matters that wouldn't matter to me at all if I were by your side, for to live or die with you would decide my fate. I have only myself now, and next to my heart beats a new heart, a ticking clock, its hands sharp as cleavers, moving second by second, dividing my self.

Royer has hinted that he has something for me. It's something from you, I hope. I am about to give him anything he wants. What do I care about the consequences of my body now—what's done is done. I will grovel for a scrap from my true love. Isn't this terrible? Isn't this a hideous thought? But what are my shallow thoughts against these black-and-white days, where people disappear into their own shadows, terrified of their potential cowardice. Terrified they will walk the wrong road and find a dead body left from the night before, when the shadows leapt out and actions spoke where words could not.

This is to tell you I found a woman lying in the road to Ville Rouge. Flies buzzed around her body sprawled on the ground. I don't know what made me go to her; she was obviously dead. What could I possibly do? She could have been me, for I walk this same road to Ville Rouge every week. It could have been me in her tattered dress. I looked around. There was no one. The hillsides were barren. I stepped toward her. I had to see her face. I just *had* to. I knew that sometimes these dead bodies were booby-trapped with trip wires and hidden explosives, to blow apart the inquisitive enemy. But who was the enemy? Who was this woman?

I knelt at her side, reaching out my shaking hand, my fingers touching her cold flesh, sending a hot shock through me, my own body convulsing with a shiver, a deep shiver to my soul. I took her by the shoulders and pulled. Her mouth was gagged and she bore no wound except the one that had bled her to death. A sign to all those who rose to resistance in the night, a clear signal that their actions had been discovered and were being dispatched back with a message. If the dead resistance fighter was a man, his left testicle would be smashed. If it was a woman, her left breast would be cut off. How curious, the French Revolution never ended. Even when another country invades us we are all too ready to turn our weapons against each other. I rolled the dead woman over. Her left breast had been cut off. She was my age. I reached out and held her hand . . . I feel it still. The smooth flesh of her hand in mine. We steady each other in these terrible winds of war blowing around us, blowing around the stone walls of my cottage as I write this.

LOUISE

Village of Reigne

No one knows I am pregnant. I hide it beneath layers of skirts and sweaters, dresses and coats. But I cannot hide it from everyone, and so I confide in you. These letters, written by candlelight late at night, are the only window through which I can be observed. I write them hoping to expose myself to you, and perhaps to myself. The joy we shared dims with each day I don't hear from you. The buzz in my blood, caused by your distant touch, grows fainter. I try to force myself—oh I don't want to lose you! I try to force myself to remember. Once we sought all life in each other, in each moment, each breath, each bite of food, each sip of wine, each caress; the sacred mornings when I brought coffee and toast to our bed, your eyes melting on me, butter sliding through your fingers, a suck of kisses to wake up by, kisses to live for, kisses to die from. The things a woman remembers. All the sacred mornings.

Now I awaken to a cold room. A bed with only one person in it is an empty bed. I instinctively reach for your slickness, to feel you rising between my closing fingers. A new morning. The sun sheds light on my empty bed. The floor is icy to my feet. I am almost out of firewood. I am almost out of absinthe. It is absinthe that keeps me warm at night, absinthe that glows in my gray moth's body. There is nothing else to drink here in the country. The times of fancy cognacs and heady wines are over, disappeared from store shelves, siphoned off for the ubiquitous officers and cozy politicians. All that one can find, if one is lucky, is the local crude absinthe. Absinthe may have been illegal before the war, but the locals considered its outlawing a Parisian conspiracy to keep those who worked an honest day tilling the darkest earth from dreaming of their own destiny, weaving their own art, making their own laws. In this provincial place the locals are condescended to by outsiders, who consider their customs quaint. But these people are not quaint; their customs are carved in stone by the predictable realities of natural seasons passing over the land. Simple as that.

So absinthe can be had for a price. If you sometimes suspect that my letters are a little too flowery or vague, unlike the way I would normally talk, then think of absinthe's golden-green honey sliding off my tongue and opening a new throat through which I can cry— and oh, I hope, sing. I am a bird singing her song. But it is my song, with its bits of chirping and trilling, a woman's thoughts—that is all. I ask myself, do birds dream? They obviously find it difficult to write, as I do. You may even require a translator when reading this. Forgive my poor letter.

I am almost out of absinthe and I am going to get some more today when I see Royer, who hints of news from you with mincing smiles, and some secret "thing" he wants to "show" me. As if I don't already know what it is! But I am desperate to hear from you. All I have to live for is my past with you, because that is a certainty. My future is already divided.

LOUISE

Village of Reigne

My Darling,

Seeing Royer today was what I expected, but also what I had not expected. As usual I went to the post office in Ville Rouge late in the day. Royer was at his desk, industrious in his paperwork and taking the odd citizen's complaint. The citizen standing before him when I arrived was a distraught woman waiting for a letter from her son, who had been conscripted into the army and disappeared in a troop train heading east. She had heard nothing from him; she didn't even know what country he was in. Perhaps there had been a mistake with the postal authorities and his letters were misplaced? That is not to say that she didn't have the highest regard for the competence of the postal authorities, and most of all the highest respect for Monsieur Royer. Surely he could help her, since he alone had the power to contact the head office in Marseille, and Marseille could contact Lyon, and Lyon could contact the capital, Paris. The missing letters could be found, waiting to be handed over to the dear mama. Certainly Monsieur Royer could accomplish that.

Royer smiled smugly. He informed the tearful mother that it was true he wielded considerable power within the vast postal system, and luckily for her, he also had a cousin who actually worked in the Lyon post office. Things could be done, actions undertaken, mountains moved, rivers straightened, and with luck, voilà—an avalanche of the good son's letters could fall on the saintly mother's head. The mother hugged Royer with gratitude. He assured her it was nothing. All in the line of duty. What else is a public servant for, other than to serve?

What else, indeed, I thought.

The relieved mother turned to leave, but Royer summoned her back.

"Do you know, Madame, what one longs for during these perilous times?"

The mother was confused. "Longs for? I only long for the safe return of my son. That is all I want."

"Yes, there are such longings, all justified of course, the grand hopes for which one prays to God each night. But then there are mere mortals like me, toiling in the obscurity of public service, deprived of the simplest of pleasures."

"Simplest of pleasures?"

"A lamb stew."

"Lamb stew?"

"As simple as that."

"But lamb is almost impossible to come by! The newspapers report that the men hiding in the mountains, making trouble for us all, have killed every lamb, every goat, every hare. Those men eat everything, that is why there is no meat in the butcher shop. Even when one has a valid food ration book, one cannot get so much as a tiny lamb chop."

"Precisely." Royer rolled his tongue provocatively along his lower lip. "That is why one longs for huge chunks of lamb, steeped in steamy fig juice, swimming next to islands of sweet onions."

The mother placed her hand to her heart. "I don't know . . . it's so difficult, almost impossible."

"It is also nearly impossible to move mountains, to shake the sky, all for a letter from a mother's only son."

"But lamb! Gracious, I haven't had lamb for a year. I haven't had *any* meat for six months!"

"Think about it, Madame. Think about how savory it is. Think of your joy in preparing the stew as I talk to my cousin in the Lyon post office about the nasty army censors who are cruelly withholding a son's most intimate thoughts from his dear mother. Think of this, Madame, as you are cutting tender lamb into thick slices."

The mother shook her head in bewilderment as she walked out the door, mumbling, "Lamb and letters. Letters and lamb."

Royer locked the door behind her and turned to me. Before he could say a word I cut him off.

"The last time I was here you told me to come back in three days, that there would be something for me."

Royer moved behind his desk with a secretive expression, speaking softly, as if passersby outside in the street could overhear him.

"My dear, you look so flushed. Your face is always so red, but red in a good way. Red as the wine in a duck sauce, lips as crimson as a raspberry sorbet."

"I didn't come here to hear you read from the menu. I want my letters."

"Letters?" He smiled slyly. "I think you need something more than that."

"I need nothing more than that."

"Ah, but a pregnant woman is in need of many things." He stopped, waiting to see the impact of his words. I said nothing.

"A pregnant woman is most in need of a man."

I realized he now had two things over me: his knowledge of my physical state and the letters from you. I needed somehow to find a way out of this dilemma, to disarm this man who held such power over my life. I opened my mouth to speak, to explain all, to try and stop the damage this man could do. But he spoke first.

"Yes, your color is like a field of burnt-orange squash flowers blooming in springtime. My niece in Nice is eight months with child. She has that color too. Not a color really, but a blush, a blush of happiness, of expectancy. What is it Madame Happy calls that condition? Oh yes—*the bloom before the blossom drops.*"

"I—"

"Then I realized, Louise is not pregnant! That is not the nature of her lovely bloom. No. I realized that each time you were here, and I have an educated nose for such matters—a nose that can separate the *bouille* from the *baise*—well, I caught the scent of dried wormwood and copper, crushed herbs, and the very sweat of those who till our own beloved Provençal earth. And I realized—" He rolled his eyes like a schoolboy, trying to look up into his brain for some remembered homework as he stood before a demanding teacher, trying to pull down from his memory some lost final piece of the puzzle. "I realized," he pursed his lips and let flow:

> "With Flowers and with Women,
> With Absinthe and with this Fire,
> We can divert ourselves awhile,
> Act out our part in some drama.
> Absinthe, on a winter evening,
> Lights up in green the sooty soul;
> And Flowers, on the beloved,
> Grow fragrant before the Fire.
> Later, kisses lose their charm . . ."

He looked at me blankly, trying to recall the rest of the poem.

I knew the rest, knew it well, for this was one of your favorite poems, "With Flowers and With Women." How often I lay in your arms as you softly spoke those words after we had made love, tears forming in your eyes. And I thought: What a melancholic romantic Spaniard you are. But it was a Frenchman who wrote the poem. You are all impossible romantics!

Royer kept gasping, trying to find the missing words to complete his triumph of memory. I helped him:

> "Having lasted several seasons;
> After mutual betrayals,
> We part one day without a tear."

"That's it!" Royer was excited his words had provoked my memory.

"No, that isn't it."

Royer looked at me quizzically. "What do you mean?"

"There's more. Surely you remember there's more?"

Royer shook his head. "No. I don't remember any more. I remember only, 'We part one day without a tear.'"

"But it's much more interesting than that. To part without a tear is so trite, and it is never true, for if the tear is not shed on the outside it will make a cut on the inside."

"Well, that's the end of the poem. I'm certain of it."

"No, it's not. Maybe for your own reasons you have lost the last two stanzas of the poem."

He didn't like being proved wrong by a woman. He fell into silence. If I were to recite the last lines his shame would be even worse. Suddenly his eyes lit up. "Now I remember, I have something for you!"

All else slipped from my mind. At last I was to receive your letters.

Royer went behind his desk and unlocked a drawer, sliding it open with great solemnity. As he reached down I peered over his shoulder. In the drawer were bundles of letters. How many of them were from soldier boys huddled in the rain thinking of their sweet mamas?

"Ah, here it is." Royer fished around at the back of the drawer and withdrew a large packet wrapped in plain brown paper. Before he could hand it to me I took it from him and clutched it close.

"Go on," he beamed. "Open it."

I did not want to open it. I did not want his eyes to see your handwriting on the envelopes, handwriting moved by the emotions of your heart. "I'd rather wait to open it."

"Wait? Wait for what? Do you think I haven't seen what is inside? Who do you think put it there, you silly woman?"

"I don't understand."

"Open the package then."

My fingers couldn't move. I couldn't betray you.

"Open it or leave it here."

"I can't. Please let me keep it."

He grabbed the package and slit its string knot with a knife. He tore off the wrapper and held in his hand a bottle filled with thick liquid.

I tried to hide my disappointment, my despair at having played his little game. I heard my words coming weakly, as if from a distance. "I thought you had letters for me. That is why I came here. That is the only reason."

Royer uncorked the bottle and held it beneath my nose. "I know all about you. I know you are not pregnant. I know the glow on your face is not a prenatal flush. No-no! It's the flush of an absinthe drinker. You are a lush!"

He pressed the bottle against my cheek. "Here. Take it. It's better than what you've been buying in the back room of the pharmacy when you coyly ask for 'something to cure the grippe.'"

I took the bottle and slipped it into my basket. I looked him right in the eye before leaving. "You're despicable."

"Now-now-now, watch where your pretty tongue goes. It might not get you what you want. It might get you into trouble."

I spun around to go but his words came after me.

"I might have what you want."

His words stopped me. I turned around. "You have letters for me?"

"I said *might*."

I turned to go again.

"Wait! I have something stronger than might or maybe."

I turned again.

"I have a premonition."

"A premonition?"

"That tomorrow, letters from the great painter are going to fall from the sky. I can taste this premonition. I can taste it on the back of my throat. Can you taste it on your tongue?"

"No."

"You must want it badly enough to taste it, badly enough to do *anything* for it."

"I won't."

"I'm not asking you to do *that*."

"What are you asking?"

"Two things." He ran quickly and pulled down the window shades so that we were in semi-darkness. "The first thing is . . . I want you to let me look."

"At what?"

"You! You are always bundled up in so many clothes that one cannot tell what is underneath. But I know what is underneath. I saw it last Bastille Day when you danced in the plaza. You had on a very thin dress. It didn't hide a thing. It didn't conceal the shape of your charms."

"It was summer then. It's winter now, too cold for a thin dress. Too cold to show you what you want."

"How about a peek then? A teensy peek. That's all. No touching! Just a hint of summer."

"Exactly what is it you want me to do?"

"I saw your great painter slip and fall in the plaza, drunk with pleasure. And you danced over him, lifting your dress. There wasn't a man in the plaza who didn't see that. There wasn't a man in the plaza who will ever forget his glimpse of heaven."

"You aren't my lover." I heard my angry words, but I did not move to go. He had your letters. I had to do something. This was no time for indignation. Those letters were your flesh and blood; without them I couldn't survive. I stepped back into the shadows and placed my hands at the sides of my long woolen skirt.

Royer sat on his desk, unable to conceal his smirk of anticipation.

Slowly I raised my skirt. I could feel it brush above my boots and expose the curve of my calves. I could feel his eyes on me as my skirt rose upward; his gaze was like a filthy tide creeping up my legs. My skirt came to just above my knees and stopped.

Royer's words panted into the gloom.

"Potato dumplings."

His filthy tide kept rising.

"Higher!" he demanded.

My skirt came up to my thighs and he shouted, "Vanilla custard!"

I could not bear to look at him, the little rodent. I thought . . . I thought of not betraying you, of the ends justifying the means, of the last stanzas of the absinthe poem:

> We burn letters and bouquets,
> And Fire takes our bower;
> And if sad life is salvaged
> Still there is absinthe . . .

My skirt went higher, stopping short of what schoolgirls call "on the edge of the flowers."

> The portraits are eaten by flames,
> Shriveled fingers tremble,
> We die from sleeping long
> With flowers, and with women.

I dropped my skirt in disgust. "That's it! That's all!"

"You can't stop now, we're only at the appetizers! I want to see the main course and the delicious dessert!" Royer peered at me, glassy-eyed. "The painter got to see more than me."

"He is my *husband.*"

Royer jumped up from the desk. "Francisco Zermano is your husband! My God, I didn't know you were married!"

"In a secret ceremony. Private. Almost no one was there."

"My-my, I was unaware! I must apologize. I thought you were an unmarried woman, a . . . you know?"

"A loose woman?"

"Yes . . . I mean, no. I mean, forgive me. I would never have insulted the wife of the great master if only I had known."

"Now you know. So give me my letters."

"But there is one more thing left for you to do. We had a bargain. Have you forgotten? There were two things for you to do."

"Quickly then. What is the second?"

Royer slipped a key from his pocket and opened another drawer in his desk. He took out a sealed envelope and handed it to me. On the face of the envelope were scrawled directions.

"What am I to do? Deliver this?"

Royer winked slyly. "You could say that. Yes, let's say that."

"Well, I can't do it until tomorrow, it's almost dark."

"That's the point. It can only be delivered at night."

"I can't deliver something at night, there is a curfew in effect. There are roadblocks, there are patrols of militia and police. They will throw me in jail or shoot me."

"Don't be so dramatic—they will only shoot you if you run."

"But why would I risk my life to deliver this letter, when I don't even know what it is?"

"Because if you deliver this letter, you will receive a letter from your beloved Zermano."

"Then tell me please, who am I delivering this letter to?"

"That is the mystery, my dear. It is better you do not know. If you did, and you were captured, and they tortured the information out of you, then you surely would be shot. Under no circumstances should you ever open this letter."

Village of Reigne

My dearest man, forgive the abrupt ending of my last letter, but I had written late and my fingers were so cold. The absinthe was gone, the fire had died down. I thought I felt the baby move. How startling these times are. How I want to be with you, but there is no turning back now, as there was no turning back when I agreed to deliver the letter Royer handed me in his office. Had I not become at that moment an accomplice? The worst kind of all, the one who will ask questions, but be satisfied with no answers. To whom was I to deliver that letter? Friend or foe? You see, I was guilty of complicity on either side. I was like all the others who made secret compromises in order to survive.

Where was I headed that night after leaving Royer's office? I'm not quite certain of the streets and roads I followed, though they were all mapped out on the front and back of the letter Royer gave me to deliver. Because I had to avoid roadblocks and police patrols, I did not arrive at my destination until well past midnight. When would the person come to whom I must give the letter? I had not been told. I thought of all the possibilities that could befall me. That after passing the letter on I would be shot. That the militia might find me and torture me to reveal the identity of a person I did not know.

There was no moon. Low clouds obscured the stars. Not even a barking dog could be heard from distant farms. All was darkness and silence. I had only the absinthe to keep me warm on such a cold night, and my thoughts to keep me company. I thought of you with your knees smashed on the Day of the Bees. The Bee Keeper lifting you from the ground and carrying you to a car he flagged down on the road. He carefully placed you into its back seat and then walked away into the fields. I thought of your moans, and how they weren't from your own pain, but from the pain inflicted upon me, as if you were unaware that your knees were broken and useless. I told you, as I held your hand while the car sped along the mountainous road toward the nearest hospital, that there was nothing to worry about, that I had been saved by the bees, that they protected me.

And you said, "What bees? There were no bees! Only those bastards on the motorbikes! I will kill them all if I have the luck to see them again!"

I assured you the bees were there. You couldn't see them because you were blinded by tears of rage.

"No, Louise," you insisted. "There were no bees. But I think I heard a buzzing."

A silence came between us and slowly filled with humiliation. We felt violated at the center of our souls. I realized that no doctors would be able to make your knees good as new. I realized that I would never be able to make you see the bees. My mind hums with their memory. Those bees separate us with their golden cloak. I try to put my hands through the cloak, reaching out to you, to touch your face. But I am spun deeper inside the cloak, the lavender light from the fields that gave birth to the bees shines ghostly on my skin. There is bee pollen in my hair. Honey fuses me with the earth. I try to lift my feet, move my arms. I cannot go forward to you. I find no release. On that Day of the Bees I lost my way. I did not fail as a woman, but was being punished for my happiness. Why couldn't you see the bees?

Is it the honey sticking me to the earth, or is it the absinthe coursing through my veins? I hear you calling to me, as you did so many times before: "Louise, lavender light of my life." I hear your voice so clearly. You are seated at the little table beneath the spreading branches of an olive tree. You are shirtless and laughing, waiting for me to bring the rabbit I have cooked. Rabbit is your favorite. You couldn't wait for the scent of rosemary on its grilled skin. You tore the rabbit apart with your hands, its flesh steamed. You fed us both, searing our mouths, the taste of burnt meat on our tongues. We could not stop laughing with such simple pleasure. Your grease-smeared lips covered my face with kisses. You pushed the table aside. You stopped laughing. You bowed your head between my thighs. Your lips touched me through the thinness of my summer dress. I murmured above you, "My tiniest man." My fingers tangled in your hair. Tears fell from my cheeks onto your bare shoulders. It was the first night we realized we were a couple. I suppose if I had thrown my head back in joy I would have seen the stars shake loose from the summer sky, streaking in a brilliant descending path across the cobalt horizon and out of sight. But I did not.

I just felt tears falling, a raining premonition that the romantic is impossible, that truth is impossible, that such happiness cannot exist—and no one ever does believe it, except the couple. Like every couple, we thought we were different, exempt.

Did you not know when I cooked the rabbit I was cooking you? The oldest trick in the book of tricks that every French girl learns at her mother's knee. How easy are the lesser weapons of love. I should know, I used every weapon against you in order to win you.

But now I was left unprotected, watching the night slowly fade into morning around me. As the darkness became visible I saw that what I thought were barren hills were actually steep mountainsides planted with rows of cherry trees. The pale trunks and twisted bare branches transformed the trees into macabre people, watching me, mocking me. Rubbing my eyes fully awake, I rose from the pebbly ground where I had fallen asleep. As the day shone more visibly I felt where I was, where the map scrawled on the envelope had led me. It was familiar, a place I had visited before. Then I realized exactly where I was: on the road between Ville Rouge and Reigne. The map had led me to the exact spot where I had found the dead woman one week before. I gazed around at the stark trees. They were moving in on me. I grabbed the envelope from my basket and tore it open.

Why was I led here? What game had I been forced to play? What deadly ruse had I been fooled by? I pulled the letter out and unfolded it. The entire page was blank, except for one small line inked in at the lower corner:

I told you not to open this.

Village of Reigne

Francisco, can you imagine my fury with Royer for playing such a cruel trick on me? Can you imagine his toying with my vulnerability, my willingness to do almost anything to get word from you? If you knew of this incident you would come here immediately. But then, you can't know of this, for I cannot tell you, I cannot be found by you. I must remain hidden. I must find devices of my own to overcome the Royers of this world, those petty and self-serving ones who sometimes wear the face of the clown, sometimes the face of a civil servant or a general.

I did not go back to my cottage after awakening that morning at the side of the road where I had found the dead woman. I went straight back to Ville Rouge to confront the man who likes to play with his food.

In the post office, Royer had a long line of people in front of his desk, all hoping that letters sent to them months before had finally passed through the censors. He saw the look on my face as I barged into the line. He hurriedly jumped up, pulling me off into a side room where he locked the door and spoke in a nervous whisper.

"Control yourself, you look like you're going to explode. You'll get us both thrown into jail, or worse."

"What are you talking about?"

"The letter I gave you to deliver."

"What could possibly be troublesome about that letter? It said nothing."

"You opened it?"

"No one came for it. I could have been murdered out there."

"It was very important that you not open it. What did you do with it?"

"I burned it."

"Burned it . . . *burned it!* How did you know that it was not written in code?"

"Well, what good is a code if no one gets the message in the first place?"

"I gave you that letter to see if you could be trusted. To do as you were instructed."

"No one came. I had no instructions for that. So I destroyed the letter."

"How do you know no one came?"

"Because I was there all night. I did as you instructed."

"Did you fall asleep?"

"Of course."

"You can never fall asleep in this situation. You must always remain awake, you must remain vigilant. That is the lesson of last night. You fell asleep—and so you could not be trusted."

"Well, no one came."

"Are you certain?"

"I awoke with the letter still in my basket. But . . ."

"But?"

"But the bottle of absinthe you had given me was gone from the basket. I looked for it in the bushes, thinking perhaps I had dropped it. But that couldn't be, because I had had a few sips of it trying to keep the cold off."

"And did you ever find it?"

"Yes, on the way back here. It was in the middle of the road, smashed by a rock. There was shattered glass and a damp spot in the earth."

"So you see, someone was there. You were being observed the entire time."

"What kind of foolish game are you playing?"

"It wasn't me who took the bottle from your basket as you lay sleeping. I was at home snuggled in my bed with my good wife all night long."

"Then who?"

"That is a question you must never ask. You must never ask anything. You must do only as you are told. Do you understand that now?"

"Only if you give me my letters from Zermano."

"*One* letter. One letter for each message you deliver for me."

"This is blackmail."

"No, this is war. You must decide which side you are on. We all must take sides."

"I'm not for any side that uses violence."

"You no longer have that luxury. You must ask yourself—are you motivated only by your love for a man, or will you serve a higher purpose?"

"There is no higher purpose than love."

"You are quite right about that. And there is no higher love than for one's country."

"There is for me."

"Well then, if you want to save this love, you must serve your country."

Village of Reigne

Dearest Francisco,

The sanctity of love's innocence is a candle that burns only once. One prays the candle will continue to burn after the short night of innocence breaks to a new dawn. Such a violent hope to hold. We are so violent.

Finally . . . finally! I hold in my hand a letter from you. I've reread it and reread it. It seems we have cried an ocean of tears for each other. If only we could swim to the middle of that ocean and embrace, drown in each other's arms, into peaceful oblivion. We cannot—it's a poetic notion that shall never come to pass. But what we had still burns bright in your letter, that candle of hope I hold. In its glow I can still see the apples of the morning through your eyes, the swallows over the vineyards dipping to warm currents of wind, the lizards preening themselves on the rock walls dividing freshly tilled fields, the colors of the grasses changing with the passing sun of each day. I cling to this, I caress each word on the page you have written to me. I cannot help but swim to you in this sea of memory, created as much by laughter as by tears.

My mind goes back in an endless whirl of dampness and heat. The moldy scented air of the abbey the morning after the Bastille Day dance, the naked children of the château laughing beneath the clock tower. I still hear their laughter. We were on the road from the cherry orchard to the dance in Ville Rouge. I wanted to show you the ruins of the Marquis's château, tilting like a broken crown atop a steep hill. We parked the Bearcat in the village below and walked through the coolness of a narrow cobblestone street winding upward. The end of the street curved away from us as we climbed, our final destination continuing to elude us, disappearing from sight. High stone walls on either side prevented us from seeing into the houses we passed. We could hear the murmur of conversation as families sat on their patios having lunch. We could hear birds chattering in the branches of fig trees. The scent of peaches and cold strawberry soup permeated the air. Each step we took unveiled another sensation. Higher we climbed, until we were above all the houses and had a view down onto the private lunches on the patios we could only sense as we walked by. Everything was normal; it was the kind of Provençal scene that postcards love to celebrate and city sophisticates love to deride. But what we witnessed next was not normal.

It was as if we had been led to that spot to glimpse the original Garden of Eden. That garden was before us, an apparition, like a play enacted only for our benefit. The play was so intimate and innocent it seemed we were part of it; yet it was something we both knew we could never convey to others, for they wouldn't believe us. Others would think that the two of us, so in love, had projected that love into a forbidden fantasy garden beneath the crumbling stone columns of the Marquis' notorious château. What we saw was not perverted. It was spontaneous nature: naked children.

From our angle of vision we could see the children, but they could not see us. They were playing in the back garden of a stone house out of sight of their parents, who lingered over the remains of a long lunch, laughing at family anecdotes. There were two sets of parents at the lunch table, one French, the other from a northern country, their accented voices unself-consciously loud. The children around the corner paid no heed to their parents; they were more interested in exploring their exotic differences.

The girl was French, about six years old, in a splashy colored sundress, her hair perfectly braided down her back and anchored with a blue bow flaring out like the wings of some extraordinary bird. Her tiny toenails were painted bright pink and flashed as she moved her exquisite feet in open-toed sandals. She was every mother's darling, the apple of every father's eye. She was confident in her skin and her eyes sparkled with devil-may-care coquetry. She knew that her supple body exacted from others a kind of supplicant obeisance. She did not yet know why this was, but it was. If she turned her leg just so, and her smallish hips jutted just so, and if her lips pouted in just such a manner, well then, she was just too cute for people to stand. So people wanted to hug her, or tickle her, or run their fingers through her hair, or lick her up like vanilla ice cream. In her mind there was nothing wrong with this, nothing unusual, and certainly nothing sinful. She was simply and knowingly, in her heart and gestures, the prize of the universe; a powerful angel that could light up the world and make it sigh and cry over perfect innocence.

And the boy? Oh Francisco, you remember how he was? He was her opposite: awkward, uncertain, and fascinated by her power. He was caught in a web that had begun to be spun centuries before he existed. He was seven or eight years old, taller than she, dressed in shorts, T-shirt, and sandals. He didn't have a clue how she could leverage the world with her provocative cuteness. He didn't understand at all why she was such a *drama*. There was an air of mischief, mystery, and play about her that seemed to bubble up from some subterranean spring deep within her.

If he had any idea of who Eve was, he would have run. Even with no idea of Eve he was still nervous and shy, not knowing if he was going to be sheared like a lamb or shot like a rabbit. For there was great danger in what this girl was whispering to him in their play, the two of them half hidden in shadows of an arched stone doorway. Their parents called out to them from around the corner, making certain these prized possessions hadn't wandered off or been swooped up by a jealous sun.

The little girl spoke in quick whispers, close into the boy's ear. He was nervous at being so near to her. The look on his face was a mix of incomprehension and incredulity. Perhaps he was taken aback by what she was suggesting. Perhaps, unlike his parents, he didn't have a complete understanding of the French language, and thought he had misheard what she intended. She slipped off her sandals and continued to whisper to him. His face finally registered comprehension. He slipped off his sandals too. She laughed and stepped into his sandals. They were too big on her delicate feet as she spun around in a little dance of glee before him. She was wearing his shoes now— and she insisted he wear hers. Obediently, he struggled to pull her sandals on, but they were too small. She prodded him to continue, and he did, breaking the sandal buckles as he forced his feet in. He stared down at this oddity, his feet constrained in girls' sandals. He was teetering on the edge of the absurd, the edge of a girl's world. He gazed quickly around. He was out of sight of his parents, but he had an expression of being exposed, caught in the act, as if the mates at his all-boys' school were seated at their desks, watching him parade around in girls' sandals, their laughter a chorus of male mockery.

She was not through with him. She stabbed him with more whispers. Now his expression was just plain dumbstruck. He stepped back into the shadows as she stepped out into the sun. With a quick laugh, she pulled the sundress up and over her head. She stood before him in a naked glow, except for his sandals and her high-waisted little-girl panties. She swung the dress back and forth, taunting him. How could he let this little girl out-dare him? He was a big boy. He was not afraid. And besides, no one was *really* looking. No one could see. No one would tell. That's what she promised with her hot smiling whispers. He slowly pulled his T-shirt off. She was fascinated by his bony white chest, and the two flat pinpricks of pale nipples. She pinched one of the nipples and he held his breath, not wanting her to know its effect on him as she studied his face with the delight of a novice scientist staring into a microscope for the first time, watching protozoa split.

She whispered for him to go further. After all, she was not ashamed of what she had to offer. Her legs were lean, her belly was taut, her shoulders were smooth, her flesh was firm, it was all just her. If he wanted, he could feel her, the scientist didn't mind being dissected. But he kept his hands to himself, not fully comprehending her game. She swung her dress again before him in another dare. She was down to her panties; it was his turn now.

He unbuttoned his shorts and pushed them over his white underpants. The shorts fell to his ankles and he kicked them off. She was delighted. He really was brave. They eyed each other warily, two armies on either side of the divide. She reached out and touched her finger to the center of his chest, then drew it down to his navel. So perfect to have a real live doll to play with. Then she froze as she heard her mother call her name.

The boy's eyes widened in terror. Was her mother about to get up from the table and discover them? He trembled. The girl called out to her mother that all was okay in the garden. The two children waited for the next intrusion, but it didn't come. They were safe. She whispered that she wanted everything off him. He shook his head in a firm no. She whispered again. He was not to be moved. She, with all the nonchalance of one squeezing toothpaste out of its tube, hooked her thumbs under the elastic of her panties and slipped them off. There she stood, the perfect little statue in all her glory—and, like a statue, incapable of inhibition.

He was astonished. Not that she was naked, but that she had the courage to do it. She was younger and smaller than he, yet she led the way. She belittled him by her action. He might as well have been standing there in a raincoat and rubber boots compared to her. How had he gotten himself into this predicament? He tugged at his own underpants indecisively, then pulled them off before he could think better of it.

I held my breath with that little girl as she stared in wonder. There wasn't much between his legs, that wasn't the wonder. It was that she had mastered the art of seduction. She had persuaded him to follow her. This created a new charge between them, a lick of lightning exposing anarchy, their flesh set free, their spirits floating. That is why she did what she did next, quite quickly and without thinking. She pulled on his underpants and whispered that he put on hers. He did, struggling with the small elastic band, but finally succeeding. There they stood, two statues with the roles reversed.

She gazed at him with such compassion and reverence. He had actually followed her lead; now she was him and he was her. Swiftly her expression changed, became a blank. Suddenly she slapped him. He was stunned. And as if she had no control of her hand, she smacked him again. He wanted to cry but he couldn't. He was a little man and could not admit the pain of humiliation. She slapped him again, so hard his whole body shook. She laughed. For he had followed her too far with too little resistance. She no longer had respect for him. If she could so easily get him to be her, then what need did she really have of him in the end? As she laughed a strange surge came up from his loins and stiffened between his legs, causing a swell in the ill-fitting panties. He wasn't hard, he was too young to be, but he was aroused. Aroused by all the confusion she had created around him and all the confusion she stirred in him. She touched emotions he didn't know he had. His flesh responded with sensations he had never felt before. A shudder of shock went through him as she pointed at the swelling between his legs, pointing her finger at a fresh source of vulnerability—vulnerability for both of them. She somehow knew that her inexplicable cruelty toward him had evoked a swelling that one day would stand at attention barking demands of its own. Neither of them would be safe then. This abstraction was like a hammer hitting a crystal ball: she shattered into uncontrollable giggles.

Francisco, I squeezed your hand so hard. The clock tower, which rose above the tiled rooftops behind the children, chimed the late afternoon hour. The children's parents called for them, getting up from the table, chairs scraping back. The children hurriedly pulled on their clothes over each other's underpants—surely there would be some fancy explaining to do later. The parents came into the garden to collect their treasures. The children whined disagreeably that the afternoon had to end so soon, especially since they had been so good and not caused an unpleasant moment. Then they were all gone. Vanished.

The two of us were left standing alone, staring into the empty garden. We had witnessed something so private and primal that we knew we could never share it with anyone else, just as the children knew that they could never share or speak of this to others—that one day, when they had forgotten each other's names and faces, they would remember only the sensation, the feelings they caused in each other without knowing why.

But I knew why. As we moved to leave I looked down. There, behind a blooming lilac bush, was the truth, hidden from the little boy the whole time he was ensnared in a game he could never win. On the ground were pots and pans in neat rows, each filled with mud drying in the sun. Delicious dirt pies and cakes, sprinkled with flower-petal frosting. It was the little girl's kitchen, her play place where she practiced for the future expected of her. Little did the boy suspect, despite all the enigmatic excitement the girl represented, that where her world really was headed lay behind that fragrant bush. She had created a home in her heart long before she would invite any man to share it with her.

We stood above the garden, holding hands even more tightly to prove to ourselves that what we had seen was not a lovers' hallucination, but real. The clock in the tower chimed again, startling us back to the present, reminding us that time is love's executioner. But we were reluctant to let go. We had become the children. Their spirit had entered us, or awakened what was always there. I was a girl with you. Isn't that what most women want in the beginning, to be a girl with her boy, so she may grow into a woman, giving all, reinventing herself inside a larger self? I held your hand like a girl. A schoolgirl walking with her burden of books, dreaming dreams that dare her to risk all. I wanted my clothes off. I wanted you in me everywhere so I could completely surround you. I did not want to be invaded by you, but desired to include you anywhere my body could receive you. You in me, for me to be you, being me. My mouth full, my heart kissing, my soul sucking. No sweet surrender, only a seed sowing. Couldn't you feel? I held your hand like a schoolgirl with breasts burning under her blouse. I was so open to you, no woman could be wider. I was a sea for you to swim in. I dip my hand into the sea's current, its scent on my fingers, on my breath, on my tongue. I want the taste of your unsuspecting boy stiffness in my mouth. Waves of heat crush over me from a cloudless sky. My fingers tremble. Between my lips the tip of the flame burns brighter. I make a thousand cuts on my body for you to enter. I feel the prick of your boy stiffness in the crease of my soul. Such is a woman on the furthest edge of desire.

And now I am left in isolation, alone in my bed with memories of the children. My head bends, my mouth touches my breasts, my lips taste a spot of milk on thickening brown nipples. I want to suck, to feel what will flow. Only my own sobbing comes, not the gentle sigh of a baby nursing. It is my own breath of life, exhausted when I turn from your phantom kiss.

I am haunted by children—all children. The sun burns a hole through my nightdress, through the thousand cuts where you once were. The hollow moon blinds my eyes. I will tell you now, as no one else can hear and we are all alone, I am frightened, terrified of what's to come. But I shall go forward.

Love is not about going back, but moving toward something. We have both been broken, we must grow new wings. I kiss the stumps of your new wings. I am flying now in this bed of memory. The bed moves beneath me, rattles and spins, moving into the clouds, ascending up above the world where no one can see my red laughter, blue tears.

Louise

Village of Reigne

Darling Man,

I must be very circumspect. Even though I am not mailing these letters to you now, as they could be opened and examined by censors, I am still fearful of putting down everything that happens to me here, as it involves others, and their lives could be placed in danger. How hesitant I am even to write these words. I have devised a place to hide these letters: the false bottoms of my knitting baskets. Knitting is a solace to me, since there is so little time left before the baby arrives. I have knitted clothes and blankets, my fingers never stop moving. This is good since my mind is restless and wanders easily. Did I tell you I am teaching in the little village school? There was a notice one day posted outside the town hall that a teacher was needed. Certainly my father, who sacrificed so much for my university education, never intended that I would end up instructing children in the third and fourth grades. But these are times in which we all are occupied in ways never imagined before. At first I only taught third grade, but the teacher disappeared one night, perhaps because she was Jewish. It is now forbidden for Jews to be teachers. Who knows? When people disappear the reason is almost never given. Were they sent east to work in the munitions factories? Were they conscripted and banished to some forlorn outpost? Were they shot for running contraband? Were they one of those never found after gunfire was heard in the mountains at night? Were they among those who wear the yellow cloth star sewn on their jackets and are driven away in trucks by armed guards? It could happen to anyone, and it happened to many at the local school. I am a teacher and so I have a little money to get by with.

I can hear you now saying, "Why don't you sell the art I left with you? That is what it is for!" I cannot sell it, for then suspicion would form as to who I really am. Also it would be a trail leading you to me; you would track me down to this small village. Besides, even if I could sell the art, I wouldn't, for the only ones with money to afford it have the blood of betrayal on them. I don't want that blood to touch my hands or the milk that my baby will drink. So I teach. I make a small difference with small lives. Mine has become a small life, and I like it that way. So many people have so little, have lost so much.

This countryside was never a place to make a person rich. It has always been a place of hard work. There is no reason that my life should be any different. I make do. I have your letters. Oh yes, I have them! Sometimes one a week. For now Royer is coming through, true to his word, trading me one of your letters for each message I deliver for him. And that is what I have been reluctant to write to you about, what it is that Royer does, what it is that I do. As I said, it involves other people who could be put in jeopardy if my letters were ever read by the wrong person. Even though now I do not see faces, I see only darkness and shadows on moonless nights. On nights with moonlight, I see hat brims and woolen caps pulled down to obscure faces. You do not know what I am talking about, do you? I am speaking in riddles.

Let me tell you that I was wrong about some things regarding

Royer. Wrong about him in the most important way. He is a man who loves his country and takes great risks. And now I assist him. I am a small link in a larger chain. My assistance grew from my love for you. I will admit that in the beginning I was afraid to become involved, but it was the only way to get your letters. So my love for you led me on a path I otherwise would never have taken. I must speak in riddles of what I do, and even then I might divulge too much. I hope not. But I think you will understand how I have become what I am.

At first Royer continued to give me sealed messages to deliver. I followed the directions mapped on the outsides of the envelopes. I had to elude armed patrols for I was always out at night after curfew. I did this again and again, reaching my appointed rendezvous point, then waiting for someone to come. But no one ever did.

After a while I began to suspect that Royer was continuing to play some kind of game with me, to string me along and make me risk my life each night for a letter from you. I thought of him in his warm bed as I slept on the stony ground. I could see him snoring next to his plump wife, his extended belly gurgling and digesting whatever meal she had drugged him with that evening at dinner. I know she cooked him feasts. He bragged about the steak-frites he ate, the shoulders of pig, the breasts of chicken, the goose pâtés, the duck soups, the good wines he drank, the bottled Vichy water he brushed his teeth with. All of this at a time when many people are starving, when meat rations are often useless because there is no meat in the shops, when half the children in my classes are fading away from malnutrition, when many of the farms one walks by have no more barking dogs because the farmers have killed them to give their families a decent meal. Almost the only ones with dogs are the uniformed patrols roaming the countryside, guarding the main roads and important public buildings. When one does hear a barking dog it means trouble to steer clear of—or one will be met with suspicion, forced by uniformed men holding the dogs to show identity papers, prove one's existence, explain one's movements. In the center of all this is Royer, a well-fed postman coming and going with impunity. A man highly suspect, a man with whom I collaborate in order to get your letters. So what does that make me?

Is not everyone who compromises a collaborator? There are no exceptions. This is what I told myself as I slept on the stony ground night after night waiting for the rendezvous that Royer promised but never came. Would he himself spring from the shadows to accost me—at the mouth of a cave, or on the twist of a mountain trail, or on a small wooden bridge crossing a torrent? Me there alone, waiting, shivering, with not even a sip of absinthe to keep me warm. Since that first night when I was sent out by Royer and discovered my bottle of absinthe smashed the next morning, I have never touched it again. That smashed bottle was a sign that I had to face my demons and fears alone. My baby shouldn't be polluted by my weakness. I have to survive my hallucinating pain in order to prevail. I need your letters for my survival and my baby needs me for its survival. So who cares what it takes for me to survive? Who cares if I collaborate with Royer? In the end it is really a conspiracy of nature for my baby to be born, but it is up to me to make sure that it be born healthy.

Another knock on my door. Is it the mistral? Where have I heard that knock before? Is it you? Is it someone to take me away? I'm afraid to look. I place my hand on my stomach instinctively to protect what is there. If I hold my breath, listen hard, and stay quiet, whatever is out there will think no one is home. My windows are heavily curtained because of the blackout restrictions. No one can see in. The knock comes again. Is it day or night out there? Maybe I should take this letter I'm writing, all the letters, and throw them into the fire so as not to incriminate myself, or others. I'm not sure . . . not sure. I think I feel the baby move. Could it be moving so soon? If you were here I would open my dress so you could kneel between my legs, put your ear to the mound of my stomach, and listen for the little heart beating. Or is that the wind beating again outside? I'm not going to answer it. Hear it? Little heart or big wind? Makes no difference now. If I let the fire die down, whoever is out there will think no one is inside any longer. They will go away.

I pull a blanket over myself and my baby, and I think back to when I was a little girl. I had my first cat and treated it like a baby. I used to make a bed of flowers in a straw basket. Then I'd put the cat in and rock the basket. That cat never wanted to stay in that damn basket. Later, when I was a teenager—and this is the truth—I put another of my cats in a basket, but this time it couldn't get out because I danced with that basket as if its handle were the hand of my Prince Charming, swinging around and around. That terrified cat couldn't get out until the ball was over and the pumpkin coach showed up. What music was it I used to dance to then? Oh yes, Billie Holiday! Now *that's* a woman who knew how to keep a pussy in a basket.

Am I asleep yet? That damn knocking. Trees swaying, cradle rocking in the treetops. Who smashed my absinthe bottle while I waited with Royer's first letter? Someone watching me? Watching over me? Are you really here, my darling? Am I dreaming? I like to think that my baby and I have the same dreams. Maybe we dream of the milky breath of goats on our bodies. Maybe we dream of silkworms. Do silkworms dream? Do they dream they will one day end up as a holiday tablecloth folded up in a dresser drawer every day of the year but one, when they are brought into the splendid light? Do they dream of being a bride's finest undergarment, carefully constructed, painstakingly woven, silken perfection of such chaste intentions, only to be so hastily discarded on the wedding night? Do they dream as they circle and cloy, swimming upstream, already spoken for by sly haberdashers and coy handmaidens? I will never have a wedding day. I will never have the honeymoon night.

Am I crazy or dreaming with this loud knocking in my head, as if the golden green honey of absinthe still singes my brain, sings a different kind of holiday jazz? Go away, whoever, whatever is outside my door! There's no one in here, don't you know? No one except a pregnant woman with a bundle of letters in her hands. She's ready to throw the letters into the fire.

Village of Reigne

My Lost Man,

Last night I woke up in the cold. I was alone in the forest. The camp fire had gone out. Something was nudging at the back of my neck as I lay on the ground shivering beneath my blanket. I came out of my groggy sleepiness, feeling that nudging. Then I realized what it was. A damp nose, a breath that smelled of earth and new-born lamb. In my terror I knew I had one moment before I was dead. I had to be very still as the last nudge pressed into my neck, searching for the softest spot to bite. I swung around with my elbow striking straight into the teeth of a wolf. It glared at me with its yellow eyes, then ran off, disappearing into the night. I looked around. Where was my baby? Did the wolf take my baby? I felt my stomach. There was a hole in it. A deep hole gnawed away, a bottomless pit. I had fallen asleep. I was not a good mother. I was not a protector. I was not on guard. I had fallen asleep and the wolf ate the baby out of my belly.

That was my dream, and I remembered it clearly as I came awake. I felt my stomach. My baby was still there. My nipples ached, the skin of my breasts swollen with the job they will have to do. Your letters? Did I burn them? I looked at the fire. It is out. I am cold. I am shivering. Scattered at my feet are your letters. I did not burn them. There is no more knocking at my door. All is silence. Is it still night? I don't know. I open the thick blackout curtains. It is day. The passing mistral has polished the sky a diamond blue. All the distance glitters in sunshine. Mont Ventoux, kilometers away, seems just beyond the tips of my fingers. Its plateau is smoothed with snow, like the pure white wing of a sleeping swan.

I must start a fire for my baby. I stir what few coals are left in the fireplace. I kneel to the coals and blow. A few flames come up and I toss on some sticks of olive wood to snap and sparkle with heat. This is my life, the beginning of a day, simple things. Simple things without you. Like the thunder in the distance last night. For some reason I have always been afraid of thunder, even as a child—especially as a child. You thought it funny when my body tensed as booming thunder unfolded across the sky. But you loved the way I curved to you, seeking shelter in your arms, my lips finding safety in the soft nest of your chest hairs. Last night it thundered. My body moved to the space you once filled, but you were not there. I felt the swell of my belly, the baby beneath. I am no longer afraid of thunder.

I open my front door. The little cobblestone lane is empty. No clouds, no thunder, no people. I hear something knocking against the other side of the door. I step around and see that on a nail pounded into the door hangs a basket by its handle. I look up and down the little lane. There is still no one. Should I open the basket? Who knows what could be inside. A torn piece of a flour sack covers the top of the basket. There could be a bomb inside. I carefully take the basket down from the nail, step back inside my house, close the door, and bolt the lock.

I place the basket on the table. It must have been what was knocking against the door all night in the wind. Royer said he was going to send me another communication to deliver. Is this what he meant?

But then he doesn't know where I live, I'm certain of that; I always elude him when leaving Ville Rouge. Who could this basket be from? Carefully I pull off the cloth cover.

Wrapped in oak leaves is a bar of handmade soap. I pick it up and smell it—honey and lavender. Soap is precious; as you know, it is rationed. There is cheese, a smooth goat cheese bound in grape leaves, just the thing to make my baby's bones strong. And there is sausage, a dark slab of cured boar meat with the scent of truffles and wild herbs. I sit down at the table, overcome as I dig deeper into the treasure chest. At the bottom of the basket is a large jar of honey with a label pasted on it, which reads: *Honey of All the Flowers*. Where have I seen that style of jar before? That kind of handwritten label? Then I remember the honey we bought from the Bee Keeper. I recall that market day in the street with you, next to the Bee Keeper's stand, was the stand of the little lady we called "the nun of cheese." She always dressed in a starched convent-style blue dress and wore a broad-brimmed straw hat with a thin veil protecting her face from the sun. She had her jewels spread out on a damp linen cloth, round eucharists of cheese, all in service of Our Lord of the Goat Cheese. She was tiny, but stood erect with dignity, never taking her eyes off the perfectly lined rows, a true saint serving in the holy order of the curdled chèvre. Could she have left the basket? How could she know that these things were what I cherished most, for my baby's health and my own cleanliness?

Then I suddenly thought that *you* had left the basket for me. That you had found me. Once in Paris you gave me honey lavender soap for my birthday, to remind me of my Provence childhood. Such a simple and true present, the thoughtful one, not the expensive one. I remember bathing with that soap for the longest time, running its sweet scent on my skin. Then I brought myself to you, glowing and naked, a country girl wanting to be corrupted by your city kisses.

But no, you didn't leave the basket. If you found me you would take me away with you, of that I'm sure. I have made certain that you cannot find me, for within my womb is the ache for life that all women have, an ache denied or accepted. Deep within there is still a war between us. The life of art is creation, the creation of woman is life. If you returned to me now I would be mere putty in your hands, the golden light of the muse transformed. But you cannot get your hands on me. Perhaps one day, my love, I can give myself to you that way again. A day when all the wars between men and men, between women and men, are ended. But as for this day? I must admit, I don't have a clue as to who left the basket. So now I am concerned with only two things: to eat cheese and take a long bath in honey and lavender.

I have not had a bath like this in such a long time and as I bathe I think of my new-found treasures. It would take six months' worth of ration coupons to obtain what I now have—if it were available at all. Maybe some black marketeers left the basket on my door by mistake? Will they come back to get it? Perhaps the police will break in and accuse me of being a smuggler? Who cares. In my bath the water is creamy honey, the lavender tickles my nostrils. I run the smooth bar of soap over my skin. I feel myself as you feel me. It's been so long. My swollen breasts are like those of a strange woman. My hips are now broad and my buttocks rounded by new muscles from carrying the weight I've gained in my belly. You would hardly know me. Would you still want me? More? Or less? It has been so long. I soak and soak. When I get out of the tin tub my skin glistens. I see myself in the mirror as I run the towel over my body. This is not the body you have sketched, drawn, and painted so many times, in so many ways, from so many angles, as if I were a mathematical problem you were trying to solve, as if I were an amorphous weight in the universe that you needed to shape in order to secure earth's gravitational balance. I see the bright gold ring in the shadowed V between my thighs. It burns a pretty color as I move my legs. No one except you knows the meaning of this ring. You have never painted me with it. No one knows its origin. It is our secret.

How well I remember when the ring was embedded in my flesh. It was cold. It was Paris. It was not the Paris of light, it was silence and darkness. An occupied city. A city mourning for itself. But still you painted. You painted in a fury. You painted as if all life depended on it. As if you sought to revive with a counter-energy all the life of the streets that had been strangled. Your studio filled with work, stacks of completed canvases. The smell of turpentine and oils permeated the air, your hair and skin. There was a light you were trying to seize, a light that had died out of the city.

Then you read in the papers that it was going to be a hundred years since the ashes of Napoléon were brought back from St. Helena to Paris. The memory of that day, a century before, still excited Parisiens. Never had there been such pomp and glory as the ceremony when Napoléon's ashes were deposited in the tomb of Les Invalides. By comparison it made the ticker-tape parade in New York, celebrating Lindbergh's first airborne transatlantic journey, seem like a mere high school graduation in a tiny village. Now, to commemorate the anniversary of Napoléon's triumphant posthumous return, the new emperor of occupied Paris was returning Napoléon's son's ashes from Vienna, where they had been interred in a crypt of the Capuchin church among the tombs of the imperial Habsburgs. At last father and son could be reunited on French soil after the historic consequence of tragic separation. At first the papers reported that there was to be as much fanfare for the return of the son as there had been for the father. But then the papers were controlled by the new emperor, so who was to know the truth? As suddenly as news of this great day appeared it seemed to disappear. No one quite knew when the son was to be brought back, and whether the public was to be invited or just the great generals who served the new emperor's armies. But you found out that the son was to arrive at night by a special armored train to the Gare de l'Est. His coffin would be carried through the streets to Les Invalides. You wanted to paint that scene. Not the literal scene—the pomp of a cavalry escort of plumed horses and uniformed men, the *caisson* wagon draped with the French flag rolling along cobblestone streets, the flaming torches throwing flickers of illumination up the walls of massive buildings. No, not that. You wanted to capture the mood of light that played in men's hearts. You were not a figurative painter in search of a passing landscape. You were a madman who dragged me into the darkness with you, even though the streets were heavily guarded because of the curfew. You pulled me through shadows, up alleys, along narrow passageways, stopping beneath the arch of a stone bridge spanning the river. The sound of horses' hooves and the mournful beat of military drums drew closer, until we heard the snorting horses and marching boots above, crossing the bridge with the *caisson*. This is what you had come for, what you had risked our lives for. Or so I thought, until you pushed me against the wall of the tunnel and kissed me, as if you could find the light you sought inside of me rather than on the surface of the river glittering from torchlight around us. I raised my skirts to you, feeling the cold stone wall on the back of my legs as you pressed against me.

You whispered, "Will you marry me?"

"When?"

"Tonight?"

"Impossible. How can we be married tonight?"

You didn't answer. A strange look came into your eyes as you nearly shouted, "The Duke of the Reichstadt is passing by and we are making love in front of him!"

I pressed my lips to yours to silence you. Over your shoulder I saw a young man stop before the wall on the opposite side of the river. He quickly scrawled in red paint across the stone: KEEP YOUR CORPSE! GIVE US BACK OUR MILLION PRISONERS!

From the bridge above came the sounds of shouting, gunning motorcycle engines, and squealing tires. You pulled me closer, your words insistent.

"You'll never regret marrying me. Trust me."

You kissed me before we ran into the shadows and gunshots echoed along the stone wall where we had been standing.

It took us until dawn to make our way undetected through the heavily patrolled streets, around sandbagged guard posts manned by steel-helmeted soldiers with machine guns.

When we finally climbed the stairs to the atelier and were once again safe I surprised myself by saying, "I want a church wedding."

"A church wedding?" The expression in your eyes was one I'd never seen before, a disfigured cynicism, as if you were peering at me from the phantasmic depths in one of Goya's night paintings. "A church wedding!" You put your head down, a bull ready to charge. "Louise, you don't understand anything. I know what they are going to do. I saw it all in Spain where they practiced for this war. Starving men covered with lice sleeping naked on the frozen ground. Men having to squat from a log over a pit of shit to relieve themselves—if they slipped they would drown in excrement. All of Europe is drowning in its own shit."

"Then why do you want to marry me, if it's all shit?"

You fell to your knees before me, you said nothing for a long time. You held both my hands in yours. I felt the calluses of your palms, the strength of your fingers, and I heard your voice.

"Because you are the only thing between me and them. Without you, I know in my soul, I would cross the line and join them. Every man has in him an ancient blood feud that drums in his ears, that makes him want to tear off his mask of civility and just take what he wants—not work for it, nor earn it, just take it and kill any other man that stands in his way. Only a thin veil of light keeps me anchored on this side of the line, and you are that light. Otherwise there is too much pain, even when I'm painting. The only thing that makes it tolerable, keeps me living on this earth, is your light."

"Where's the wedding ring?"

"Then you'll do it?" You jumped up, alive with joy. You opened a drawer in your big mahogany dresser and pulled a velvet box from beneath a jumble of clothes. You popped the lid of the box and a gold ring glowed inside. I held out my hand.

"No." You took my hand and kissed my wedding-ring finger. "This is not where you will wear it. No one can know we are married. It's too dangerous now. We have to wait to tell the world."

"I won't wait. I've been waiting too long. I'll be your wife, but I won't remain a mistress."

"Yes, I am going to marry you. Only the ring is not going on your finger."

"Why?"

"Because we can't trust the future. We can only trust what is between us."

"Then we should get married in a church, if this is only between us and God."

"No, a church is not strong enough. They will burn all the churches down. They will burn everything to the ground before this war is over." You held the ring up delicately between your thumb and forefinger. "But this they will not get. This will remain hidden. Only you and I will know of its existence. Only you and I will know, every time we make love, it will be there—our ring for eternity."

"What do you mean? Every time we make love?"

You pushed on the ring with your fingers and it unclasped, exposing an arrow-sharp prong that held it together.

"Lie back, Louise. It's the only way. One day you will understand why it must be this way. On that, I give you my solemn word."

"And what about you? Where are you going to be pierced with your gold ring?"

"It's too dangerous for me to have a ring. It will mean there's a wife, and if there's a wife, they might come looking."

"I still don't understand."

"You don't have to understand. You just have to believe in our love."

I lay back on the bed. I did trust you, with my heart, with my body.

I heard the sound of water filling a tin bowl, then the smell of gas from the stove, a striking match, a burning flame. I heard the ring being dropped into boiling water. You pushed my thighs open, and tenderly, you rubbed at my very center with cotton soaked in alcohol. The scent of alcohol filled the room, alcohol burned my skin.

You got up and came back with the ring, holding it up to the light bulb over my head. I could see the sharp prong intended to cut through my skin and into the clasp, piercing through me to complete a perfect golden circle. The prong was no bigger than the beak of a hummingbird. This would not hurt, and we would be married. I was lying to myself.

You reached between my legs.

"This is going to hurt, Louise. Think of something beautiful."

"Why are you doing this? Who are we really hiding from?"

"Something beautiful. Think . . ."

"I think I'm mutilating myself for you."

"Love is always a mutilation of the self."

"My God, it hurts."

"Think beautiful."

"Francisco it's hurting!"

You kissed me. I bit your lip. You kept your mouth on mine. My cry was muffled. The pain did not go away. Not *there*. Not in the center of my vulnerability. I thought of something beautiful. Provence in the winter. The singularity of it, the harsh, abrupt season dying such a public death so that all would know the price that was being paid for something to be born. I saw the winter grapevines, rows and rows, marching over hills and across broad valleys, stitching the earth together so that it holds against the bold mistral wind that would blow it to hell. They say that when Christ was dying on the cross it was a windy day too, that each tear he shed was whipped in the fury and carried over the Mediterranean Sea to fall like a translucent purple pearl on the barren earth of Provence. Each pearl turned to a seed, and the seed to a vine, and the vine to grapes. They say that is why wine is the blood of Christ, and each autumn raisin is sweet, because Christ's tears were not from his pain, but from his joy.

As blood trickled down my thighs onto the sheet I heard your voice. "Don't cry, darling. We're married now. I will always love you."

"We're not married."

"What do you mean?"

"Who do *you* belong to?"

"Why you, of course."

"For how long?"

"Forever."

"That's not good enough."

I looked over at the sink. Your pearl-handled straight razor gleamed on the porcelain.

"Bring that to me."

You didn't say a word. Your eyes followed mine to the razor.

"Bring it."

You got up and went to the sink. You picked up the razor, a quizzical look on your face.

I raised myself painfully on the bed.

"Take your shirt off."

You pulled your shirt over your head and let it drop.

"Come to me."

You stepped up next to the bed.

"Kneel down. Kneel the way you would before a priest, as if you were taking Holy Communion at your own wedding mass."

You knelt, confused.

I took the razor from you and flicked its blade out.

"Think of something beautiful."

You looked at me even more confused.

"Think of something *really* beautiful." I touched the edge of the razor to your skin. There was a guarded look of fear in your eyes. I pricked your skin with the blade. "What are you thinking?"

"I'm thinking . . . thinking of you on the first trip to Provence, about the field of flowers we drove past, and you wanted me to stop the car. I knew what you were going to do. I had seen you do it so often. Wherever you went flowers appeared and you gathered them in bundled bouquets. I think it is something in your Provençal touch. If you went walking in the Sinai Desert you would come back across the parched sands with a miraculous bouquet."

I drew the blade swiftly down on your chest, cutting a straight line.

"God, that hurts!"

"Keep thinking beautiful."

"I stopped the car. You got out. You went into the field and excitedly picked flowers. Some you broke off with your fingers; others, with stems too thick to break, you bit off. One broke your tooth, but you were so intoxicated you didn't feel the pain. You kept gathering flowers and filled the whole back seat of the Bearcat with them. A perfume engulfed us as we drove along, and I thought to myself, where does God make women like this, whose nature is to be surrounded by flowers? Does he have a special little room in heaven where he creates them? Oh Jesus that hurts!"

I pulled the blade deeply through your skin at a right angle. You winced, but did not cry out again. I folded the blade of the razor into its handle.

"Now, my darling, we are married."

I pressed my lips to your chest, tenderly kissing the blood from your wound. It would heal perfectly, and until your dying day there would always be, carved above your heart, a perfect **L**.

PART FOUR

Fool of Love

CERTAIN THINGS OCCUR in life and one keeps circling back to them. When fate brought Louise and Zermano to the cherry orchard in Provence on the Day of the Bees was such an event. From that day forward they would never again be free of each other—not through war or peace, fame or obscurity, even exile or death. My accidental discovery of their letters pried loose an enigma concealed for half a century. These personal writings, raw and unadorned, were never intended for other eyes. Sometimes as I read I was shocked out of an exquisitely shaped insight into naked revelation, where desire's anarchy overruled rhetoric. Peering at these private pages was a distinctly voyeuristic act. Often I placed my hand across a passage that appeared too explicit, asking myself: Do I have the right to know this? Eventually I would lift my hand and continue reading, but not without guilt. As I read further I questioned the ethics of exposing these letters to others. Should they be locked away? Should they be made available only to scholars researching Francisco Zermano's art? And then the ultimate question: Should they be destroyed?

There are other compelling questions. Zermano is still alive and does not know what happened to Louise. Do I not have an obligation to give her letters to Zermano and set his tortured mind at rest? These issues take on a power of their own, and I must confess there have been times when I wished I had never discovered the letters. I have become an unwilling player in the drama, unable to resist making an erotic identification with the two lovers. I have to be honest and ask: Am I obsessed with their story? The answer is yes. But if Louise had not intended for the letters to be found she would have destroyed them. She would not have left such a complete map unless she wanted someone to chart the course to her heart. So I decided I must follow the route she set down. The letters existed. It was my obligation to take them to Zermano, to make certain their message was delivered.

This decision was more easily made than carried out, for Zermano has not been seen in public since that day in 1969 when the American astronauts landed in the moon's Sea of Tranquillity. Around the world people watched that extraordinary event on television, unaware that at the same time one of the twentieth century's most important figures was disappearing. It was as if Zermano had departed for the dark side of the moon. He could not have become more "disappeared" if he had been one of those political dissidents in Latin America who are suddenly snatched from their daily lives and lost in oblivion.

Oblivion was not to be Zermano's fate. The world eventually demanded to know his whereabouts, or whether he was still alive. But his family and the Spanish government refused to give any information about him. No hospital records existed, no death certificate. Only his paintings remained; and as with all great artists after their passing, an inevitable aura of semi-divinity surrounded them. His art seemed not to have been constructed by human hands, invention, or force of will, but conjured up—no more to be questioned than the shape of a cloud.

The debate about Zermano's disappearance continues, entertaining the public and fueling endless books and biographical television broadcasts constructed on speculation and outright deception. There are those who say he is dead, or assassinated as a collaborator in World War II. Some posit that the Spanish government executed him, since his fame for exposing war's demonic proportions in his paintings could make him an embarrassing political liability.

Before my discovery of the letters I had my own theory about Zermano's disappearance. I deduced that Louise had resurfaced after decades and Zermano had abandoned his family for her. In order to avoid the shame and hysterical scrutiny such an action would provoke, the family denied any knowledge of Zermano after he disappeared. My belief in this theory was what took me to Provence after Louise died. I needed to determine if her death had been faked to mislead everyone. Now I know there is another story.

After Zermano completed his antiwar mural, *Archangel Gabriel Flames Down the Sky,* he quickly departed Paris. A dangerous voyage by fishing boat took him from a small harbor south of Cassis into the Mediterranean Sea, where patrolling warships were intent on sinking any vessel not flying their country's flag. That he survived an eight-day journey, eventually making it to the Balearic Islands, is something of a miracle. The other miracle is that the *Gabriel Flames* mural survived. Twenty-two feet long and eight feet high, it had been painted on a canvas bolted by its stretcher boards to a wall in Zermano's Paris atelier.

Once the mural was finished he built another wall in front to hide it. On this second wall he painted a mural depicting the industrial area along the Seine by night. In the painting, illuminated by malevolent energy, a dusty pall of ash is cast over the Seine as it flows past dilapidated factories. Fires burn on the banks of the river, spotlighting garish women who advertise their naked bodies with provocative thrusts, while behind them a conveyor belt transports an endless line of shadowy men to hell.

This work, unlike any other Zermano painting, bears an improbable title, *Nude Walking Her Man on a Leash.* Much has been written about it, and all the usual interpretations and condemnations have been applied. Some think it is a sexual metaphor for war; others that Zermano is a misogynist declaring war between the sexes. The painting remained in Zermano's atelier after the war because the city of Paris commandeered the space as part of its effort to relieve the housing shortage. The family living there prudishly placed large storage closets before the mural. Also, at this time many, from those in government to those in the arts, including Zermano, were being accused of collaboration with the enemy, so the embarrassing mural was better off forgotten.

And forgotten it was, until the atelier was removed from the public domain and sold as a private residence. The new buyer knew Zermano's work was being favorably reevaluated in America. He had the mural detached from the wall to be shipped to New York and discovered the masterpiece behind it, *Gabriel Flames*; he sent that off too. The French government, citing an obscure Napoleonic law, seized both pieces of art when they were declared at customs. The Spanish government also claimed ownership, asserting that Zermano, a Spanish citizen, had been forced to abandon his art due to "inhumane and incomprehensible duress during times of intense international conflict." A vicious court battle ensued. The ultimate disposition of the art did little to enhance the pride of either nation. The court ruled that both works belonged to the atelier's owner, so the art finally went to the highest bidder in New York.

I believe the explanation for Zermano's abandonment of Paris was simple. The loss of Louise was too painful; to him, she *was* France. He saw her in the color of the changing sky, in the sun setting on the Seine. He needed to escape. He did not want to be a painter who recorded only the devastation of the heart and the war—for that there were poets and photographers. He did not flee to America, as had so many other artists with the fire of Europe at their backs. He was not seeking to rebuild himself, he was already solid. He sought rootedness in simplicity. He returned to where he had begun, the island of Mallorca. The music, the stars, the light on the sea would again be his companions, and they would not speak to him of Louise. Zermano needed to survive; he cannot be condemned, as he has been by many agenda-driven socio-art critics, for returning to a country that was fascist at the time. If he had to live in a brutal world, then he would choose Spain, for there war had its origins in family battles, brother against brother, before it became religious dogma against secular ideology. He understood that; he could paint the psychology of that.

Zermano's return to Mallorca during the war attracted no attention, for the world stage was crowded with far more compelling characters. But when the war ended, and making money from making art could be tolerated and talked about by former combatants gazing at each other across the rubble of Europe, then Zermano was rediscovered. When Europe became prosperous again a parade of media appeared in Mallorca, waiting in cities, beach towns, and cafés to ambush Zermano with microphones and cameras. It was logical that one day he would disappear from Mallorca as quickly as he had disappeared from Paris. When his Spanish wife died and his children were grown, he vanished.

I spent an entire year of my life trying to contact Zermano. After going through the obvious channels like gallery owners, museum curators, and French and Spanish cultural officials, it became clear that the only way to Zermano was through his adult children. I repeatedly sent copies of my books on Zermano to the lawyer who represented the children, with the urgent message that I had something of importance to deliver to their father. I received no response, and the packages came back unopened. What I could not do was to inform anyone that I had the letters, for my ownership of them would be challenged by private and public entities; I could lose the letters in court and never know if they reached Zermano. Also, the furor they would create in the press, given their political context and erotic content, would make Zermano distance himself further from me. The last thing he wanted, I knew, was to have the most dramatic and intimate events of his life revealed at a time when his seclusion was paramount and his life growing short. There was only one recourse: I had to go to Mallorca and see where his footsteps led.

Day of the Bees

I applied for a sabbatical from my university and left the moment it came through. I wanted to see Mallorca as Zermano had fifty years earlier, arriving by sea, so I took the overnight ferry from Barcelona. On the deck of the ferry at dawn I was startled by the light. It was not the lavender light of Provence, nor the eye-splitting brilliance of North Africa so close by; it was a healing hue of gold, as if I were observing the world from within a glass bowl smeared with honey. Mountains rose up to form a vision of a jagged coastline that seemed to have been torn from a brochure advertising a timeless Mediterranean tableau. Quickly this vision faded. The ferry steamed closer to the island, and white concrete collars of high-rise tourist hotels choked once-paradisiacal coves.

Then the sweeping shoreline of a vast bay appeared. Beyond it loomed an architecture of Arab fantasy and gothic excess, stone spires and turrets of castles and cathedrals. The distant city of Palma glinted in dreamlike splendor. One could envision an Arab sheik in flowing white robes, or a Christian Crusader in shining armor, riding on horseback down from the mountains above, ready to enjoy the fruits of life after fighting a long war. This is also how it must have appeared to Zermano fifty years before, when the population of the city was one-tenth of what it was today, before the onslaught of cars and jets, a time in its way closer to the rhythms of shepherds and fishermen than to super-discos and hyper-markets.

In Palma I went directly to the Ministry of Culture to present a letter of introduction from my university confirming my credentials as a scholar. I thought I might find someone there sympathetic to my cause, willing to drop a hint as to the great artist's whereabouts. Indeed, I was received respectfully and given access to the Zermano archives, which filled three full floors. There wasn't much in the archives with which I wasn't familiar. The only thing different was to be able to handle the original materials, rather than to stare at them on a computer screen from six thousand miles away. The one surprise was a large number of previously untranslated lectures regarding the influence on Zermano of Ramón Llull, a thirteenth-century messianic mystic.

Ramón Llull lived variously as a Don Juan, a hermit, the tutor of a future king, the founder of Mallorca's first Franciscan monastery and Europe's first school of Oriental languages. His protean outpouring of over two hundred books, fired by his neoplatonic philosophy and his radical belief that Jews, Christians, and Moslems were all of one faith, resulted in his martyrdom in North Africa. Llull's death instigated one of history's first conspiracy theories. Revisionists still joust over whether he was killed by ignorant tribesmen or set up by the three organized religions who wanted him out of business. Llull's best-known work, *The Book of the Lover and the Beloved*, is rediscovered each year by students who regard it as the equal in significance to the *Song of Solomon* or *Das Kapital*.

The aesthetic connection between Llull and Zermano, Mallorca's native sons, was one I had never taken seriously. But Llull, the outlaw philosopher and first liberation theologian, is considered in some quarters to rank between the Pope and Christ, while Zermano fits between Velázquez and Goya. Even so, I had no reason to pursue the parallel theories of these two men any further. I abandoned the archives and queried Ministry officials as to where they guessed Zermano might be. This was frustrating, since Mallorquins are notoriously indirect. Their wariness is the result of centuries of domination, from the Vandals to the Spanish. So I was dealing not only with the cover-up of Zermano, but the island's paranoia.

The outside world has always posed a threat to the Mallorcan paradise; deception has been its best defense. From the Roman chariots that thundered across the inner plains, and the invaders from the Maghreb storming the coast, to modern mass tourism, Mallorca has been under attack. Today's outsider is met with a deceptive smile, a discourse on why the remaining natural splendor of the island must be saved, and a polite inquiry as to when the traveler would be leaving. A Mallorcan folk song best expresses this subterfuge: *"I went I know not where and met someone I don't remember. He asked me something I didn't understand so I can't recall my answer."* Everyone I queried about Zermano's whereabouts might just as well have sung me that lyric in reply. I was constantly asked when I had to return to my university, and assured that if documents pertaining to my search for Zermano were found after my departure they would be mailed to me. Still, I persevered.

In the Zermano archives were listed the locations of every place he had lived on the island. These I visited, hoping to find a clue. The first, a dilapidated fisherman's cottage in a pretty little harbor, was now a fancy seaside restaurant catering to residents of nearby mansions. The second, a deserted sixteenth-century convent during the time Zermano lived and painted there, now housed a medical school. The convent's former chapel, once Zermano's studio, was an amphitheater for surgical demonstrations. And on it went, more than seventeen different sites that had since been put to other uses or demolished in the name of progress. I found nothing leading to Zermano, and time was running out. I was left with no alternative but the one I detested most, for it made me feel like a pushy paparazzo: I had to go directly to the family and plead my case.

The family was notoriously uncommunicative and protective. I needed to persuade someone within their closed ranks to break the code of silence. Which one would be the most likely to yield? Of the three children, one son was a judge and the other a senator; my chances of convincing them to talk were probably nil. The third, a daughter, might be my only hope. Perhaps I could appeal to her sense of romance, noting that I was in possession of her father's love letters. Since the letters had been written before Zermano met her mother, and since the mother was deceased, she would not be betraying her by helping me. Fortunately, the daughter was the youngest of Zermano's three children, which meant she might be less traditional than older Mallorcans, who are fond of asking: "Which is bigger, the world inside Mallorca, or the world outside Mallorca?"

I found out where the daughter lived in the most straightforward way: I looked in the phone book. There were her name, address, and telephone number. I called the number and the telephone was immediately answered by a woman. I explained who I was and asked if I had the pleasure of speaking with Señorita Serena Zermano.

"Who is calling?" she inquired.

I identified myself again and she hung up. I called back, and in the most polite manner asked if I might leave a message for Señorita Zermano.

"No," came the answer. The phone went dead.

Perhaps I had been speaking to the maid, who had been instructed to hang up on anyone with whom she wasn't familiar. I decided to wait and call later, but when I did, no one answered. I phoned the next morning—no answer. I called all day long and into the night until the woman answered again. I made my inquiry. She asked which Serena Zermano I wanted to speak with. I replied the daughter of the painter. Here was my chance, a small crack to slip through—I quickly added that I was in possession of some of Señor Zermano's most personal items. There was a long silence before she spoke:

"Personal items?"

"Yes, very personal."

"There is no Serena at this number."

"Please don't hang up! These items are more than personal, they are intimate."

She hung up.

The next day I set off for the address listed in the phone book. It was not an easy place to find. The centuries-old cobblestone streets were a maze of zigzags, circles, and dead ends. The stone facades of the houses formed three-story-high walls with locked wooden doors and window shutters. There was a solemn sense of abandonment, nothing like the sunny Mediterranean idea of half-naked children playing in the street as their laughing mothers shout after them. It was if people here expected the return of raging Moslem armies, who once again would butcher civilians and make the streets run with blood. Who's to say they were wrong? Their memories were long and the shores of Africa close. It was ironic, I thought, hearing the echo of my own feet as I passed these fortress-houses, that when death came again it would not arrive with the clamor of horses and shouting men in robes brandishing swords. It would come with a whisper, an anonymous missile that would not be tricked by the idea that nobody was home.

On a street in the gothic shadows of Palma Cathedral, I finally found Serena's house. The massive wooden door was studded with steel spikes. I banged the iron knocker. No response. I banged again. The sound of the loud knocking reverberated in the street like gunshots. Finally a small peephole behind steel mesh in the center of the door slid open. I glimpsed brown, almond-shaped eyes. I politely asked:

"Señorita Serena Zermano?"

She said nothing. The protective steel mesh covering her eyes like a veil made me feel like I was peering at the most prized woman in the harem. The peephole slid closed.

I stood there for a while, knocked once again to no avail, and left. I walked the streets of the city, its houses shuttered against the outside world. I knew I was being watched, as if the letters I had come to deliver could wreak the same havoc as that of past invading armies. It seemed as if the whole island conspired to keep Zermano hidden, knowing that someday a messenger from Louise would appear. As I walked, hollow whispers followed me. I glanced up stone staircases leading to deserted plazas, where old Moorish fountains dripped faint splashes of water. I looked up at the sky, caught in rectangles of blue above narrow passageways that were once crowded with hooded men in black cloaks carrying crucifixes and swords. I stared at dusty palm fronds stirring in the wind and listened to the whispers.

The next day I returned to Serena's house. This time I went at two-thirty in the afternoon, a time when I knew she had to be home, when everyone was home, enjoying the day's major meal behind locked doors. I lifted the heavy knocker and let it drop. Footsteps sounded on the other side of the door. The peephole slid open. Brown eyes peered out, not the brown eyes of the day before but those of an older woman. Her words were spoken in Spanish, which fortunately I understood.

"She's not here! Leave before I call the police!"

The peephole closed. Footsteps faded away across tiled floors beyond the door. I could smell food, the scent of heated olive oil and saffron. Serena was in there. I pressed my smallest finger through the steel mesh over the peephole and slid the wooden slat back. Enough of a space opened up so that I could crane my neck and peer inside. It was another world, an immense patio surrounded by Moorish columns of pinkish marble. Sunlight streamed down on a verdant landscape of tropical foliage—flowers bloomed and vines cascaded. Behind two marble columns was an arched opening into a grand salon, where a painting hung in a gilded frame. I had previously seen pencil sketches for this painting, though I didn't know then if the actual painting existed. The sketches, entitled *Swallows Looming at Midnight*, were thought to be Zermano's attempt to capture the moment of epiphany when Ramón Llull, after fasting and praying in a remote mountain cave, received the Holy Spirit. To see the completed painting was stunning—not just the bravura of its execution, but to realize in my own small epiphany that Ramón Llull was the answer. He would lead me to Zermano.

I went back to the archives and with a new eye read through the texts linking Zermano to Llull. I also secured biographies of Llull, including the earliest, published in 1311 while he was still alive. It was difficult to separate legend from fact, to distinguish the reality of his life from the deluge of material offered by his apologists and propagandists. For this reason, serious scholars outside of Spain looked on any connection between Zermano and Llull with a jaundiced eye. To go down that path had about as much validity as proclaiming that Santa Claus and the Easter Bunny had an affair and Jesus Christ was their love child. What is known for certain is that Llull was the son of a Barcelona nobleman who sailed in the armada to Mallorca that recaptured the island from the Moors. The father was rewarded with land and social position. His son, at the age of fourteen, was a page at the court of King James the Conqueror, and later became a tutor of James's son, the future king. Llull traveled throughout Europe, flourishing in the privileged life of royalty. He reached adulthood in a rarefied world of palaces, armored knights, falconers, troubadours, and painted ladies in silken finery. He became a polished and dissolute courtier; his friend, Prince James, tried to tame him by arranging a marriage. The marriage resulted in a son, but could not prevent Llull's slide into adulterous delights. He himself wrote about this period, "The more apt I found myself to sin, the more I allowed my nature to obey the dictates of my body. The beauty of women was a plague and tribulation." His conquests in royal boudoirs and houses of pleasure were so well known that women sought him out to determine if his reputation as a skillful seducer was justified. By all accounts it was.

The celebrated incident that changed Llull forever—strengthened his refusal of carnal delights and opened him to spiritual inquiry—happened, not surprisingly, in his pursuit of a woman. It is here that Llull crossed paths with his near-contemporary, the Italian poet Francesco Petrarch. Petrarch, another legendary seducer, fell eternally in love when he glimpsed the beautiful Laura de Noves in Avignon Cathedral. For ten years Petrarch held no one else in his heart but Laura, a young married noblewoman whose bed he was never to share. She died of the plague that swept through Provence in the fourteenth century. All that Petrarch held in his heart spilled out in songs and sonnets, a passionate outburst that would outlast not only the plague but his own death, and which shone the light of love's promise across Renaissance Europe. But the death of Llull's love sent him on a very different road. It ended with his death in an African desert as he stood preaching with a Bible in one hand and a radical philosophy of universal religion in his heart. He was turned upon by the indignant population.

Like the woman with whom Petrarch fell in love, the woman who changed Llull's life—Ambrosia de Castillo—was also married. Unlike Petrarch, Llull was not stopped by this. When he saw Ambrosia he did not try to hide his passion. This was astonishing, for Ambrosia came from one of the nine noble families that dominated the island, and a rigid code of behavior was imposed on the aristocracy. Perhaps Llull's ties to King James allowed him license to pursue his prey without regard to social consequence, or maybe he had finally found the woman for him. He attempted to seduce Ambrosia not with calculated charm and mysterious midnight promises, but with the naked longing and elegant pain of a denied lover. Word spread that Llull waited for the day Ambrosia would come to him, as her marriage had been an arranged one and her husband was in ill health. At first Ambrosia rejected Llull's advances, no matter how fervent they were. She eventually allowed him a friendship, which meant, in the convention of the time, that he could see her in daylight hours when she was chaperoned by other ladies of her station. It is written that Ambrosia, defying social custom, would sometimes release the lacy mantilla she wore over her head and unpin the coils of her black hair, her eyes gazing at Llull with a longing of her own.

The royalty of Palma followed this courtship closely and it became the source of salacious gossip until one day Ambrosia disappeared. Some said her husband locked her up, others that she committed suicide by jumping into the sea, but most said she had been sent to a convent in France. Llull followed up on every rumor. He broke into her husband's five houses after dark and searched the rooms for her. He traveled to France and scaled the walls of convent cloisters in hopes of finding her cloaked figure among the praying nuns. He never gave up hope and never looked at another woman. After a year passed, everything changed again for Llull.

On that fateful New Year's Day, Palma was alive with a festive commemoration of Mallorca's liberation from the Moors. Boys ran through the streets tethered by ropes to the tails of young bulls; virginal girls smashed clay urns said to be filled with the Devil's evil thoughts; men on stilts, costumed as gaudy demons, stalked the plazas attempting to snatch terrified children from their mothers' arms. At night warships sailed along the harbor's massive fortified sea wall, the ships' rigging hung with thousands of lanterns. Soldiers disembarked from the ships. On the stone ramparts mock battles raged between Christians and Moors. Llull watched all of this from horseback. Then he saw Ambrosia. At first he thought, because of the long day and the night lit up by spinning fireworks and ships firing cannons, that he must be hallucinating. But it was indeed Ambrosia, in a flower-bedecked carriage.

Llull followed the carriage, and when he drew alongside he called Ambrosia's name. She turned, startled, hiding her face behind a fan. The carriage driver whipped his horse and the carriage lurched through the parting crowd. Llull followed as the carriage twisted through narrow streets and stopped before a church. He called to Ambrosia as she climbed from the carriage, but she did not stop, running up the steps into the church. Llull was not about to lose her again. He spurred his horse up the steps and through the church doors left open by Ambrosia. The horse's iron-clad hooves echoed in the vast church as Llull rode down the center aisle. In front of the altar he spun his horse around. In dim candlelight he could see that the rows of pews were empty. He jumped from the horse. There was only one place she could be. He strode to the wooden cubicle of the confessional and yanked its door open. He stood face to face with her. Ambrosia shuddered and pulled back, her thin body huddled against the wall. Llull spoke softly. He said he had not come to harm her, only to profess his undying love. Why had she abandoned him? He saw her tears through her lace mantilla, her lips quivering. He gently touched her in reassurance. She cringed. Her fingers went to her neck, undoing the clasp of the cape she wore. The cape slid off her shoulders. She unbuttoned her blouse and removed it. A gauzy cloth bandage was wrapped around her chest. She tore the bandage away, exposing her once perfect breasts, now hideously ulcerated and scabbed. She shouted:

"See, Ramón, the falseness of this body that has won thy affection! How much better hadst thou done to have set thy love on Jesus Christ, of Whom thou mayest have a prize that is eternal!"

Llull turned away and vomited on the marble floor.

After this incident it is recorded that, like Petrarch in the next century, Llull devoted himself to describing in verse the purity of love lost to early death. In the tradition of his time, Llull tried to compose a troubadour's song that would ring with truth. This vain exercise drove him to suicidal despondency; he sought sanctuary in the great agony and sorrow of Christ crucified on the Cross. Llull was a sinner who had loved the beauty of flesh over the beauty of the soul. He had to reinvent himself in order to redeem himself. The rest of his life would be an act of contrition.

Llull sold his possessions to support his wife and children. He dressed in sackcloth and let his hair and beard grow. He was determined to go out into the world and preach to the unbelievers. For this he needed to learn their science and philosophy. The unbelievers were Moslems; Llull had been taught that their Arabic voices spoke in devilish tongues. He was determined to master their language and conquer the knowledge that stood behind it. To speed his studies he hired a black Moorish slave who, before the Conquest, had been an educated merchant. One day the Moor derided Llull's idea that the religions of man were actually one and could be merged. Llull went into a rage, beating the Moor into cowering submission. Two days later, as Llull sat reading in a chair, the Moor attacked him with a knife. Llull wrestled the knife from the Moor and tied his hands with a leather rope. Llull could have had the slave executed, but he did not. He locked the Moor in the house and went to church to pray for guidance. This was Llull's first test: to find a way, a spiritual path that would convert the unbeliever. Llull returned home from prayer and found the slave had gotten free and, with the leather rope, hanged himself. After this Llull left Palma. He set off on foot for the sacred mountain of Randa.

I decided to follow the route Llull had walked eight centuries before. I rented a car and drove out of Palma. Once past the airport and its immense parking lot lined with tour buses, the road wound through wheat fields, then groves of carob and almond trees. Solitary Mount Randa shimmered ahead in the hazy heat. When Llull made his pilgrimage the mountain was considered sacred. It was the only place on the island feared by the Moors, who thus never settled on it. Driving closer, the steel skeletons of radar and radio towers on the high peak came into view. The serpentine road I followed up the mountain was paved, but Llull's path had been steep and stony, strewn with boulders and thorny bushes. The road ended at a tiny chapel built into the base of a cliff. I got out of the car and looked up. The cliff leaned toward me at an angle, creating the unsettling impression that the mountain was collapsing. The cliff was riddled with swallows' nests. As I walked gravel crunched beneath my feet, startling the swallows. The birds swooped down in a rush of wings over my head, careening off the side of the mountain toward the smudge of blue sea on the horizon. I turned back toward the cliff. I had seen this place before: it was the inspiration for Zermano's painting, *Swallows Looming at Midnight*.

I stopped before the pretty stone chapel. Next to it a rusty Coke machine with an old motor groaned away. At the chapel door was a box with pamphlets telling Llull's story. A small donation was requested. I made my donation and thumbed through a pamphlet. On the last page an illustration indicated the trail Llull took to a cave where he could see both the sun and moon rise. I found the trail and followed it until it ended at a stone wall. A sign warned in five languages that it was dangerous and illegal to proceed further. I jumped over the wall and down onto the other side. There was no longer a trail, just a rutted path. I climbed higher and was surprised by a breathtaking view—the granite spine of the towering Tramuntana Mountains, slicing down the entire length of the island from sea to sea. Somewhere in the distance the tinkle of goat-bells floated on the wind, unseen animals herded by a ghost shepherd.

There was no path beyond this point, just thorny bushes and bladed cacti between the rocks. I looked around, trying to get oriented. On the slope above centuries of rain had ripped open a ravine, and at its top, half-hidden in shadow, was the dark mouth of a cave. I scrambled up the ravine. A treacherous slide of stones gave way under my feet and I grabbed hold of bushes, pulling myself up on hands and knees to the top of the steep incline and into the cave.

It was here that Llull had retreated, fasting and praying. From this vantage point he saw the confining world of his island and knew that his fate lay beyond the sea. He later wrote about this time: "Say, O Fool, perilous is the journey that I make in search of my Beloved. I must seek Him bearing a great burden with all speed. None of these things can be accomplished without great love."

I settled into the cave, sitting cross-legged and gazing out over the dramatic landscape, thinking of how great was the burden of guilt that Llull bore: he had provoked the death of a slave whose God went by a different name, and he had shamefully turned from his love when she exposed in the confessional her naked breasts, disfigured and killing her with a curse that didn't yet have the name *cancer*.

The panorama before me glowed as the sun set. Darkness closed in and the perfume of wild plants drifted up from the plain below. The sea glinted as the moon showed a crescent of its orb above the horizon. I heard wings: swallows were rising to the full moon's false day. The silver light behind the birds lit up their movement, as if they formed the pendulum of an infinite clock swinging back and forth. I fell asleep knowing Zermano had seen this too, witnessed Llull's vision. Zermano himself bore the burden of having abandoned a great love.

I awoke from a deep sleep with the sun directly before me, a good light in which to navigate the trail back. When I reached the chapel a busload of vacationing families pulled up. People piled out, dizzied by the heights and the optical illusion of the cliff above about to crash down. Some of them ran to the Coke machine while others hurled stones at swallows nested in the cliff, trying to startle the birds into abandoning their eggs. This was no longer the world of Llull or Zermano. Their world had gone out of fashion. Love had made them believers and desolation delivered them, two hearts that gambled. Had it not been for them I would have given up on delivering Louise's letters. I too might have picked up a stone and hurled it at the birds with all the other cynics.

I returned to Palma and went directly to Serena's house. I banged the iron door knocker. I heard footsteps from within. I heard shallow breathing on the other side of the door. I banged again. I tried to keep my voice steady, nonthreatening. I had to make my case.

"I don't mean any harm to you or your father. I have something that belongs to him. I'm the one who wrote you from California. I know you think this is a trick, but it's not. The truth is—"

Footsteps sounded from within, walking away from the door.

"Wait! Just give this note to your father! Give it to him and he'll know!"

I slipped my note through the sliver of an opening at the bottom of the door. I waited. There were no more footsteps. I went back to my hotel room. Had I done the right thing? I picked up an old leather-bound book of Llull's contemplations that I had found in a Palma junk shop. I reread the passage I had copied on the note left for Zermano:

"Say, thou that for love's sake goest as a fool! For how long wilt thou be a slave, and forced to weep and suffer trials and griefs?" The answer is only one: "Till my Beloved shall separate body and soul in me."

This passage was one Zermano would recognize. He would know that a messenger from Louise had arrived and he could not die until he understood the truth of his Beloved. I waited the rest of the day in the hotel for his answer, for I had also included my phone number on the note. I was afraid to leave my room in case the call came through. No call came that day, nor the next. I ordered all my meals in, sleeping fitfully, and finally the phone rang. I grabbed the receiver:

"Señor Professor?" inquired a man's voice.

"Yes!"

"This is the hotel manager. We would like to know if anything is wrong. You haven't left your room for days and refuse to let the maid in. This is most unusual. We must maintain hotel standards."

"If she has the vacuum cleaner on I can't hear the phone ring."

"Excuse me?"

"The goddamn vacuum cleaner! Tell her she can't use it!"

"How much longer do you intend to stay? Perhaps we can arrange another hotel?"

"No!"

"Another room then, so that we may clean yours?"

"Impossible. I must stay in *this* room."

"One moment, please."

The phone clicked. I didn't know whether he wanted me on hold or was on his way up with the hotel detective. I stayed on the line until the phone clicked again. The manager spoke.

"Sir, the operator informs me there is a call for you. Shall I put the party through?"

"God, yes!"

The phone clicked again and a woman's voice asked calmly:

"Are you the American professor?"

"I am!"

"My name is Señorita Serena-María Zermano. Can you come to my house today at three in the afternoon?"

"I will, and—"

The line went dead. I put the phone down, opened the balcony doors, and stepped outside. Before me was the palm-lined waterfront; yachts cruised in the bay among cargo ships steaming toward the docks. On the boulevard below, cars raced and honked their way around a circular traffic island. In the island's center stood a bronze statue of a powerfully built man in his later years. He was barefoot, his long hair and beard flowing. He wore the cloaked habit of a Franciscan monk and his left hand held an open book. He seemed to be directing a higher traffic, a traffic of souls. It was Llull, facing Africa across the sea, as if to say to those who killed him: *"Won't you let me read these words I wrote, just one more time."*

I returned through the maze of streets to Serena's house and knocked on the door exactly at three. I heard footsteps inside; they stopped and the peephole slid open. The sensuous brown eyes I had glimpsed once before peered through the protective steel mesh as locks were being undone. The door swung open.

Serena-María Zermano was a slight woman, her black hair pulled tightly into a knot at the back of her head. She wore no makeup, black pants, and a white blouse. She had the no-nonsense stance of a female toreador, on guard against the next thrust of the bull's horns. Her skin was that particular white of Spanish women who respect the omnipresent sun and shelter themselves from it. Even though she wore no jewelry, it was clear that on this island, in another time, she might have been bought for a fortune or stolen at great risk for a harem. She offered no gesture of cordiality, only a simple nod of her head as she closed and locked the door behind her, then led me through the verdant patio and into a formal living room with massive antique furniture. Covering one wall was a watercolor copy of the mural Zermano had left behind in Paris, *Nude Walking Her Man on a Leash.* Zermano had obviously done the watercolor from memory, a reminder of a lost time. The women in the watercolor, standing above the glow of fires burning along the Seine, all resembled Louise. Was Serena aware of this?

How ironic of Zermano to name his daughter Serena, knowing that no daughter of his would ever be a docile bundle. Serena was anything but serene. He knew she could withstand all the seduction, duplicity, and fraud with which children of the famous are besieged. She would not abide those who felt that rubbing up against her would cause her father's greatness to rub off on them; or those who would stroke her with flattery, so that later they could preen at dinner tables or stand behind lecterns, feigning self-deprecation: *"Oh yes, I was a friend of his . . . family. I have so many confidences I'd like to share, but since I'm on the inside I'll have to obey the higher calling of discretion. I can only tell you about the severe emotional scarification of growing up the child of a megalomaniac."*

There was nothing I could say to Serena that would ever impress her, nothing that would dissuade her from the notion that I was just another one hoping to get close to her father in order to validate my own superior aesthetic. No matter what I said, it would sound wrong. But she didn't allow me the refuge of polite silence. She asked me bluntly:

"You are the same professor who called stating he had *intimate details* about my father's life?"

"Excuse me, I didn't mean to imply that I myself had intimate knowledge, only that I had come into possession of items belonging to him."

"Where are they? You come empty-handed."

"They are safe."

"I suppose you are willing to give them up for a price?"

"I want to give them up, but only to him. I don't want money."

"Do you have a small camera or a hidden tape recorder on you?"

"No."

"Let me be frank. I don't like you. I don't like what you represent."

"I don't represent what you think."

"My housekeeper gave me the note you pushed under the door."

"I'm sorry I had to do it that way."

"She was going to throw it away, it made no sense to her."

"Ramón Llull made no sense?"

"Not to her. Outsiders like to romanticize that everyone in Mallorca knows the work of Llull by heart. In fact, Llull is thought of as a quaint antiquity, when he is thought of at all. It's not like the days when his ideas were actually fought over to the death."

"They still do fight over him in universities."

"Those people will fight over anything. All of this nonsense about not being able to understand the soul of the Mallorcan people, nor even the Catalan language, unless you understand Llull! It's like saying you can't understand the French unless you understand Thomas Aquinas. I think you can learn more about the French by watching them make salads."

"Your housekeeper gave you the note and it made sense to you?"

"No. I took it to my father."

So Zermano *was* alive. It became even more important that I did not alienate this woman. Perhaps he was upstairs.

"And what did your father say when he read the note?"

"Nothing. A few days later he sent word that he wanted to meet the person who felt that quote meant something to him."

"I wasn't certain it would. I was taking a chance."

"You still are. What do you *want*?"

"I want only to return what is his."

"Give it to me and I will pass it on."

"I can't do that. He might not get it."

She was silent. I could see she was thinking that if I was telling the truth, and had something to reveal to her father, did she have the right to keep it from him? She continued:

"You said it was intimate."

"Very."

"And you won't trust his own daughter to give it to him?"

"No, it concerns Louise."

"Louise? Louise who?"

There was no reason why Serena would immediately think of Louise. She probably kept Louise out of her mind—the great love of her father's life before he met her mother. Perhaps I shouldn't have mentioned Louise's name. The last thing this daughter wanted was to disturb her father with something so volatile. But I had to tell the truth.

"The Louise I'm speaking of is Louise Collard."

"She's dead. How could she give you something for my father?"

"It's something she hid, something she protected her whole life."

"My father is in ill health. This mysterious something you speak of could overwhelm him, even kill him. Why should I take the chance?"

"Because he told you to. That's why I'm here."

"Yes, I never would have allowed it."

"There's something else. A favorite saying of your father's, translated from the Arabic by Llull."

"Since I was a small child I was always in my father's studio when he painted. He used to talk and talk, often forgetting I was there, perhaps even forgetting who I was as he painted. There's not much he said that I didn't hear, especially a favorite saying."

"It's a simple one: a blind man goes to a gypsy and asks, 'Do you have anything for a broken heart?' The gypsy answers, 'Broken hearts are my specialty.' 'So what do you prescribe?' The gypsy says, 'The same for everyone.' 'And what's that?' asks the blind man. The gypsy smiles, 'You will see. If you are patient you will see.'"

Serena stared intently at the mural on the wall, as if it were the last reel in a movie. She turned to me, but not a muscle moved, not an eyelash flickered. I did not know if it was over, whether I had convinced her, or if I should get up and leave. She turned again to the mural, took a deep breath, and spoke:

"My father said, after reading your note, 'Serena, bring the professor to me. This fool wants to see.'"

PART FIVE

Night Letters

Village of Reigne

My Darling Francisco,

Another week has come and another mysterious basket filled with rare treasures has been left on my door. Can you imagine? Who can be doing this? In any case, I am keeping everything. This time, besides the wonderful food and soap, there were even ration coupons for cloth. Cloth is what I need, and it is very hard to come by. I am making all my baby's clothes, it is another way I can save money, for I certainly cannot afford to go to Madame Happy's shop for miniature Coco Chanels! But even she has a limited stock and sells only what she had on hand before all these troubles began. Two years ago there were fur coats on sale in the stores. Now materials are so scarce they're even making women's purses out of wood and rope. The trick is to conserve. What extra items are in my basket I can take to my school and share with the children. So many of them have nothing, their fathers having been among the million or so soldiers taken prisoner in the first spring of the war. The children come to me so proudly, asking me to read the letters from their fathers that they have received. It doesn't take me long to read these "letters," for they are the official Correspondence of Prisoners of War, little white postcards with enough space to write a few lines, open for all to read. The messages are nearly all the same, such as: "My big boy, you must obey mommy and study hard. Your papa believes in you." Or, "My precious girl, daddy is coming home soon and he has a pretty present for you." This is about all they can say, or are allowed to say, painfully prosaic words to convey an aching avalanche of emotions. But emotions are one of the luxuries that everyone is learning day by day to do without. Like the signs in the store windows that say: NO MILK TODAY. The children know this means there can be NO TEARS TODAY. Everyone has to be a big boy or girl. And when I read the flimsy postcards to those eager faces watching me, I feel the tears within. In the short words I read to them a Victor Hugo novel is playing out in their minds, and they see strong Daddy, rising up valiantly among his foes and marching home. Because even though there can be no tears today, there must be bright hope for tomorrow.

These children have lost so much and that is why I give them what I can, everything out of the baskets that is not absolutely essential to me. I even break up the soap bars into pieces and wrap them as presents. How proud the children are to take these home to their mothers, who themselves have so little to make do on, what with the government distributing nice cookbooks to us women entitled: *How to Cook Without Meat*, or *How to Cook Without Butter or Oil*. Maybe the next book can be, *How to Cook Everything You Need with Air*.

I worry about you my darling, how *you* manage to eat. You were never one to cook, not wanting to spoil the magic of it all, as you used to say. You had a reverence for cooking not unlike that which you had for your painting, a respect for the soulful magic of it, the blind science, the problem solved not by trying to find the right answer, but by intuitively discovering the right solution, measure for measure. I can't imagine how you cope with these endless ration cards for vegetables, cheese, bread, a coupon stamp for everything. And everything weighed with those damn metal ciphers, as if they are weighing out the blood of a country, one gram at a time. And to top off the insult no alcohol is allowed to be sold three days a week. You must have drunk yourself through the wine cellars of all your friends by now.

I worry about you. I worry about the reports of tuberculosis in Paris, how rampant it is. Even here, many of my children have it. They should be in the hospital, but hospitals are for soldiers. I try as best I can to keep my schoolroom warm, using my own ration coupons for coal—one precious lump can go a long way. I try to keep myself warm as well, since the poor children are always sick with this and that, many of them dressed in pathetic rags. I would give them the clothes off my back if it weren't for my baby, and if it weren't for my baby I wouldn't give a damn about tuberculosis. But I must stay healthy.

Today at school a girl came to me in hysterics. She couldn't be consoled and it took me the longest time to coax from her what the great calamity was. She tearfully confessed that the boys told her that the Eiffel Tower had been torn down and made into tanks. A thoughtless prank on the boys' part, but it could be true, the way they want us to save the scraps of anything that can somehow be transformed into a weapon. Maybe they will tear down the Eiffel Tower to make more of those badges with the image of Marshal Pétain in full military regalia stamped on them. The badges are given as rewards to the children who memorize the recent books about the new French state, extolling the secular virtues of school, work, family, and most important, allegiance to Pétain the father. People must return to the earth and plant their gardens for the ultimate victory. All good children should plant potatoes so farmers can use their time making hand grenades. The Marshal is everywhere, in his red cap, gold-braided uniform, and chestful of medals; his framed picture hangs in every classroom. His face is on calendars, clocks, thermometer gauges, even stitched into commemorative honeymoon pillows—not by mandate, but by patriotic fervor. There is nothing more dangerous than an old warrior unless it is a young fool. I teach my children what I am instructed to: the importance of family and state. But in my small way I try to make them accountable to each other first, that no selfishness goes unpunished, that no selflessness goes unrecognized. They ask for so little, these children. They have been handed the suffering of so many. It is important that they understand how all this came about.

It is also important for me to remember how this came about, that I am here because of you. I do what I do with Royer because of you. I pass many houses with tables newly placed outside, covered by black tablecloths and set with burning candles, bowls of bitter olives, open books of condolences to be signed by family and friends of the recently deceased: a soldier imprisoned last year in the East, a sister taken months ago to Lyon for questioning, a child who began spitting blood days before. I have to keep reminding myself how simply this all came about. It's not the swirling morass that people claim it to be. It is a small pinprick of recognition that life will go on with or without us, but the steps we take on the road we walk will echo long after our passing.

Now I will tell you what road I have taken, but it will be written in a kind of shorthand, a code, if you will, for what I do is actually part of a code that no one person fully understands. As for using real names, I will not, for their protection. They all have, already, aliases and *noms de guerre,* but I will change them again, in the event these letters are ever discovered. I will also change the locales where things happened. But they did happen, that I can assure you. And those on the other side, soldiers, militia, secret police, does it really make any difference if I name them? What difference does it make to a rabbit if it is hunted by an eagle or a weasel? The only name you already have is that of Royer, and let us say, for the future, since he has not ever been described as being involved in anything criminal, that he will be appropriately designated. When I write to you of these things you will not know my voice, it will be the voice of the night letters. Do I write these night letters to you alone? No. Because we are no longer alone. Divided or not, there is a child. So these night letters are written for my baby as well. When you next hear of certain matters the names of the participants will be shielded, and my name will be Lucretia. What happened to Lucretia is not opera. There is no orchestra, and all the singers are without tongues. Lucretia is the nightingale, her sound rises from the earth to the sky in a song not of her making but only of her hearing, resonating through the long winter of occupation in the garden that was once called Provence.

LOUISE

Lucretia?

Lucretia?

Lucretia, do you hear me?

The train to Nice rattles through the winter night as cold sweat beads on my brow. What is in the basket I carry balanced precariously on my knees as I sit in the crowded train compartment? I am the only woman. Is that why the men avoid me with their eyes? All of them look at me by not looking *at* me. If even one looked at me, then I would exist, flesh and blood in a skirt and sweater, big gray coat with a woolen scarf wound around my neck. I'm not showing any skin, except my face. My face is exposed and on it I think they can read me, their gaze collectively pulling away the skin to the bone of truth. And what is their truth? All are in uniform; most speak the language of the new emperor, a language I can't understand. Would I feel less violated in my own country if I understood their language? Or would I feel even more betrayed? Do they see in me the field where wheat once grew and the earth now lies fallow, its farmer far off in a foreign prison, or dead as a turnip, or working in the factories once worked by the uniformed men surrounding me? If one of them looks at me then they all will, so no one dares. They know I am Lucretia, they know they have already raped me and torn the soul of my country.

The train rattles, it is like the chattering of teeth. There is a faint ticking. My heart or my baby's heart? Can I really hear it, or is it a ticking in the basket? Does the basket have a heart of a bomb timed to explode on this train full of soldiers before I ever arrive in Nice? Royer said, "Here are your instructions. Do not question them, do not ask, only obey. Take the train to Nice. These are your papers, false identification, all in perfect order. You will be asked to show them along the way, but you will pass through with no problem, because you have the proper authorization to travel, because you have an innocent face, because you are a woman. They will ask you what is in the basket and you will answer, a loaf of bread. They will say you are not supposed to have a loaf of bread, that the bread ration is less than two ounces a day per person. You will answer that you know this, and you know that cakes and croissants and brioches are classified as luxuries and are illegal to have. But you have only a loaf of bread. You have saved up two ounces of flour a day for weeks to bake a loaf of bread for your sick mother in Nice and you are taking it to her. You know that this is not strictly legal, but you hope they understand. They will not understand. They will demand to see the bread. You will pull back the cloth and they will see a lovely loaf, baked to perfection, snuggled in its basket content as a baby pig. And they will say, okay, you may pass. And they will watch you, still suspicious. But they will leave you alone because you have an innocent face. And you will keep your face turned to them at all times, shining like a beacon, your skin scrubbed and faintly pink with a pearlescent glow, and this face will shame them from investigating further, for they know its truth, they know the pain it masks, and they will let you continue unmolested, so they can claim they never laid a hand on you, or threatened with a violating gesture. So that they can go home at night and pretend they are not guilty. Even though they are *all* the ones who raped you."

I was stunned. How did he know I had been raped?

"Because," he answered, "after you proved you could be trusted with matters demanding the utmost secrecy, when I told you that a new name was required—a name for the night world where all move anonymously to protect the true identity of the collective resistance—you chose the name *Lucretia*. You chose the name of a woman who was raped in ancient Rome. Through history this tragedy shook the guilt of all men. They wrote poems about Lucretia, staged plays, sang operas, all to prove they were not the guilty ones."

What he said was true, but I quickly reminded him that Lucretia killed herself after the rape. *I* was still alive.

He smiled. "There is still time. For what is war but a mass unconscious desire for suicide?"

"It's not so simple."

"Everything is simple; the lie is the truth."

"So everything you are asking me to do has another purpose?"

"Precisely, which is why you must always follow my instructions, never veer from the lie or you will derail the truth. The fly hunts the eagle."

"Flies don't hunt eagles."

"And eagles don't hunt flies . . . in a normal world."

"Tell Lucretia what you want her to do."

"Here is the basket of bread you will take to your sick mother in Nice."

"I don't have a sick mother in Nice."

"You do now." He handed me a slip of paper. "Here is her address."

"And what do I say to her?"

"The fly hunts the eagle."

"It's a lie."

"It's the truth."

*   *   *

THE TRAIN CONTINUES to rattle. Is it an even louder chattering of teeth, or a ticking in the basket balanced on my knees? Do the
uniformed men around me hear the ticking? Is that why they avoid
looking at me, afraid I will blow up their compartment if they approach? The train lurches to a squealing stop in the Nice station. I
still hear the ticking. My heart? The soldiers must hear it too. They
stay where they are, not moving, letting me make my way down the
narrow aisle between them. I feel like a little girl walking in a forest
of tall trees with a picnic basket of poisoned food. Red Riding Hood
carrying a bomb?

I am not prepared for what I encounter after I manage to push
my way through the crowd in the train station. This is no longer the
Nice I remember. No longer the glittering Baie des Anges, with its
broad sandy beach and hotels frosted with pink stucco. In winter
light a grey film coats everything. Windows are painted blackout
blue, walls are covered with thick camouflage netting, coils of barbed
wire block the seaside promenade. Menacing concrete and steel
struts line the shore, and spoked black balls of surface mines float in
the sea.

The city streets are not filled with fashionable summer visitors,
but with the homeless seeking shelter, a restless mob with everything they own tied in pitiful rag bundles or suitcases held together
with rope. The air echoes with accents from all over Europe. Begging
hands are held out everywhere, dirty hands with deeply creased
palms. Men, women, and children cough and shiver in the cold. The
scent of summer perfumes and suntan creams has given way to the
stench of the unwashed, the stale sweat of defeat. Following the gaze
of downcast eyes I see shoes worn through with holes, exposing fes-
tering feet. How far have these people journeyed, walking with
blood in their shoes? Did they flee here from other countries or
from a house just around the corner? It makes no difference now. I
have been instructed not to stop nor reach out a comforting hand,
not even to a small girl, slumped alone before a high stone wall with

a boarded-up mansion behind. The girl's whimpering cannot be drowned out by the shouted pleas of others around me. I continue, still seeing the stain of urine on the dirty sidewalk beneath the girl, feeling her shivering body in my own bones.

I look at the address on the slip of paper Royer gave me. Can this be right? There are nothing but fancy hotels here, protected by banks of sandbags and patrolling soldiers. Two soldiers stop me; one asks for my identity papers. I hand them over. He reads them carefully, then hands them to the other soldier, who quickly walks away with them.

"What's wrong?" I ask, trying to keep the alarm out of my voice.

The soldier does not answer. He looks down at my basket as he puts his hand on the holstered gun at his hip.

The other soldier returns with a tall blond man. The man wears a leather trench coat and expensive dress shoes shined to a high gloss; he is not a soldier. When he speaks I am relieved that his language is not foreign, but French.

"Madame has a reason for traveling so far from home?"

"Aren't my papers in order?"

"Travel in this area is restricted."

"My mother is ill. I've brought her a present."

"A present? May I see it?"

"I have nothing to hide. Nothing at all."

"I'm certain you don't."

"Look." I pull the cloth cover off the basket.

The two soldiers draw their revolvers and point them at me.

My hand stops, but I cannot prevent my fingers from trembling.

"Madame is nervous?"

"No . . . no." I continue to pull the cover back, exposing the loaf of bread.

"Ah, Madame has only bread! She has saved her coupons to get enough flour to make her sick mother a present. How quaint."

"It's only bread. I assure you of that."

"May I," the blond man bends over and touches the crust of the loaf, "just have a closer look?"

"Yes, of course."

He pulls the loaf from its basket and holds it above his head, looking underneath as if expecting to see dangling wires. Could he hear a ticking from the loaf, or was it the pounding of my heart? He spins the loaf around, assaying it from every angle, verifying its shape and weight like a judge in a baking contest.

He hurls the loaf onto the sidewalk. It hits with a hollow thud and smashes into crumbs at my feet. I am surprised the loaf contains nothing inside, that he has taken such a chance. But was it a chance? He must have known the loaf was harmless. He hands back my papers.

"Madame should be aware that she has only one hour before her permission to travel through this area expires. She must be on the last train leaving today."

"Yes . . . I'm aware."

He turns and walks rapidly away with the two soldiers on his heels.

Surrounding me is a sudden clatter of grey wings and deep-throated gurgles as hungry pigeons descend in a rush to the crumbs on the sidewalk, pecking and jostling. Then, just as quickly, they fly up as children gather around, stomping their feet to scare off the birds. The children fight one another for the crumbs, snatching bits of bread and shoving them into their dirty mouths. Among them is the girl I passed earlier, the little rag doll slumped in her own urine. I want to reach down and stroke her matted hair, to soothe her pain, but my time is short. I am not to call attention to myself, even though my loaf has been lost; I have instructions to follow and a rendezvous to keep.

I glance again at the address written by Royer. I am surprised to see the number is the same as the gilded gold number above the ornate entrance of a hotel. Can this be right? It seems a mistake. But I am to follow instructions. The hotel attendants swing open the heavy doors, bowing solicitously as I pass.

I feel I have entered the grand salon of a luxury ocean liner at sea, so far removed is this world from the one outside. I am transported into another reality as I step onto the plush carpeting. Glistening marble walls soar upward; the crystal brilliance of chandeliers high overhead casts an expensive glow onto a shadowless realm. I become lost among the velvet-flocked pillars of the vast lobby. I search for a way out. Royer must have given me the wrong address. Or is this another test?

"I can assist you."

The words float toward me through the forest of pillars. I try to adjust my eyes to the rich light. Then I see a man dressed in a black tuxedo and white shirt. He stands on the far side of a granite counter; behind him rises a wall of message boxes holding silver room keys. How can he assist me? I see him looking at my basket. My basket! I carry no luggage; I must be someone to be quickly ushered out.

He comes from behind the counter and beckons me to follow: "Right this way." He leads me down a broad hallway lined with potted palms and stops at the entrance to a formal dining room.

An imperious maître d'hôtel, standing guard at a desk with an open reservation book before him, glances at me skeptically. "Is this she?"

"Yes." The man in the tuxedo nods and walks away.

"Your table is ready." The maître d'hôtel picks up a leather-bound menu and starts into the dining room.

"Wait." I grab him by the sleeve. "Who do you think I am? I can't possibly afford to eat here." I look around at the linen-covered tables where people in fancy clothes speak in hushed tones, pretending not to notice my shabby appearance. The perfume of flowers in Chinese vases makes me feel even more light-headed.

The maître d'hôtel pushes my hand away, whispering, "Follow me and don't ask questions." He glides off among the tables and stops at one with a silver stand on it. The stand holds a card: RE-SERVED. He slides out a silk-covered chair and motions for me to sit.

"I told you, I can't afford—"

"You have the right address. Sit."

I sink into the silk chair with embarrassment, like an impostor queen being seated on a throne.

The maître d'hôtel bows and glides off. A waiter appears with a bottle of champagne in an ice-filled silver bucket. He pops the cork and pours champagne into two crystal glasses, then hurries away.

No one at the surrounding tables makes eye contact; only the murmur of low voices comes to me. I am afraid to drink the champagne. Maybe I am expected to pay for it! I push the chair back to leave, but a stern-looking man wearing a brown suit and wire-rim glasses sits down opposite me. He picks up his champagne glass and raises it in salutation.

"To your health." He smiles.

I don't touch my glass.

"Are you afraid it's poisoned?" He sips his champagne and licks his lips. "So, you are the woman men write operas about."

I wanted to say no, that I was a school teacher from a small village. I say nothing, because he knows who I am. How? I remember my instructions from Royer: not to speak unless I hear the right words, not to engage in conversation because the enemy might discover my identity. But this man may not be the enemy. How am I to know? I finger the stem of my champagne glass.

"Have you met the Fly?" he asks.

I do not answer. I pick up my glass and drink.

"The Fly hunts the Eagle," he continues.

I swallow hard. Now I can speak. "Flies don't hunt eagles."

He refills our glasses. "And eagles don't hunt flies."

"Not in a normal world."

"This is not a normal world. What's in the basket?"

I look around, afraid to be overheard.

"Don't worry about them; they are busy with their own conversations. They are all butter-and-egg men."

"Butter-and-egg men?"

"Black marketeers. Who else do you think could afford to eat in this mausoleum?"

"And you? Who are you?"

"I work here. Now, what's in the basket?"

"Nothing," I whisper. "They took the bread."

He slides a silver room key across the table. "I want you to meet me in this room in five minutes."

"I told you, they took it. There is nothing left. I have no reason to meet you in your room."

"Yes, you do."

"Why?"

"Because your name is Lucretia."

I PACE the Persian carpet in the hall before the room of the man I am to meet. Each time I pass his door I listen for sounds inside, but there are none. A DO NOT DISTURB sign hangs on the doorknob. On the door itself is a bronze plate engraved with the words HOTEL DOCTOR. Finally I knock.

The door cracks open. The man in the brown suit pokes his head out, looking up and down the hall. He sees no one else and pulls me into the room, locking the door behind us.

There is dull blue light in the room. What am I doing here? He takes the basket from me. I tell him again, "They destroyed the loaf. There is nothing for you! My trip was a waste. I must get to the train before my right to travel expires. If they catch me without proper papers I can be arrested."

"If you are arrested we will have to kill you."

"What are you talking about?"

"We don't know what you would tell them if you were tortured."

"So what good is it to kill me *after* I've told them?"

"Because you might make a deal with them that leads them to us."

"I wouldn't."

"You could."

"So could you."

"No. I would not wait for them to torture me. I will kill myself first."

I see now the room is blue because of blackout paint on the windows. His skin is blue. He keeps talking, like a blue ghost.

"I'm a doctor. Do you want me to give you something to swallow if you are captured? That way you'll be dead before they get a word from you."

"No, I'm not going to do that."

"As long as you know the rules. They are the same for you as for the rest of us. No exceptions." He flicks on an overhead light and sets the basket on the table.

"I told you it's destroyed! Let me go to the station while there's still time."

"It's not destroyed—on the contrary, it's here."

From the basket he takes the rumpled cloth that covered the bread. He holds it up to the light, pulling both sides tightly until the material is stretched like a screen. Within the red-and-white checked pattern another pattern can be discerned, sewn into the fabric in delicate black stitches. It is a grid; within its lines numbers and letters stand out against the light.

He peers closely at the coded pattern. "You did a good job. You got it past them."

"I did?"

"You did indeed."

"Then I must go."

"That's right. We don't want you to be captured."

I turn to leave but he grabs my arm.

"Wait one moment."

"I haven't much time."

"No, you don't. That's why I want to examine you. You're pregnant—you can't hide it from me, I'm a doctor."

"I'm in a hurry, I'm leaving."

"Do you want to jeopardize your child's life?"

"Of course I don't!"

"Then let me examine you and make certain you're all right. Have you seen a doctor since you've become pregnant?"

"No."

"Then for the sake of your child this must be done. You don't want any complications."

"Complications? I just learned that if I'm captured I'll be killed! And you are talking about complications!"

"If I had known beforehand of your condition I wouldn't have used you. I can tell you are pregnant from the way you walk and the pupils of your eyes."

"What else do you see in my eyes?"

I stare at him angrily. Can he see the tears I have not shed? Can he see the fear I've tried to hide? Can he see that I have no reason to trust him? But if he really is a doctor, I should let him examine me.

"I see a woman who needs to trust someone."

"No! I don't need to trust. I need to know if my baby is healthy."

"You'll let me examine you then?"

"Yes. But now that you know I'm pregnant, and I understand the risk I'm running, I don't want to be used any more. I want to protect my baby."

"You won't be used any more. We can sympathize with your condition."

"Let's do it; I must go."

"Take off your clothes and lie down on the bed."

"You don't have an examining table?"

"This is wartime. Everything I used to have here in my office has been confiscated. They left me nothing but this." He snaps open a black leather doctor's valise and starts pulling instruments from it.

"I heard most of the doctors in the country have been forced into the military. How do I know you are not a veterinarian, a common cat surgeon?"

"You don't. But who better to examine you—a trained veterinarian, or no one?"

I disrobe and lie on the bed, shivering from my exposure to a stranger. To be naked in front of a man is one thing; to be naked and pregnant is quite another. I feel misshapen and vulnerable. In the blue light my blue skin makes me look like some marine creature tossed ashore by the tide and left abandoned in a tangle of seaweed. But it isn't seaweed I am tangled in, it is the swollen blue veins of my belly and legs. I am just a big blue swollen thing, but inside is something beautiful, this I must believe.

His hands touch my cheeks. He presses his thumbs beneath the bones of my jaw, feeling my lymph nodes. He puts the cold metal tip of a stethoscope beneath my breast, listening to my heart. It is quiet in the room, just his breathing, and then my own as he tells me to inhale and exhale deeply. He slides the stethoscope over the mound of my belly, listening even more intently.

He drops the stethoscope back into the valise, takes out a rubber glove, and draws it tightly onto his right hand. "I'm going to have to ask you to pull your knees up and spread your legs."

Is he really a doctor? I am doing this for my baby. I spread my legs. A cold finger comes into me. Is he a cat surgeon? I shudder.

"There, there," he assures me as he prods. "It's just a routine examination."

"Hurry. The train."

He removes his fingers from me and pulls the glove off with a loud snap. "I'm concerned about you down there."

Dread shoots through me. I feel impending death rattle every cell of my body. "Don't tell me there's something wrong with my baby!"

He takes my hand between his and holds it sympathetically. "Your baby seems fine. But you are anemic and too thin. You must eat more."

"We all need to eat more."

"You especially. I'm going to give you some pills for the anemia. They are hard to get. You must take them."

"I will."

"And—"

"What?"

"You must have this baby in a hospital."

"Why?"

"Because you are very small down there. I'm afraid there could be complications."

"Don't treat me like a lamb. What are you saying?"

"You have a narrow birth canal. Without proper medical care things could go very wrong."

"You mean I could lose my baby?"

"And your life."

"It's the baby I care about!"

"That's why you must deliver in a hospital."

"I will."

"Good. Now get dressed."

He turns away as I hurriedly put my clothes on. When I finish he is standing at the door with the basket. He hands it to me. It feels heavy and has a new cloth cover. He smiles. "I put another little something in it. I don't want you to go away empty-handed. So many people have gone to so much trouble to get you here."

"I thought you weren't going to use me any more."

"Oh, don't worry. This just needs to go to the hotel entrance."

"What do you mean?"

He looks at his watch. "In six minutes you will be at the entrance. A black Citroën will pull up. There will be a commotion. The Fly will hunt the Eagle. You will see him. Do not panic. Be firm. Set the basket behind the Citroën and walk quickly away. You will have just enough time to catch your train, the last one out before they seal the station off."

"Why will it be sealed off?"

"Because of the commotion."

"But what about the basket? They will search it again at the entrance."

"No, they won't. They have already searched it." He taps his watch impatiently. "Now *go*."

Should I thank him? I don't even know his name. Is what he says true, about my being small down there? Is he a quack or a double agent? I have one last question.

"Who will be in the black Citroën?"

"Don't worry. Just a butter-and-egg man."

He smiles and opens the door. I step into the hall. Before I can turn around the door slams and locks behind me.

WHEN I STOP outside the hotel entrance I glance at my watch. I want to keep going to the train station. Why should I wait for a black Citroën that might never appear and make me miss my train? The two soldiers who challenged me earlier spot me on the steps. They come directly to me, demanding to know why I am still in the area. I assure them I am going home. I show them my train ticket with its departure time just minutes away. I tell them I must run to catch my train. They insist that I stay. They want to search my basket again. The tall blond man in the trench coat approaches, shouting angrily at the soldiers that the basket has already been searched, that no one is to be in front of the hotel but authorized personnel.

I thank the blond man and walk away. Around the corner in front of me comes a man on a motorcycle. He is dressed in black, his head completely covered by a leather helmet strapped under his chin. Bulging glass goggles hide his eyes. He looks like one of the insect men on motorbikes on the Day of the Bees. Is he coming for me? I turn back just as a black Citroën screeches to a stop in front of the hotel. The blond man in the trench coat stiffens to attention and salutes those in the Citroën. The two soldiers at his side also snap to attention.

The man on the motorcycle roars by, pulling a gun from his black leather jacket and firing straight at the blond man, whose hand drops from his forehead as blood sprays from his face. The soldiers fall to their knees and take aim, shooting at the motorcyclist.

I set the basket down on the curb beneath the back bumper of the

Citroën and run, not knowing where the gunfire is coming from as its metallic cracking echoes along the street. As I reach the corner an explosion thunders above the gunfire. A concussive whoosh of air pushes at my back. I turn to see the Citroën in a twist of steel, windows blown out, flames engulfing the interior.

I hurry to the train station. Everything is still normal. Word of the explosion and killings at the hotel has not yet reached here. I push through the crowd and climb into the train as it starts to roll away. The train whistle blows; in the distance police sirens wail. The train lurches. Is it going to stop? It picks up speed, rolling quickly out of the station. Through my window I see the streets fill with speeding truckloads of soldiers, their rifles pointed at those they pass.

The world seems gray and cold with a dull frenzy at its center. My hands are clutched between my knees, trembling. Then I remember. The doctor forgot the pills for my baby. Maybe he was a cat surgeon. He never gave me the pills for my anemia. Instead he gave me a bomb in a basket. The train picks up speed, its iron wheels clatter on the track. I lay my head wearily against the glass window and fall asleep.

How long do I sleep? Am I dreaming? Something jolts me awake. I rub foggy moisture from the window. A motorcycle is racing alongside the train. A man in black is crouched over the cycle's handlebars, leaning into the wind, a leather helmet on his head, goggles obscuring his face. He looks like a fly. Is he now hunting me? The train goes into a tunnel. Everything in life or in a dream is blacked out. At my very center I hear the dull frenzy, and faintly, in the unseeable distance, the distinct beating of another heart.

Village of Reigne

Darling Francisco,

So many things left unspoken. Even though I now feel we shall never see one another again, I must say these things before they are sealed within my wounded heart, locked away with the passing of time. You are still so real to me, so close. I place your hand between my legs, now as then. I give you the most precious object, love; this delicate threat, obsession. You can press your fingers into my skin, play all the notes of my joy and sorrow. In my soul, I never betrayed you. His heart belonged to his queen, my heart belonged to you. You must understand that before it is too late.

"What," you may ask, "are you *thinking* of?"

The answer is what I fear most to tell you.

"Speak up!" I hear you shouting. "Speak up in your little stone cottage so that I may hear you. Don't be afraid. The object of love can be smashed, the heart broken, but the spirit cannot be destroyed."

But Francisco, how can I describe my naked feet bound at the ankles, wrapped by barbed wire and thorny roses? My lacerated white skin bleeds. Can I ever tell you how this came to be on the Day of the Bees, during the storm in the lavender field with bees buzzing and lightning striking?

"What are you talking about, Louise? There was no storm that day."

So you still do not see. You still do not recognize the lightning that electrified my heart, the storm that defiled my body.

"I see that you do not write to me, though I write to you."

That is true. You cannot see these thoughts I put on the page because I hide them. When I write these letters I feel myself merging with you, my voice no longer mine, sounding like yours, uttered from the same tongue. That is why I can speak to you like this.

"Then why can't you tell me of the many things left unspoken?"

Because if you promise to love someone until you die, and then you cannot, you die inside yourself.

"I am alive, waiting for you."

Sometimes as I walk back from Ville Rouge I pass through a long lane of sycamore trees, their leaves dispersed by winter wind, the sun coming through the high branches and caressing the bare trunks. The smooth bark of the trees is so voluptuous, like the skin of a newborn baby's bottom, and I allow myself to hope.

"Why are you crying? If you would only let me hear these things from your own lips, you know I would take you in my arms. I would be your tree, your strong oak, my branches encircling you."

How do you know I am crying?

"I can feel the dampness of your cheek in the darkness between us."

You could light a candle. You could come to me.

"I did, but you were in hiding."

In mourning. That's different.

"I mourn for you, Louise. I will for the rest of my life."

That's not good. It will kill us both.

"You leave us no alternative."

No. I . . . I'm alone here and the wind howls.

"The war?"

The war was once inside me. Now I am empty. There is only echo. Footsteps going nowhere.

"Think of something beautiful, Louise."

Do you remember the children of Château-Colline?

"How could I ever forget them? How could I ever forget the way you came to me after?"

The smallness of that little girl's intentions was so enormous. A woman does not go out into the world to find a man and make a home; she prepares a home in her heart.

"Yes, you told me at the time."

She builds her heart-home with twigs of memories, makes mortar of passion, constructs walls from clouds of detail. Only when it is finished docs she invite a man inside to share it.

"And now your heart is wounded, sealed forever against me. Is that what you are trying to tell me tonight?"

No. My naked feet are bound by rusted wire and thorny roses, red blooms press against my ankles.

"Are you drinking absinthe again?"

Do you remember my white feet, the toenails painted red?

"Of course I remember! I'm the one who always painted your nails. Those were my ten greatest masterpieces. When the paint was dry I parted each toe like the petals of a blossom and—"

You kissed them.

"Sucked them. But you're trying to distract me. Answer. Are you drinking again? You know you must not do that because of the baby."

What baby? I never told you about a baby.

"You did—in the letters you never sent to me. Now you're confusing me."

Lucretia doesn't drink absinthe.

"And what about Louise?"

Day of the Bees

She's drunk and the wind is at her door.
"What about the baby, Louise?"
Do you hear the howling?
"Tell me before it's too late! I'll come! Let me into your home!"
There is no baby.
"What do you mean? What are you saying?"
Howling.

Village of Reigne

The wind stopped.

Francisco, did you actually speak to me last night as I was writing to you? I thought I heard your voice. I hid the letter after writing it, hid it so well that even I can't find it this morning. I'm not sure now what you know about me—what I have or have not told you. Did I tell you Madame Happy spat on me?

I was on my way to meet Royer. It was late and I was trying to avoid being caught out after the eight-o'clock curfew. I passed Madame Happy's shop just as she was locking up. She turned and caught a glimpse of me by surprise. Many others were rushing around, trying to beat the curfew as well. I did not want to appear rude by hurrying past without a polite hello to Madame, so I stopped, smiled with a courteous bow, and inquired as to her well-being.

"*Slut,*" she hissed. The people on the street were startled.

My first thought was that she could see I was pregnant, despite my layers of bulky clothing. After all, Madame Happy made a living off expectant mothers. But from the look of her own clothes—once regal, now frayed—it was apparent she wasn't making much of a living at all. In a land where the economy feeds the death machine, people don't have the means to lavish their meager savings on clothing for an uncertain future.

"*Slut!*" She shouted so loudly this time that curious bystanders moved quickly away, not wanting to give her a fresh target.

I couldn't move. I felt shamed. But why? Why should Madame Happy, a pillar of bourgeois respectability, act so vicious? Was it because she knew I was pregnant, yet wasn't buying anything from her shop? Did she think my failure to do so would put her out of business if others followed suit? I wanted to tell her that I would love to purchase my baby's first clothes from her shop of exquisite finery, but I couldn't. I had no money. I had to make everything for my baby, even though I had no skill at sewing. As a matter of fact I often looked into Madame's shop window after closing hour. The fuzzy booties and colorful cashmere gowns, I wanted them all. But my child would have to make do with clothing I made myself. Of course I couldn't say any of this to Madame Happy, because I was still guarding the secret of my condition. I sympathized with her fear that "modern" girls like me would put her out of business, but I resented her for humiliating me.

It seemed strange for her to call me a slut, yet it fit with the tenor of the time, the war, and the need to take control of the personal— for the impersonal could not be controlled. One simply had to choose a side and stick to it, preferably in public. So she tried to shame me. I turned to leave; there was nothing left to say.

Before I took two steps she caught me by the arm. I spun around to give her a piece of my mind. As I opened my mouth to speak she slapped me. The force of her hand against my cheekbone nearly knocked me down.

"*Slut!*" She spat on me and walked away.

No one in the street offered to help. They kept their distance, their heads bent down as they shuffled away.

Why? Why had Madame Happy gone out of her way to insult me? Was it simply the frustration of the war? Had she just heard that someone close to her had been killed? No. I knew the answer: she was choosing her side and making a public display of it. Somehow word must have reached her about my resistance activities. She despised me for them. She despised the Lucretia in me. I hurried along the now deserted street, with its shuttered windows, to my meeting with Royer.

When I reached the post office it too was shuttered. I tried the door, but found it locked. I stood there, not knowing what to do. I had come so far; I couldn't just leave. Then from behind the door I heard the muffled sound of a single voice, followed by the roar of a crowd that thundered as if from a great distance.

What could this be? Was Royer having a meeting behind closed doors? If so, he must have half the men of the village with him, given the volume of muffled chants and yells rising again. I pounded on the heavy wooden door. It was after curfew and I would have to make my way back to Reigne in the dark. What was going on? Was Royer having a meeting and locking me out? Why were so many men inside? Never in our meetings were there more than five, seven at most. This was crazy; they were making no attempt to keep their voices down. I pounded one last time. The sound of voices from inside died away. I heard footsteps, then a key in the lock, and the door opened. Royer stood in the narrow crack of light, holding a finger to his lips. But why should I be quiet? All the noise was coming from inside. He pulled me quickly in and locked the door. I looked around. Where was everyone? There was no one here except Royer. Did I really hear what I thought I heard?

Royer was silent. He slipped a cigarette package from his jacket pocket, tapped one out and lit up. I could tell from the scent that it was not one of those ersatz cigarettes everyone choked on, trying to pretend they were inhaling real tobacco—this *was* real tobacco.

Royer sighed and blew a pungent cloud of smoke into my face. Where did he get real cigarettes? They were impossible to come by. Probably one of the mothers whose son's letters had been lost gave the cigarettes to Royer, hoping for a miracle. I really did despise him. And if we had not been thrown by chance onto the same side in this mess of a war, I certainly would have indulged my temptation to end his odious existence. But as it was I knew the risks he took, his bravery. Maybe after the war the statue of himself that Royer wanted so badly would be erected in the town square.

"You're late," he whispered.

"You're lucky I'm here. They told me in Nice I wasn't to be sent on missions until after my baby was born." I looked around the post office again, thinking perhaps those whose voices I had heard earlier were somehow hidden behind counters and desks, just waiting for the word from Royer to reappear.

"You believe all we want is to use you. On the contrary, I thought you might be interested in retrieving the packet of letters I have for you."

"From Zermano?"

"Yes, of course. Who else knows you're hiding here? Come with me." He led me back into his office and took the letters from a drawer in his desk. He handed them over. "You've done a lot for us. You deserve these. You've earned them."

"You almost got me killed more than once. What if I had waited by that Citroën in Nice after setting the basket down?"

"I knew you would follow the orders exactly. You've proven you can do that. It was very simple really."

"Try it yourself sometime."

"There's nothing you've done that I haven't done."

"You didn't do it while you were pregnant."

He blew another blue cloud in my face. "So you've met the Fly."

"Quite an introduction."

"Do you know where he is?"

"How could I possibly know where he is? I don't even know *who* he is."

"No one knows who he is."

"I think he followed me."

"When?"

"After Nice. He was chasing my train."

"That's unlikely. Why would our most important agent risk capture by following your train right after he assassinated—"

"Who? Who did he assassinate? Who did *I* assassinate?"

"It's not important who the players are."

"It's important to me."

"Keep your focus. The *who* is not important, just the *why*." Royer watched as I tucked the packet of letters into my basket. "That is your *why*. You've already made your choice."

"Love."

"Then why aren't you with your love?"

I turned to go.

"Wait, I've got something."

"And I told you I'm not doing any more missions until my baby is born. I won't risk it."

"It's just a message to deliver, but it's important. First let me show you something." He flipped over a newspaper that lay on his desk. A blurred photo on the front page showed a man in black on a speeding motorcycle; a helmet and goggles obscured his face. The headline read: *Reward for Captain in Army of Crime.*

"I'm astonished to see this. Normally our exploits pass unmentioned in the newspapers. Even if we blow up a troop train they keep it a secret, trying to deny our impact. Why this?"

"Because the Eagle hunts the Fly out in the open. How embarrassing for the Eagle."

"Why?"

"They show their vulnerability. We are hurting them."

"We hurt them and they scream—yet they cut off our arms and legs and we cannot shed a tear."

"They must not know they hurt us. That is what makes us strong."

"I don't want to be strong. I just want to go home."

"All of France wants to go home, Louise. The trouble is that it's not our house anymore."

"Don't give me a patriotic speech. I told you, I'm out for now, I won't be used."

"A shepherd always begins his journey on a full moon."

"I told you, *no*. I'm not going to be at one of those drops again. It's too dangerous."

"A shepherd does not graze his flock in the same pasture every day. You don't have to be *there*. We want you to be near. To report that everything went all right. That the lamb has fallen into the shepherd's arms."

"Wherever I am it's too near, I'm always in the middle. You've proven that."

"I promise you—this time you will not be in the middle. You will be on your own, there will be no others. Your job is just to wait, watch, and report. In fact, under no circumstances are you even to speak to anyone. The only person you may speak to is the Fly, and only if something goes wrong."

"The Fly is the shepherd?"

"I can't tell you that."

"How will I know I'm talking to the real Fly? All his features are covered. He even wears gloves; no skin shows at all."

"Don't worry, even I don't know the true identity of the Fly. But I know the code."

"I'm not saying I will do as you ask. But if I do, if a shepherd begins his journey on a full moon, what must I know?"

"THUNDER IN MARCH MEANS GOOD ALMONDS."

"And how will he respond?"

"WHY DO YOU HUNT CICADAS?"

"And what will I say?"

"BECAUSE THEY SUCK THE SAP OF THE ALMOND TREES AS THEY SING."

I fell silent. Now I knew the code, but I did not know if I would ever use it.

Royer watched to see if I would give a sign of assent. He noticed the drip of spittle that still clung to the front of my coat. "How did you get that?"

"Madame Happy. She just approached me in the street, called me a slut, and spat."

"I can't imagine her doing that. She's the most conservative woman in town."

"Maybe that's why she did it. Maybe she suspects my involvement with the cause. Maybe she fears I'm a threat to the town and will bring reprisals down on the heads of everyone."

"Impossible! If she knew of your involvement, then she would know of mine."

"Maybe she has already informed on us."

"We would have been arrested."

"Not if they were trying to get to the leader. Not if they were trying to get to the Fly."

Royer sucked the last of his cigarette down to an ember between his nicotine-stained fingers and mumbled, "As if I don't have enough to worry about already! How could that old pot of bone marrow have found out? There's not a move we make that isn't somehow betrayed." He seemed to forget I was there. He reached down and turned up the volume of the radio on his desk.

The strange muffled roar I had heard earlier leapt back into the room. A crowd was chanting intoxicated approval of a piercing voice that rose higher and higher, chasing its own cadence to a breathless summit. When the voice reached the summit, the crowd went wild again. The voice continued, powered not by breath but by audacity of will. I couldn't understand the language the voice was speaking, but I visualized the hysteria exploding each syllable as the voice urged the crowd to follow.

Royer was transfixed. Obviously he understood the language spoken by France's new emperor. Why was he so involved with the speech? I quietly let myself out, closing the door against the ranting crowd, and started walking the darkened streets. Of course, Royer had to listen to the speech in order to know what was coming. Even more clever was the fact that he listened without trying to hide it. By doing so he knew that some townspeople would consider him a traitor. But others, like Madame Happy, would think, "If Royer listens to the new emperor he surely can't be sympathetic to the resistance. Royer is not a man to be spat upon!"

Village of Reigne

My Dearest Love,

I don't know what is happening, but suddenly I get so tired. Last night I fell asleep over your letter with my pen still in hand. I was trying to tell you something important. Be patient, I'm almost there. It is such a difficult story to tell, a confession really.

Before I fell asleep I was talking of Royer and his pressure on me to stay involved. That he gave me the treasure of your new letters, and did not try to bribe me with them, came as a surprise. Perhaps he is appealing to my patriotism. It could be that he wants to see if I will act without being motivated by my love for you—to get more letters. Perhaps he needs to know how far I will go, how far I can be pushed, how much I can be trusted, so that he can use me in some ultimate sacrifice.

Certainly no one else seems to trust me. Sometimes I think I am the only one in the middle, while conspiracy swirls all around.

But am I truly in the middle? Probably only for the children who are in my charge at school. They turn to me for calm and guidance, unaware that the same woman cries alone at night, reading your letters over and over—as if that very act could make you appear, arise and walk from the words on the page, into my home, into my bed.

The children cling to me. When the Officer from the cherry orchard arrived at our school with his armed soldiers, the children looked to me for courage. The Officer himself looked upon me, not at me, without acknowledging we had ever met before. He stared suspiciously at my chalked lesson notes on the blackboard, studying them as if they were coded directions on how to assemble a sten gun. The children were afraid to look at him, I think both because of their intrinsic fear and because of the jagged red scar covering his right cheek. It was the scar I left when I bit his cheek on the Day of the Bees.

He commanded the children to stand and empty their pockets. I could not protest, for to do so would certainly arouse suspicion. I clapped my hands, startling the children who were frozen with fear, and turned the Officer's request into a game.

"Whoever has in their pocket a photograph of Marshal Pétain shall be given an extra chocolate ration."

The Officer glared at me. "That's not what I'm looking for."

"Don't worry, children. It's what *I'm* looking for."

The children rose and hurriedly emptied their pockets, giggling with expectation. It is funny how children are: even though they know they don't have what you want they still believe in their own magic, so they go through the exercise certain that somehow they will miraculously produce the searched-for object. Out of the children's pockets and onto their desks poured all kinds of oddities, trinkets, and keepsakes—yellowed marbles, smoothed stones, small crucifixes, and a Star of David pin.

The Officer walked between the aisles as his men kept guard along the wall, their fingers on the triggers of their rifles as if expecting one of the children to pull a grenade from his pocket and toss it at them.

The Officer looked down at every desk, surveying the secrets from each pocket. He stopped at the desk of the child with the Star of David and picked up the shiny pin. The boy at the desk fixed his terrified eyes on me; I was his lifeline to safety.

I threw the boy a rope. "The pin doesn't belong to him."

The Officer turned to me. "I suppose you are going to tell me it belongs to you."

"Yes."

"Yes, you are Jewish?"

"No. But I gave it to him. We are studying different religions in our history class."

The Officer fingered the pin with disdain. "What right have you to teach this kind of subversive history?"

"The right to teach the Bible. It's not on the list of censored books."

The Officer stepped up to me, his face flushed, the red scar on his check stood out prominently. "You think you are very clever. Maybe I should pin this star on your chest."

I quickly unbuttoned the top of my sweater, exposing my neck. "Go ahead. It will go with this."

He looked at the crucifix hanging on the thin gold chain around my neck. He slipped the Star of David in his pocket. "I'm taking this as evidence. It will go into the report." He leaned closer to me. He seemed to realize, for the first time, my condition. "Don't think just because you are pregnant you can get away with anything."

"You should try it sometime. You'd be surprised what you can get away with."

My words made the flesh around his scar redder. He raised his hand to hit me. I did not know if his rage stemmed from simple hatred for what I represented, or if he finally realized that he could well be the father of my child. The room was silent except for the soft whimpering of a few frightened children. He dropped his hand

and strode to the blackboard. He erased what I had written earlier and in bold letters chalked out:

FATHERLAND
OBEDIENCE
VIGILANCE!

The children stiffened, as if facing a strong wind. Alert, they waited for the Officer to speak, to make his speech about how they should be suspicious of all, even their own parents, and must report immediately any inappropriate behavior. But the Officer said nothing. He motioned to his men and they followed him out the door.

That night when I returned to my cottage there was another basket hanging from the nail on my front door. Once more I had honey and sausage and soap, and even some cloth to make a small gown for my child. Someone was keeping watch over me, but who? I turned on my radio, and through the cat-yawling static I was finally able to tune in the faint frequency that broadcast from London. I listened to the litany of codified language, odd as it was, a nonsensical chant offering meaning only to the few: IT IS DIFFICULT FOR AN ARMY TO MARCH IN A MISTRAL. IT IS BEST AN ARMY ATTACK DURING A SIROCCO. WHY EAT BEANS WHEN IT RAINS ORANGES? NANCY LOVES SNAILS, ROGER EATS NAILS. These secret messages, even when I was not listening for one myself, gave a kind of comfort, alone as I was in the cottage. They allowed me to enter a clandestine world, a strange underwater garden where radio static forged a fantastical language constantly shifting its shape—a phantom language of the night, a language of love, of war. Nonsensical. And then I heard: A SHEPHERD DOES NOT GRAZE HIS FLOCK IN THE SAME PASTURE EVERY DAY.

The code! So much had happened that I had almost forgotten. I opened the door and looked at the sky. It was unusually bright. "A SHEPHERD ALWAYS BEGINS HIS JOURNEY ON A FULL MOON."

I knew the rendezvous point. I had been there for the past two full moons, but the sky on both occasions had lowered gray during the day, and by night there was no moon; one could not even see one's hand before one's face. And here was brilliance all around me, everything glittered. The shepherd was on his way. What was my role in this? I could go or stay. I was not expected to participate, only observe. Surely the risk could not be too great.

In these situations there was always risk. I had heard the story of a woman who, like me, was asked only to observe because she had a baby. She was not to take part in the action, so she went. But she was spotted by a patrol with attack dogs; she ran, and the soldiers unleashed their dogs. The dogs caught up to the woman, snarling and biting at her legs, jumping up and ripping away the small baby clutched in her arms, then tore it to pieces. This woman, they say, is inconsolable and wanders the roads at night calling for her child. Yet the child does not answer, so the woman wails for the dogs to come back and devour her, to put her out of her misery.

Why do I think like this? My child is safe within my body; it is the world outside that is unsafe. If I want to change that for my child, then I must act. I cannot afford to dwell on thoughts of dogs ripping children from their mothers' arms when the real threat is the enemy that walks among us, tearing our husbands and brothers, daughters and sons from our arms. I must act to change that. A SHEPHERD ALWAYS BEGINS HIS JOURNEY ON A FULL MOON. I must act, but that does not mean I am fearless. It is quiet. No dogs howl at this full moon.

Lucretia, where are you going?

I go where the shepherd kills all his beloved lambs because the invasion is coming and he does not want the enemy to eat them.

But we have already been invaded.

I have been invaded, but I will not kill my lamb.

Are you drunk on absinthe?

No, I am drunk on pain.

Do you know what you are doing?

Of course! My heart is not a stone tablet on which to carve the word forgiveness, it is flesh and spirit. I am fighting.

What are you fighting for?

I am walking. It is night. I am going. That is the act.

Do you hear the dogs?

Yes, but they cannot stop me.

Do you really think they are dogs? They are so far away. Maybe it is the sound of a plane. Listen more carefully.

I'm listening.

Stop. Hold your breath. Your own breath is what you are hearing. That is what pursues you.

I have walked a long time. I will stop.

What do you hear now?

A plane. I'm certain it's a plane.

Do you see it?

No.

What do you see?

I'm on a high plateau. I can see the whole valley before me, and the dark edges of villages on hilltops, but there are no lights; all the villages are under blackout orders.

But there are lights in the sky. Perhaps a plane?

No. Stars. Winter stars. And above the silhouette of Mont Ventoux the moon hovers, full and brilliant, with a cobalt ring around its edges.

Are you afraid?

Always.

Do you hear dogs now?

No. But I see new light.

What kind of light?

Flickers of light. Flashlight beams on the plateau across the valley. There are specks—it's people standing in a field. They are forming a huge **L** of blinking lights, marking the place on the field for a plane to land. Or maybe there will be a parachute drop of weapons and wireless radios.

Do you wish you were with them?

I have been with them before. I was told to be at this spot to observe. I don't feel guilty.

What is your biggest problem, then?

My feet are cold. No matter how much I stamp them, despite my boots, I can't get them warm. I can't stop shivering.

Do you hear a hum?

Engines.

Where?

On the ground and in the sky. The ground rumbles, the sky whines. I see the plane, and a line of trucks coming up from the village below to the plateau across from me. The trucks must have been hidden in the trees until the plane was sighted. Truckloads of soldiers. Those on the plateau can't hear the trucks. The wind is blowing away from them, blowing in my direction, and it blows clouds that suddenly obscure the light. God has put his hand over the face of the moon. I hear the plane droning through the clouds—it has lost sight of the twinkling **L** on the ground, it banks and circles. There are rifle shots from the plateau, yelling and screaming, high-pitched whistles, and . . .

What else?

Dogs.

Really?

Vicious dogs, barking.

You should leave.

I can't leave. I was instructed to stay and give a report. I'm not in danger. The people on the other plateau are the ones risking their lives.

Can you see them?

Now I can. The clouds have parted again. I see the plane, it is circling over me.

What's happening to the people?

The soldiers are after them. Gunshots.

Get away.

I can't! The door of the plane is opening. I can see it in the moonlight, shining like a beacon. Something falls from the plane. THE LAMB FALLS INTO THE SHEPHERD'S ARMS. I can't tell if it's a person or a long metal canister. Why doesn't the parachute open?

If something is being parachuted onto your plateau the soldiers will be coming. Run.

It might be a person falling from the sky.

*I don't think that plane ever intended to land on the opposite plateau. That lighted **L** was a decoy to draw the soldiers. The real*

drop will be on your plateau. You are the shepherd. The lamb will be
falling into your arms. The soldiers will be coming. You must get
out!

The parachute is opening in the sky. The silk chute blossoms over
my head. It looks like someone is dangling from the cords, trying to
guide the chute away from the oak forest where the wind is blowing.
I'm running on the ground, looking up, hoping somehow that I can
keep the parachutist away from the trees. I can't believe this is happening. All this work, months of planning, and now the parachutist
is heading straight toward the bare winter oaks with their sharp
branches waving in the wind. He can't stop. I see him pulling frantically on his guide lines. The wind has him. Branches crack in the
night—or is it the breaking of bones as the chute drags the man
across the treetops?

Is he alive?

When I get to him he has fallen through the trees. I stand above
him, gasping for breath. He lies on the ground, his clothes ripped, his
face torn. He is a bloody pulp. There is nothing I can do to help him;
it's over.

What do you do?

I unsheath the knife holstered at his belt and begin to cut at the
silk chute. I have to work fast before the soldiers get here.

What are you cutting the parachute for?

My baby. This is a treasure. I can make silk clothes for my baby.

Can't you help the man?

He's dead. I already stripped him of his identification. I know
what to do. This silk is so hard to cut . . .

Who's that coming out of the trees?

I don't know. Two men with guns pointed at me. All I have is this
knife. I stand up, holding the knife in the most menacing position I
can. I want to be shot standing up, not on my knees.

Don't move. Maybe they won't shoot.

Another parachute is coming down.

A man?

No. A long steel canister. It is crashing through the treetops as it heads for us. The men are watching it.

Run while they are not looking.

It's too late. The canister is falling in the clearing between me and the men.

It could be a bomb. The first parachute was to draw you in; the man was already dead when they threw him from the plane. The second drop could be an incendiary bomb and you might die in the flames.

In flames or from the men with guns.

What are they doing?

Running after the canister. It hits the ground hard and is dragged toward me by the fluttering parachute before it stops. One of the men bangs on the canister with a wrench. They try to pry it open.

Now is your chance to get away.

No.

Why? They aren't looking.

The man with the wrench is the Cat Surgeon from the blue room in the Nice hotel.

Him? He almost got you killed. Leave!

The other one is dressed in black leather—pants, jacket, boots, gloves. His face is obscured by a leather mask pulled over his head, and dark goggles cover his eyes. It's impossible to tell who he is.

The Fly?

The barking dogs are getting closer.

You know what to say if he is the Fly. Say it! THUNDER IN MARCH MEANS GOOD ALMONDS.

They unload the canister. Inside it are plastic explosives, money, a field radio, sten guns. They are trying to fit all this into the packs strapped to their backs.

Give the code so they know who you are and don't shoot you as a witness.

The soldiers are coming through the trees with dogs. The two men stagger quickly toward me beneath their heavy loads. They see the knife in my hand, pieces of cut silk in my other hand, the dead parachutist at my feet. The Cat Surgeon shines his flashlight beam in my face, then clicks it off. "I know you. The opera woman."

I look at the man next to him dressed in black. "THUNDER IN MARCH MEANS GOOD ALMONDS."

The man in black says nothing. The Cat Surgeon speaks for him. "The Fly won't talk. If he talks people will know who he is."

I stare into the goggles covering the Fly's eyes, but I can't make anything out. How do I know I can trust these men? I give the code and they answer nothing. Maybe they are trying to trick me into talking before the soldiers arrive. I glance back at the Cat Surgeon and repeat, "THUNDER IN MARCH MEANS GOOD ALMONDS."

He looks at me and smiles in recognition. "DUCK LOVES MOS-QUITO."

I stare at him blankly and keep my mouth shut.

"Oh shit," he grumbles. "That was the wrong one. How am I sup-pose to keep it all in my head when it changes by the hour?" He snaps his fingers nervously, trying to recall something. "Yes, I've got it—cicadas. WHY DO YOU HUNT CICADAS?"

"BECAUSE THEY SUCK THE SAP OF THE ALMOND TREES AS THEY SING."

"Then it is you, Lucretia. We were told you would be here. Is the Englishman dead?"

I look down at the bloodied man. "Yes."

"Why are you cutting up his parachute?"

"To make clothes for my baby."

"Are you crazy?" He grabs for the silk in my hand. "If you're caught with this they will know who you are. It will give us all away."

I hold onto the material, trying to pull it back. "It's mine! I need it!" Tears were on my cheeks, tears of rage. He wasn't going to deprive my baby of clothes.

The Fly grabs my wrist, squeezing it so tightly I feel my bones will break. A pain shoots up my arm, forcing me to release the silk.

There is a mouth hole cut in the Fly's leather face mask. The edges of the hole, damp with spittle, flutter with his breathing.

"We've got to split up." The Cat Surgeon speaks above the insistent barking of the dogs closing in. "Lucretia, go home."

"No, I'll stay with you. We have a better chance of defending ourselves together."

"You must go home. If the soldiers go there and find you gone, they'll know you violated the curfew and were part of this tonight. They'll arrest you." The Cat Surgeon takes my arm. "Come with me, I'll get you home."

The Fly pulls his revolver and puts it to the Cat Surgeon's head.

"What's going on? Are you crazy? Why are you pulling a gun on *me*?"

The Fly says nothing, but the hammer clicks into firing position.

"Okay." The Cat Surgeon lets go of my arm. "She goes with you."

I can see nothing of the Fly's features behind the mask and goggles. Who is taking me away? The dogs are barking; behind them are running footsteps.

The Cat Surgeon tightens the straps of the heavy pack on his back. "Remember," he says to the Fly, "tomorrow morning you must make the appointed rendezvous. Be there! Too much has been risked tonight—what we've picked up here must get to its destination." He turns to leave. "One last thing. Damn, man, after all we've been through, why would you pull a gun on me? What does she mean to you?"

The Fly is silent. The Cat Surgeon hurries off into the darkness along the plateau's edge and disappears over the side into the ravine.

Suddenly I gasp, not in pain, but in utter surprise. The Fly puts his leather gloved hand over my mouth to silence me. I pull his hand away and whisper, "I think my water has broken." A wet warmth is spreading down my inner thighs. How could this be happening? I'm not due to deliver yet. Panic overtakes me. I should have gone with the Cat Surgeon; he would have known what to do.

The Fly cranes his head in the direction the Cat Surgeon has taken, listening to a distant sound. Truck engines. The soldiers are trying to surround us. The Fly quickly starts running, leaving me alone.

The wind is at my back, blowing away from the direction of the barking dogs. I realize the Fly is running in the direction from which it will be hardest for the dogs to pick up our scent. The dogs will follow the Cat Surgeon. I lose sight of the Fly in the darkness. Is he leaving me there as bait for the dogs? I am afraid to move. The wetness on my thighs thickens. I am trapped between two fears. If I stay I will be shot by soldiers or torn to pieces by dogs; if I run, I might lose my baby. Clouds swirl overhead and cut the light of the moon. I feel a hand come around my waist, its arm locks behind my back and nearly lifts me from the ground. I hold my breath, too frightened to make a sound. Then I am in the air, my feet only occasionally touching the ground as we move into the night. I feel the skin of an animal against the side of my cheek. When I turn, I see the Fly's leather mask. I am being carried, half on earth and half in the air, in flight from the snarling dogs and shouting soldiers close behind.

Lucretia? Do you hear me? Why won't you answer? Are you there?
Please talk to me.

I have to be quiet.

Where are you?

I can't tell you exactly where I am.

That's okay. Just talk to me.

I told you I have to be quiet.

No one can hear you talking to me.

I don't know—I don't know. Sometimes I think people can hear my thoughts. I think people are listening.

Is the Fly there?

He's up on the ridge. I'm not certain he's alive. There was gunfire. It's quieter now. I think he killed some soldiers and dogs.

If he's up on the ridge, then you must be low and hidden.

Yes, in a field of sunflowers. The sunflowers are all winter-dead, standing on brittle stalks. Their once bright faces have had the seeds pecked out of them by birds. It seems I am surrounded by giant pockmarked people.

How is your baby? Are you in pain?
My water has stopped flowing. Maybe it was a false alarm.
Can you walk?
I still need help. There is a pain.
What if the Fly doesn't come back? He could abandon you.
I told him to leave me. His work is just as important as mine.
You are a hindrance, a liability.
If he doesn't return, then I will crawl.
Start now. You can't have your baby in a field like a cow.
I can't have a baby—I must have a baby.
Start crawling. He's not coming back.
He's trying to lead them away from me, to keep them off my scent—the dogs can smell me.
Lucretia, this is no way to end! Push the pain down in your belly and crawl.
I'm crawling through the dead sunflower people.
Good. Keep going. Can you stand up?
Yes, but I must bite my tongue.
Why?
To stifle the pain in my stomach. My tongue is bleeding.
Keep going, it's you and you alone now. No one can save you but yourself.
Yes, I'm running. It hurts.
You're lying to me. You've stopped.
I feel wetness on my thighs again. I'm afraid.
You can rest when you are dead. Keep going.
Gunfire is all around, bullets smash through the dry faces of the sunflower people.
Is there any way out?
No. Flashes of light on the ridge, tracer bullets stream through the air, cutting down the sunflower people around me. Trucks close in, guns mounted on them firing rapidly.
You'll die if you don't start moving.
Shush. The bullets have stopped. Someone's close to me, crawling through the mutilated sunflower people.

Take out your knife and hide it in your skirts. When he gets close enough, stab him. It's him or your baby.

I understand.

Don't lose your nerve.

There's a loud blast. One of the trucks has exploded; soldier-flesh and metal are blown into the air and whistle by me. A ball of flame billows over the disfigured sunflower people. Fire. The sunflower people are on fire.

Stab the man!

I can't.

Why?

It's the Fly! He pulls me to my feet and supports me as we run through smoke and flames. The sunflower people moan and crack in the intense heat. Flames catch my skirts. The Fly beats the flames out with his gloved hands. It is so hard to breathe! How can he breathe in that leather mask? I want to pull it off to give him more air. He doesn't have to hide from me. The leather around his mouth is wet from saliva and sweat. I start to cough, choking from the smoke, the heat is burning my lungs. The Fly puts his hand over my mouth to keep me from being heard. The smoke ahead becomes thicker, a roiling cloud; from it bullets flash and dogs yelp. We plunge straight into the darkest part of the cloud.

Lucretia, I lost you in the smoke. Where are you?

I'm in my cottage.

You are safe! Maybe you were dreaming and you didn't cross a field of burning sunflower people?

No, it happened. But now there are growling dogs outside.

Oh God!

The dogs are panting, racing back and forth before the stone walls. They leap against the locked door, their claws tearing at the wood, trying to get to me.

Where is the Fly? I hope he is gone. Perhaps the dogs will give up and go after him.

The Fly brought me here. I could barely walk. He didn't have time to leave before the dogs found us.

What's that pounding?

The soldiers, banging on my door with their rifle butts.

Do you have a gun?

Yes, the Fly's sten gun, but I'm not going to shoot myself.

I didn't mean that. You can defend yourself!

How? If I start shooting they will kill me and my baby. The best thing is to stay calm, to let them capture me and take me out. They can't prove I wasn't here all night.

What about the Fly? They will find him.

He's in the cellar. They will find him, and they will find these letters hidden in baskets.

But everything, everyone, will be exposed!

The soldiers will find the Fly. That is why I must give him time to finish what he is doing. When the soldiers go down into the cellar the Fly will blow it up with plastic explosives. Everything will be destroyed.

He doesn't have to sacrifice you too. Your baby must live. Shout to the soldiers that you will surrender!

The door splinters, breaking open to the night. Black faces of dogs lunge from the dark, their mouths exposing slashes of white teeth.

Can they get to you?

No, the soldiers hold them back on leashes.

If you keep still the dogs won't attack.

Their mouths foam, their teeth snap, they're crazed from hunting me all night. They have me cornered. One voice rises above the shouting and barking. I know that voice. I seek it out. There he is, standing behind the dog handlers, his words commanding silence. It is the Officer: his face flushed from exertion, the red scar on his cheek standing out vividly.

Ask for his mercy. He saw you at the school, he knows you are pregnant, he knows the baby might be his—

I won't ask him for mercy.

You must!

He's demanding that the soldiers quiet their dogs. The animals sit stiffly on their haunches, breathing rapidly, their pink tongues dangling with anticipation as the Officer speaks.

"Did you really think you could escape me?"

"Escape what? I was here all night."

"Sooner or later, my clever Joan of Arc, you had to be caught."

"I'm no Joan of Arc. You don't know your history. She was brave. I'm just a schoolteacher."

"You are not, you are much more. The first time I saw you in the cherry orchard, I thought, I've seen this one before, I know this body, this naked body."

"Impossible."

"And later I remembered your painter friend. Where is he now, this famous man? Is he hiding under a rock, or in your cellar? Perhaps he has run away to America with all the other intellectual heroes."

"I don't know where he is. If you think he's here, why don't you search for him?"

"Then I remembered where I had seen you before: in a museum, in a painting enclosed by a heavy gold frame. I know who you are. Your body is quite famous."

"I'm not who you think I am."

"Ah, but you are, I'm certain."

"If I were that woman I would be with the famous painter. He would have saved me."

"Perhaps. Or perhaps you like to play night games in your scenic countryside."

"I have no idea what you are talking about."

"I could never discover where you lived. That is one thing you were quite clever about."

"You can't prove I wasn't here all night."

"We do not need proof to charge you. Partisans are not protected by international law. They are no better than common criminals, thieves, or murderers."

"Then arrest me, but your charge will never hold up."

"Yes it will, for there is someone waiting to step forward and denounce you."

"That is only accusation. You still have no proof that I wasn't here all night."

"But I do have proof, right here in this house. Don't you know how the dogs found you?"

I don't speak. I think of how the Fly had feared the dogs would pick up my scent when my water broke. He made us walk four kilometers in a shallow stream to put the dogs off our trail.

"You fail to answer me, but I shall not arrest you. You will not have to stand trial. You are going to die without my laying a hand on you."

I don't understand what he means. I need to get out of the house before he discovers the Fly and everything blows up. "If you have someone willing to denounce me, take me to them so I can confront their lie."

"Once again you are in a hurry to be arrested and taken away. Why?"

"To clear my name."

"But you will soon be dead. You are already condemned."

"What are you saying?"

"How do you think the dogs found you?" He points to the floor.

In the dim light I see reddish-brown spots glistening on the tiles. In my haste, in my chaotic state, I believed that my water had broken. But what drips down my thighs is not water, it is blood. I am nauseated. The pain at the center of my stomach punches like a fist. I hear a whimpering sound. I see one of the dogs licking a splatter of blood off the floor.

The Officer steps forward and unbuckles Aunt Mimi's belt, which is loosely cinched around the waist of my heavy coat. Two soldiers grab me by the shoulders and throw me onto the bed. The Officer raises my hands above my head, wraps the belt around my wrists and ties its end to the iron bedpost. The dogs strain at their leashes. Is the Officer going to let them have me? The dogs whine with expectation. I pull hard at the belt with my upstretched arms.

"There's nothing you can do to escape."

I know the Fly is in the basement. There is no way he can surprise the Officer and the soldiers, for he has given me his gun. If the dogs are going to chew the baby out of my belly I want everyone to die. I want the Fly to detonate the bomb in the cellar.

"So, my little heroine, I am going to leave you in your bed of roses. I am going to let your bastard baby be the death of you."

The pain in my stomach is unbearable. I bite my lip to keep silent. Blood fills my mouth. I want to spit it at the Officer, to color him with my rage, but I do not. I do not want to give him any satisfaction, any indication of the shame he has inflicted on me. He clicks the heels of his boots together and spins around, commanding the others to follow. The soldiers pull the leashed dogs away from the bed. In a moment they are gone.

A fire burns in the ice cave and rain slashes across my forehead. Dogs howl in the distance. I float alone on a raft in a sea of blood. The howling of dogs is the howling of wind blowing through the smashed open door of my house. My house is freezing, it is the ice cave. A rain of sweat spurts from my forehead. I clench my fists against the pain invading my body; a thousand barbed fishhooks rip at my flesh. I rise from the raft of the bed, a ghost of myself, a smear of a cloud, nearly lifeless, cut loose. I see myself on the blood-soaked bed. My baby is down there inside me, tearing the life from me, trying to tear itself free. I plummet back into my body. I can't escape this pain. I want this pain. It is the only way I know I am still alive. It is the only way I know another life lives, taking me with it as it rips and kicks.

The wind hurls around the room, an icy hand slapping my face and punching my stomach. My legs are raised, my knees are cocked, bending my stiffening body in ever-deepening pain, breaking the life from me. All at once I want to stand, to protect, to be a tree with roots refusing to be ripped loose in this hurricane blowing through my body and out my soul. But I cannot stand. Some unseen force holds me, pushes me back down. The whir of the wind beats a distinct pulse in my ear, like a small baby's fist banging at the back of my eyes. Why don't I hear the baby cry? Why do I hear only my own voice, screaming, then strangled to silence? Darkness.

The wind departs the ice cave, sucked away in bleakness. There is crying. I do hear it. It is far away. No. It is next to me. Someone else is clinging to this raft in a sea of blood. My baby! My baby has survived, my baby is with me! I reach out my hand. I feel a smooth head, but it is large. Did I give birth to something awful? I struggle to rise. I struggle to see in this room dripping blood-red icicles. I must focus. I am a mother. I am a mother no matter what I gave birth to.

I see my feet. They are naked and white, bound by barbed wire and thorny stems of roses. What is this smooth head I feel, the sobbing I hear? Something is coming clear now. I am touching the leather mask of the Fly, who kneels beside my bed. I cannot see his eyes behind the goggles, but I can hear sobbing. The Fly sobs.

I am a casualty, something has been torn from me that can never be replaced. I am a casualty of war, of those who destroy love. This I do not want to admit, even to myself, for I thought I was stronger, I thought my female nature and my secure sense of self would rise above all else.

I cannot explain the enormous emptiness engulfing me as I awake in my red room. I am still numb, not realizing wholly what has happened, not knowing completely who I am. How long have I been alone? The Fly is gone. My hands are free, I have been untied from the bed. The sheets around me are hard with dried blood. I summon the strength to lift my head and move its aching weight to look down across my body. My ankles are bound tightly together by Aunt Mimi's belt. What I had thought, in my painful hallucinations, was wire and roses binding my ankles, is really Mimi's belt. Things come back, pieces of the puzzle float through the haze. As I recall particulars of what happened my mind refuses to go there, can't go there—not across the clamoring void where the raft sank in a crimson sea. As I breathe my split lips tear even more. The cottage door is open, the winter sun scars my eyes with brightness. I don't want to live another day.

A silhouette appears against the sun in the doorway; someone in a straw hat and carrying a harvest basket, the kind of basket I found nailed to my door in the past. Maybe it's not the sun that scars my eyes, but the piercing blue light of his eyes. He enters and sets the basket on the table. I try to speak but only hollow coughing comes, choking me back to silence. He closes the door and lights a match to wood in the fireplace. The slightest heat begins. From the basket he unpacks honey, sausage, lavender soap, and powerfully scented bundles of herbs. Water boils in a pan on the stove. A warm cloth covers my brow. His eyes are near, shining down. I move my hand toward him. I thought he was so close but he is an eternity away, untouchable. My hand falls back to the bed, weakened from the exertion. I struggle to find breath to speak. "Bee Keeper, my man is gone, my baby is dead."

He speaks. I am startled that he isn't mute. His words are as direct as the countryside he lives in.

"I tied your feet together with a belt, like one of my goats in the mountains when she miscarries. I tied your feet together so all the life wouldn't bleed out of you."

He lifts my unresisting body and pulls the bloodied sheets from beneath me.

Then I say something unlike me but so true it is only natural: "You saved me."

Darkness closes in and releases me. I fall into that darkness, spinning away in a clean bed, free of blood and sweat, screams and tears, rocking away from agony. I hear the Bee Keeper in the darkness. "Mother yourself, woman. The milk from your own breast is your salvation. Your milk has the power to make the blind man see."

There is a pungent taste on my lips, not mother's milk, something different, a warm liquid fills my mouth. I swallow. A heady aroma engulfs me—basil, wild marjoram, sage and savory, juniper and mint. I am being fed the essence of the Provençal earth. The medicinal liquid of plants courses through my veins, revives my blood. With each suck the pain ebbs, with each suck another hurt falls away. Finally there are flames unseen but blessed heat felt, and unfamiliar hands caressing.

I am released, for the time, for the moment. A moment arches into hours, perhaps days. Rocking between life and death until I am succored toward light and awake to see a brilliant shape, *my baby.* Half the size of a normal baby, it is being washed gently with lavender soap, then rubbed with almond and rosemary oil, its smooth skin anointed. My baby's shiny being is wrapped carefully in a blanket, spun into a wool cocoon, and placed in the Bee Keeper's harvest basket.

I am beckoned to leave. I rise from my bed, dazed by the day. At first I don't feel my knees, nor my feet, but they are moving. I hear my breath like that of a stranger as I go further from the cottage, leaning against the shoulder of the Bee Keeper. We travel higher, leaving all time behind. My heart is confused as I enter a country I've never encountered before, a wild forest, a tangle of green, narrow paths and footbridges across streams. I fall behind. The Bee Keeper waits, standing in his rough flannel shirt and thick corduroy trousers, his eyes gleaming beneath the broad-brimmed hat. In one hand he holds the harvest basket; in the other hand he carries a pickax. I catch up to him. He tucks the ax under his belt and puts his arm around my waist for support. He could take me to jump off a cliff and I would follow. He is mine to follow now.

The Bee Keeper's solid boots dig into the earth as we continue. The forest darkens the day, the sun glides behind the vast plateau of Mont Ventoux. We climb. I hope I never see the world below again, I hope we'll keep walking across the clouds. A sound ahead grows louder. It is like a river rushing over stones, then the cascading roar of a waterfall, then onrushing waves smashing against the shore. We emerge into a meadow and the sound becomes overwhelming, a mighty buzz vibrating the earth.

Across the meadow the sheer face of a cliff looms; before it mil-
lions of orbs dazzle the air in a translucent flurry of wings—*bees*. A
world of bees such as I never knew existed. Bees swarm on the riddled face of the cliff, in and out of crevices and holes tunneled
through stone by the driving force of rain over centuries. Now the
ancient erosions are inhabited by thousands of bee colonies, a universe of bees, touching, buzzing, flying, crawling. The atmosphere
throbs. I am at the source of all humming. I stop before the cliff. I go
into the hive of myself, mother my emotions. The whir of wings
beats a fierce pulse in my ear, like a small baby's fist banging at the
back of my eyes. Why don't I hear the baby's cry? The pickax swings
in front of me, its blade slices the earth, sparks fly off sharp steel,
stones scatter. The cliff shimmers through a curtain of bees. The hole
in the earth deepens.

The Bee Keeper takes the perfect body wrapped within its wool
cocoon from the basket and lowers it into the hole he has dug. He
covers it with earth and stones to form an impenetrable sarcopha-
gus. I fall to my knees and press my ear to the stones. Now I hear my
baby cry. Now I know my baby lives. The deep hum of bees vibrates
up from the earth, filling my emptiness. My tears splash on the
stones.

Francisco, what came to me on that original Day of the Bees now
leaves me. My baby's spirit is alive, borne away in the living drone. I
hear laughter reverberating across the face of the beehived cliff. The
laughter of a thousand children, bubbling over from a thousand
fountains in a thousand towns. There is no more sorrow. There is no
sorrow when the child becomes the mother, when the mother
returns to herself.

I am healing now, the Bee Keeper is healing me, he straightens my bent spirit. He knew there was still something in my Provençal soul that would respond to the ancient Romans who once ruled here, some trickle of blood memory that would rouse me. It wasn't until my strength returned fully, replenished by the Bee Keeper's herbal concoctions and the nourishing foods of the forest, that I recalled something I had read as a schoolgirl. During Roman times, wives of the centurions would anxiously await their absent husbands. When the soldiers returned and news of the missing spread among the waiting women, the inconsolable widows wept and banged their foreheads against the ground. The only thing that could heal the widows was to take them to a place of bees, where the immense drone of the colony would overwhelm the women's burdened souls, suck their wailing grief, and disperse it in dissolving shards of light.

I feel the deep hum of the vibrating bee earth whenever the Bee Keeper is near. I watch the days sail by in a haze of pollen dust. At a certain point in life a woman surrenders her notion of passion and succumbs to the solace of compassion. Francisco, do you understand what I am telling you? I still want you, but I no longer need you. My womb is deaf to you. The ability to bear children has been forever taken from me. My menstrual periods will always be violent, in revolt against rhythms that now have no purpose, like waves crashing on a barren beach. I am not like you. You can live without love, but not without passion. So you cannot live without a woman— whether it be me, a rich socialite, or a paid model with the scent of pine in her hair.

You have written to say that what you left for me in the Bearcat at Elouard's farm will explain all; meanwhile you left me here to wait, alone and cuffed to our memory. My darling, if a woman's dress is on fire, you don't offer her a piece of cake. We have love, but we no longer have a life. You don't allow me that. Do you think I only wanted to be with you in order to share your triumphs? You insult me now by not allowing me to share your failures.

My darling, I did not betray you. I was lost to you long before the Bee Keeper found me. At night when he comes to me, I can smell the bee pollen on his skin. He is already taken, but so am I, for the rest of my life, by you. He gives me his honey, but my hive is empty. Maybe his queen knows this and that is why she is not jealous. Maybe she is the queen because she learned compassion first. I have learned that the Bee Keeper does not keep her; she keeps him. Now he keeps me from you, but his heart belongs to the queen.

He seduces me with small presents, simple offerings from the land: pots of honey, loaves of olive bread, clutches of wild flowers, hares and partridges stuffed with dried apricots. He warms my feet before a fire of grapevine wood. It was he, that long-ago night when I found the dead woman on the road, who took the bottle of absinthe from me while I slept and smashed it on the ground. He was the one who left the harvest baskets filled with gifts to sustain me. He is the one who knows that a single bee must fly over twenty-five thousand kilometers just to fill one jar of honey. He is the one who knows that a bee must visit each blossom at least eight times in one day in order for a perfect fruit to bloom. He is the one who knows that the male honey bee's genitals explode when he makes love to his queen, filling her up so that only he impregnates her. He is the one who knows that no matter how much honey he fills me with, I will never again be the sweet girl I was with you.

He is used to being calm around bees; he knows that fear will cause them to sting. He touches me gently, his fingers have the feel of light winged bodies on my skin. When I lie against his chest I hear the hum inside his heart, the flutter of bee wings fanning their nectar into a deep weave of honey. I am no longer drunk on green-gold absinthe, but on the mercurial flow of propolis, a milky secretion of bees after they have feasted on the resinous sap of trees. This royal jelly is fed only to the queen; it is her sustenance.

I bathe in the morning with lavender soap, running the sweet scent over my skin, hoping to attract my Bee Keeper. He smells the scent rising off my breasts as he walks between the purple mounded rows of lavender in the mountains. He knows that the queen is the center of the hive, keeper of the home, it is her world. He calls to me and I go. The ground beneath my feet is a white carpet of fallen almond blossoms. The clouds above pile up on themselves, creating a cirrus lace filtering the sun. I lie on the earth's carpet, the branches of almond trees overhead. I am in the queen's world where males are only guardians, pollinators of fruit and flower. In the distance thunder slaps the curve of the horizon. A buzz fills the air. The Bee Keeper lies down beside me, our outstretched hands move toward each other, through falling blossoms our fingers touch. A bee lands on his forehead, it travels over his face and down his arm, crossing over the bridge of his fingers to mine. The sensation of the bee makes me shiver as it glides up my stomach, across my breasts, and along my arched neck. I am afraid to move. Wings brush my cheek. The bee stops on my quivering lip. The sky is struck through with lightning, a sky bruised blue from suck of memory.

Francisco, I am not betraying you. The Bee Keeper's heart belongs to the queen. He deserves to come home and taste crushed berries when his lips sting mine with a kiss. I am the woman with bee-stung lips. Do you hear me cry when he kisses me? I am not certain I cry for you, or for this man attempting to release me with kindness. He does not stop when he touches the gold ring at the center of my being. He says nothing, but he knows. How cold the ring you pierced me with must feel to him. Cold as ice. How many men have gone into how many women and felt another man there? It is not that uncommon; it is life. It takes a brave man to continue, to penetrate to the center of the hive where fresh honey awaits.

Lucretia, where are you?

   I am walking through orchards of leafless trees. I am walking through barren winter fields of cut grapevines. I am true as a blind watchdog who barks only when it senses danger. I reveal less than half, exposing just the shadow. My world is light playing on stone walls, a moon at noon, a sunset at midnight, a train in a tunnel, a plane cutting through a cloud, a man parachuting into a burning sea. My reality is discovering a young girl stripped and shot, the bullet holes in her naked skin the size of the buttons on the convent dress she once wore. My reality is hiding with men in the mountains, watching them scratching for something to eat beneath the oak trees, searching for truffles, wild asparagus, tiny mushrooms, and instead finding hidden mines that blow off their faces. I have heard brave laughter at night in the mountain hideouts, the accordions squeezing out plaintive tunes for gypsies and bankers to dance together, the music inspiring petty thieves and priests to lock arms and join in. They are all strange comrades in arms, queer fellows in the bed of war. I cannot quit them, I cannot betray them.

I know some would turn away from this sorrow, judge it against more peaceful times and say, For God's sake, woman, seek your own happiness, you have suffered enough! But these are not peaceful times. Let those who are not strong enough to know of these things, much less live them, abandon me here. Let the bluebirds of optimism take flight, for this is about survival of the fittest in an unfit world. The battle is real, we are occupied by a foreign body.

It is difficult for an army to march in a mistral, so sometimes one person must act alone. The blind watchdog's eyes are a luminous red in the midday sun. The black crows in the barren fields don't even croak as I pass by. They know I can take apart a sten gun in seconds; they know I can cook up a plastique bomb faster than I can make an omelette. I keep moving in a shifting landscape.

Lucretia, are you dreaming?

No, but I think you ask the important question. Is this a dream? Maybe peacetime is the dream. Maybe we are only truly awake when there is war.

That's a terrible thought.

It's a thought I've had while destroying ancient Roman bridges. After the charge is set beneath a bridge there is the explosive blast, balanced arched stones fall into water, the poetry of purpose is erased by the need for survival. Can you tell me what is reality and what is dream?

I can't tell you anything. I can barely stand to hear you speak. Your words are filled with heartbreak. I can only hope that you are not angry with me for reading these letters, tracing your pain on the page. This is not the kind of thing I would normally read, it is too private, too intense. But something compels me to continue. Perhaps it is shame.

Shame? Who are you now? Who is reading my life? You used to be Zermano, you used to be my baby, you used to be Louise.

I can't answer that question. I can only fear for this journey you are on. I am compelled to take each step with you, to see where it leads, to bear witness.

Watch out for the bomb craters. You might step in one and break an ankle.

I will be careful.

You will be quiet. You will follow me for a long way and a long time. You will watch me go to the sanctuary. It is not quite dawn yet.

I am watching. What is this place?

The Virgin Mary appeared here in the seventeenth century: she of the exposed heart, she of the mother's grief for a lost child, she with a mother's power to heal. For ages faithful pilgrims have descended the steps into this vaulted stone crypt, where Our Lady's statue is illuminated by votive candles. In the chapel over the crypt the walls are covered with photographs of children—children lost to disease, to childbirth, to the unknown. Photographs to remind the Virgin Mother that these are missing children to be kept safe until their mothers can join them. There are alcoves with still more photographs: children on crutches, in wheelchairs, in sickbeds, in steel braces, in military uniforms. Hundreds of expectant faces stare from the walls, pleading to be saved, healed, returned.

Did you come here for your child?

No. I don't believe in this house of lamentation. We are all missing children.

You have lost your faith.

Faith abandoned *me.*

Why are you here then?

In the south altar of the sanctuary there is a beautiful Madonna with Child carved in gilded wood. I was told to go there and light a candle, so I do. The candle's light illuminates more faces on the wall. These photographs are old and yellowed, covered with dust and cobwebs, the faces faded by time. Among them is a fresh piece of paper standing out bright white, on it is neatly penned: LUCRETIA, I AM IN THE GROTTO.

Who is in the grotto?

He is. He told me to meet him here.

Who is he? The Bee Keeper?

Follow me outside and up the trail on the hillside rising behind the chapel. We can't get lost, there are crude wooden crosses staked into the ground marking the way. Don't stop to catch your breath. Here we are. A trick of the trail brings us out under a rock overhang into a grotto half obscured by ferns. In the cool dampness of the grotto is a lichen-covered marble statue of Our Lady. She is seated, cradling her full-grown son in her arms. Her son is dead from the cross, his hands, feet, and side pierced with fatal wounds. The expression on her face is ironic. If she can let Him go, if she can give Him up to heaven, then why can't we?

The sun is coming up.

It changes the color of the rocky overhang above us from gray to an ethereal milky beige.

Beautiful.

Watch as the hand of light points into the grotto and flares into another color.

It's a gorgeous rose hue.

Turn around, the entire valley below us is lighting up.

I hear church bells.

Look further, beyond the vineyards, farms and orchards. Above all is Mont Ventoux.

It's massive in this light.

That's where my baby is, where the Bee Keeper keeps watch.

There are fires in the valley.

Farmers are burning vine cuttings from their vineyards. Soon the sky will be smudged with smoke and Mont Ventoux lost in haze.

Someone is coming.

Quick, get behind the statue.

Who is it?

It's not him.

Then who?

It's the Cat Surgeon. He's calling to me.

"Lucretia, is that you in there?"

How did he know I would be here?

"Goddamn it, answer!"

I'm not answering unless he speaks the code.

"THE DOG WITH EYES BARKS AT ALL HE SEES."

He knows the code, I can answer. "THE BLIND DOG ONLY BARKS WHEN IT SENSES DANGER. Why did *you* come? I was supposed to meet Monsieur Royer."

"I have a note from him. Here, take it. These are your instructions."

"Where is Monsieur Royer?"

"There's no time for explanations, just do as you are told." The Cat Surgeon stares at me strangely. "What's that on your dress?"

I look down. My coat is open and the top of my dress is spotted with two damp stains. I can't tell him what is happening. There is no baby, but there is still milk, and even in times of danger it flows.

I am marching. I march alone, but soon I will be joined by many.

Lucretia, do you think it will ever stop raining?

At night the snails move. We move.

So dark, so wet.

Walking across these fields, with the suck of mud around my rubber boots, the rain quickly erases my steps, as if I have never been here.

There are patrols everywhere in this area.

I am grey in grey rain. I am invisible, but the sten gun under my coat is hard steel.

You have become so hard.

If the birds peck away all the soft flesh of the peach, they come to the hard stone at its center.

The rain is blinding.

The note said the meeting is tonight. I have my instructions. Everyone will be there.

Do you remember the code?

Day of the Bees

IF YOU WANT TO EAT SNAILS YOU MUST STARVE THEM FIRST.

What is this village we are climbing to now?

Its name makes no difference, its time has long passed, it is deserted. Once, other wars were fought here in the narrow streets leading up this terraced mountainside. Catholics and Protestants hunted each other, burned each other, beheaded each other, threw each other from the ramparts of the castle above us now.

I can barely see the ramparts. Are they still there?

Yes, but everything is overgrown, vines cling to the crumbling stone. It's a medieval ghost town. Rain rushes down eroded streets and through destroyed walls of houses. . . . I hear something other than pounding rain.

I don't hear anything.

Up ahead, through that arched doorway—footsteps. Someone is there, on the other side of the stone wall.

The instructions said they would all be here.

I can't be sure it's them.

Just walk through the door and say the code.

Forget the code. I'm going in with my gun ready. I'm sliding along the stone wall, I'm stepping through the doorway. So dark. What's that shuffling sound? Eyes in the night. Yellow eyes. Growling. Something huge comes at me from the blackness, clattering over broken floor tiles.

Shoot!

No, it might be them!

Shoot before it's too late!

I'm shooting. God, I'm shooting! Red bullets pierce yellow eyes. It's hit but it's still coming. It crashes out of the darkness, banging into me, throwing me back against the wall, knocking the wind out of me.

What's that strange breathing?

Not me, I'm too terrified to make a sound.

What you shot is next to you, moaning. Shine your flashlight on it.

Yes, yes, I'm switching it on. I'm shining it.

It's a huge pig!

A wild boar lies on its side, its stunned eyes staring into the light beam, blood bubbling from its black snout.

There's grunting back there in the corner.

I'll shine the light.

Baby pigs scattering, confused!

I have killed their mother. This is where she had them, to get out of the rain.

Pigs living in the houses of ghosts.

Someone's calling from outside. It must be them. I'm not waiting. I'm shouting the code. "IF YOU WANT TO EAT SNAILS YOU MUST STARVE THEM FIRST!"

A voice shouts back. "THAT'S SO THEY'LL SPIT OUT ALL THEIR POISONS."

They know the code. I'm going out. The rain slashes my face; I can't see well. Shapes in the grey. The same voice that shouted the code speaks now.

"Good evening, Louise."

My name is Lucretia. Who can this be?

"I hope I haven't kept you waiting." The grey shape in the rain steps forward. It is the Officer. "Drop your gun."

I can make out others, more soldiers with their rifles aimed at me. I drop my gun.

"That's better. Now be a good girl and come with us."

Perhaps if I act like I'm going to surrender without trouble they will let down their guard and I can find a chance to run, disappear in the rain. If I am arrested I must be abandoned by those like me who move in the night for security reasons. It will be the end of Lucretia, but not the end of the war. Lucretia must survive. I spin around and run. A swift pain explodes in the back of my head as something blunt strikes me. The rain swells up in fierce gusts and everything goes black.

The night consumes me and a dark bird bursts from my chest,

explodes from my throat, and soars skyward. It looks back, watching my every move, alive to my unconscious state as I am pulled down steps rushing with a dangerous torrent of rainwater. The bird follows as soldiers drag me through mud and throw me into the back of a truck. Rain beats down as I am driven along winding roads, past flooded vineyards and orchards, then up through towering stone columns of an old Roman gate: the village of Reigne. The truck stops in the square before the church and I am dragged out. The Officer bangs the iron knocker of the church door. A priest finally opens the door. The priest, dressed in a nightshirt, holds a lantern that illuminates his frightened face. The Officer whispers; the priest nods nervously and closes the door. The Officer motions to his men. They drag me up the church steps, press my back against the door and stretch my arms out at my sides. The Officer puts a fist under my chin and shoves up my face. I can see him as clearly as the bird above, and I can hear him.

"Normally I like to hang traitors by the neck."

The Officer motions to a soldier standing by the truck, who rushes up the steps with a canvas sack. The Officer takes a can of paint and a brush from the sack. He pries off the can's lid and dips the brush in. Above my head I hear the swish of his brush, painting words.

"This time I'm going to do something different." The Officer throws the brush down and pulls a hammer and nails from the sack.

I struggle to pull my arms free but the soldiers hold them tight, squeezing my wrists.

"Now Joan of Arc can serve her country!"

I feel a sharp nail press into the palm of my hand. The hammer flashes by my head, strikes the nail, pierces it straight through my hand into the door. My body stiffens against the pain. A second nail pricks my other palm. The hammer slams again, pounding the nail down through the bone. I hold my breath against the electric jolt of pain.

"No last words?"

I'm not going to cry out my agony.

The Officer pushes my face up again with his fist. "Your lover became famous by nailing your nude image to the walls of museums. I have nailed your body to our Lord's house for the world to despise."

I will not speak. I throttle my moan.

The Officer turns away with his men. They get in the truck and drive away.

I gaze down. The steps before me run red in the rain. Red from paint and blood.

I see myself through the eyes of the dark bird hovering above the village square. I see the rain has stopped, and in the church tower the priest rings the bell, calling the faithful. But there will be no morning mass, for the church door remains locked. The priest is doing what he was told to do by the Officer: calling the people to come and bear witness. I see through the dark bird's eyes that I am slumped against the door, hanging by nailed hands, the painted word TRAITOR still visible above my head. The trail of blood from my body leads down the church steps to the worshipers dressed in their finest for Sunday-morning mass. Some hold their children's hands. All are motionless. Not one steps forward to help or to see if I am alive. In the back of my throat is a thirst so savage it tears at me with greater pain than that in my hands, a thirst that grates as if all the sand of the Sahara fills my mouth. I am ashamed. I am ashamed for myself, and for those who cannot step forward because of fear or disgust, who cannot reach out in order to save themselves. Theirs is a complicity of silence.

As the morning moves on they begin to drift away until only a young girl is left watching me. She looks like the beautiful girl I saw that day in the garden below the castle. Is it really her? She stares, trying to divine what the woman nailed to the door has to do with her Lord nailed to His cross inside the church. The girl's mother comes and pulls her away. The girl tries to say something, but her mother places a hand over her mouth. I try to call to the girl but my own lips are cracked, my mouth filled with sand.

I cannot speak as the life drains from me, but I can think. *Think of something beautiful.* How can I think of something beautiful with holes in my ruined soul? *Think.* The wind howls through the holes. *Something beautiful.* I want to be surrounded by children. The wind blows. It's cold and I'm thirsty. *Think to stay alive.* There once was a sea captain from Provence who brought his true love back from China. On a hill he built a tower for her to watch the sea's horizon for his ship. One day he returned, only to discover that her home-sickness had outweighed her love for him—she was gone. After that the sea captain was a captive in his own tower, watching the horizon for his love to return.

Think. Francisco, I send you my love shaped like a boat, carrying kisses to you. My breath fills the sails and the wondrous boat moves on, battered by so many storms, but I will survive until the boat reaches shore. *Think.* Francisco, it was only when I lost you, and could not stop loving you, that I knew I was destined to be yours for-ever. In my eyes you saw my need, my desire: I wanted only to be looked at by you. I did not betray you with the Bee Keeper; his heart belongs to the queen and in the end he will return to her. *Think.* Francisco, in the winter of our days I keep the candle for you burn-ing, it shines through the window of my heart. *Think.* I feel my Aunt Mimi's hand on my bare girl's shoulders. I hear her words— "only if a woman knows where she is going." *Think.* The Bee Keeper takes a honeycomb from a damp cloth and breaks it in two. Honey cascades onto my skin. The wings of the muse stir after the long winter. I am in the center of the hive surrounded by the brilliant gold light of a thousand bright bodies. Specks of gleaming amber coalesce into a perfect sphere, a ball of heat. A woman must have the courage to love a man as a mother loves a child, to be naked and ruthless with her emotions. The milk from a mother's breast can make the blind man see. My milk flows. *Think.* The bird sings the beauty of the flower it has eaten; the bee transforms beauty into honey. Francisco I cling to the memory of your face. There is the scent of wax, dust, and pollen. I am buried in the Bee Keeper's gold honey but I am forever bound by the weight of gold chains you tied me with. The bird slips through gold into me, filling me, then escapes.

Above me the dark bird soars higher over the bell tower until I am a mere black dot nailed to the door below. Maybe I am dead. Maybe my heart is pulsing in the bird's throat. Maybe I couldn't think enough beauty to keep myself alive. Maybe I am lost to myself, to consciousness. Maybe what I see when I struggle to lift my head is not true. Why should it be true? Coming up the red-stained steps toward me is Madame Happy. How did she know I was here? Who told her? Maybe she has come from Ville Rouge only to spit on me one last time. She is a blur. Something in her hand . . . a hard object. Is she going to deliver the coup de grâce? She raises her hand: she is holding a hammer. She hooks the hammer's claw under the nailhead pounded down into the flesh of my right hand. She yanks the nail from the door and out of my hand. I feel nothing. My hand is numb from shattered pain. She quickly pulls the nail from my other hand. Freed, I fall to the ground.

The bird in the sky follows as Madame Happy helps me through the streets. All the houses are shuttered, no one is in sight. The secret of Reigne's silent complicity holds; the people guard their shame. Madame Happy takes me home. How does she know where I live? She lays me on my back on the bed. She puts my hands in porcelain bowls filled with warm salty water. Her stout body bends over me. Her tears fall with her words as the blood from my hands leaks into the white bowls.

"Can you ever forgive me? I had to spit on you in Ville Rouge. I had to put as much distance between you and me as I could, there could be no civility between us. I can help you because they haven't made the connection between us. They will think I am just taking pity on you. Tonight I have a doctor coming, for a hospital is too dangerous."

Madame Happy pulls my hands from the water and binds them tightly with strips of cloth. I am confused by what she says.

"The fly hunts the eagle."

She's telling me she is the *one*. She is the one who orchestrates the night moves. Working from her little baby shop, Madame Happy is the deadliest weapon of all.

"Flies don't hunt eagles in a normal world, but we do." She smooths my brow with her hand. "Someone has betrayed you . . . betrayed *us*. I will find him, and he will be no more."

I try to move my tongue to speak and to my surprise the words come, hoarse and direct. "I know who he is."

"Tell me and I will do it."

"No, I must."

"But your hands . . ." Her voice chokes and she holds back more tears.

"I can do it."

"We can't wait if there is a collaborator among us."

"It must be me. I am the only one he won't suspect, who can get close enough."

"I'm sorry to say," Madame Happy's tears begin again, "but you will never be able to use your hands."

"That would be true in a normal world. This is not a normal world."

From the window of my cottage I see Mont Ventoux. It has stopped raining. The sky has been swept clear of winter and shines with the promise of spring, pulling from the damp earth the rooted scent of plants. Green leaves burst and bright red poppies flicker across the fields. Swallows dip and dive over budding vineyards; bird's wings in the air rustle like a woman's silk skirt against her legs as she hurries to a rendezvous. Specks of young bees dot the air, drunken acrobats loaded with nectar, zigzagging with excitement.

One bee drifts up from the fields and lands outside my window as I lean gazing at Mont Ventoux, my bandaged hands folded beneath my chin. What is this bee doing here? Why isn't she in a hive, rubbing her body in the rhythmic waggle dance that tells the others where more pollen beckons? She flies up, then drops onto my bare arm. I see the throb of her overflowing nectar sacs. She has visited over fifty flowers in the past hour, and now she comes here. She buzzes up and alights on my cheek. The vibration of her body becomes more insistent. She crawls into the corner of my mouth, wedges between my lips. Does she think she has found her hive and wants to deposit her pollen? Her feet press into my flesh. She darts away, straight up, then hovers in the air and faces Mont Ventoux in the distance. She buzzes off toward Mont Ventoux where my baby is buried, where the Bee Keeper is. Something is happening on Mont Ventoux.

I try to find my way from memory across the fields, through the forests, up trails and down ravines, over footbridges and along ledges carved into the rocky sides of high precipices that plunge into distant valleys. Brambles tear my legs, ferns whip my face, but the buzz of bees pulls me forward. Ahead looms the cliff I know so well from heartache and healing. Voices stop me, strange voices floating up. Why should there be voices? Only the Bee Keeper and I know of this spot. I bend down and crawl among the bushes, inching toward the voices. A hand comes from behind a bush and grabs me, covers my mouth, and pulls me down. I stare into the face of the Cat Surgeon.

"Lucretia, what are you doing here?" he asks in a low voice, releasing his hand from my mouth.

"What are *you* doing here?"

He nods toward the cliff. Through an opening in the bushes I see soldiers with rifles standing before the cliff. In front of them is an armored truck with a machine gun mounted on top. Behind the machine gun is the Officer.

The Cat Surgeon whispers. "They followed us here after we tried to destroy a troop train. It was a trap—they knew exactly where we were going to sabotage the railroad track; someone told them. They ambushed us. That was two days ago. They've been hunting us ever since. We had to split up."

"How many of you are there?"

"Only five left, hidden in the bushes around us. One made it into the cave at the base of the cliff behind those rows of wooden bee-hives. Shhh!"

I hold my breath and hear the Officer shout. "Fly, surrender! It's impossible to escape!"

I nudge the Cat Surgeon. "We've got to help him."

"It has to be the right moment, otherwise we all die."

"Give me a gun."

The Cat Surgeon looks at my bandaged hands. "You can barely crawl, and you want a gun?"

It is true. I am helpless.

"Lucretia, you must leave because—"

The Officer's voice interrupts. He aims the machine gun at the bee hives. "I'm losing patience!" The metallic clatter of the machine gun bursts out, bullets firing into the hives, shattering the wooden boxes. Pieces of wood, clumps of honey and wax explode into the air with specks of bee bodies. The deafening clap of the gun echoes off the face of the cliff, stirring more activity from the bees hived in the rock crevices. A strong buzz fills the air.

"One last chance!" the Officer shouts into the buzz.

Soldiers run along the base of the cliff, pouring kerosene onto the shattered wooden hives.

"Surrender or burn!"

The only answer the Officer receives is the angry buzzing of bees. He signals his soldiers, who light torches, then throw them onto the kerosene-soaked hives.

An air-sucking roar explodes in a wall of flame racing up the cliff. The angry buzzing of bees turns to fury. Thousands of maddened bodies spiral out from crevices in the rock, swarming in a torrent of black clouds.

A whistle sounds from the Cat Surgeon next to me. He leaps up, firing his rifle at the soldiers. Other men jump from the bushes, shooting. Bullets whiz over my head. Soldiers fall and the men around me are struck with rapid thuds, until everyone is down except the Cat Surgeon.

The Officer on the armored truck swings the machine gun around quickly. A spray of bullets cuts through the Cat Surgeon; his body falls next to me. I grab for his bloody rifle, forgetting my hands are bandaged. I try, but I can't pick it up. I rip at the bandages with my teeth, tearing them off. My hands are yellow and shriveled, palms pierced with deep purple wounds, fingers curled inward like the claws of a dead chicken. I force one hand around the rifle, pushing a finger through the trigger hole, and jump up.

The Officer's back is to me. He is firing the machine gun at a ghostly figure emerging from smoke at the cliff's base. I try to pull the trigger of the rifle but my finger won't move. The Officer keeps firing at the figure. The ghost shoots the last two soldiers, then runs toward the Officer. The ghost is dressed in leather and his face is masked. I have the Officer in my sights but my finger refuses to bend. Machine-gun bullets hit the ghost's smoking body.

My mind screams at my lifeless finger—MOVE! Nothing. I jam the rifle butt into my shoulder, aim awkwardly, and with my other hand push the stock of the barrel toward my stiff finger in the trigger hold. A shot fires. The Officer slumps over his gun. He seems dead, but then his body shifts, swinging the gun around to shoot me. Two shots sound, hitting the Officer from behind. His lifeless hands fall to his sides but his eyes remain open, staring straight at me. Behind him the wounded ghost staggers into smoke and flames and disappears.

Village of Reigne

My Darling Francisco,

My sweet Columbus discovering the night. I know that it has
been difficult for you to read these last letters, and to see by my tortured scrawl across the pages the trouble I've had forcing my
maimed hand to write. For the rest of this war my hands will prevent
me from being anything but a bystander. My hands will heal but the
doctor says they will never be of much use. I can write by taping a
pen to my index and middle fingers, a trick I have become quite good
at. I must laugh, for what good is the muse with her wings clipped?
But I still have my school children to look after, to protect from
burning skies and bullet-ridden winds. I rejoice in these children and
how they grow in surprising ways under my guidance, for even
though my hands are crippled my mind is supple. I am consoled by
this when I attempt to knit, clumsily holding the needle between
stiffened thumb and forefinger, concentrating on the task of trying

to make something, no matter how crude the creation. You and I are alike now: me with my mending but mutilated hands, you with your smashed knees leaving you forever off center when you walk. And each of us has letters to the other that won't be read. The truth is I will never open a letter of yours again. Let me explain why.

The day after the bees were destroyed on Mont Ventoux I returned to Ville Rouge. When I did, Royer informed me that he still had many letters from you, so many that he did not feel safe giving them to me in public during the day. He asked me to meet him that night, since he was being transferred immediately to a post office in another town. When night fell I walked from the center of Ville Rouge up the hill, past the last houses and the cemetery with its skyline of carved angels and crosses silhouetted in the moonlight. The hill I was climbing ended abruptly. Before me was a precipice hundreds of feet deep, an immense pit created when the hill was half eaten away by ochre mining.

I sat on a bench overlooking the pit, a place where schoolchildren were brought during the day to see a marvel. This giant abyss was the work of Roman slaves who were lowered by ropes to fill buckets with precious red dirt that was loaded onto donkeys, carted to Marseille, and shipped to ports around the Mediterranean. The pit was so enormous that the cathedral of Notre Dame in Paris could be slipped inside it and buried. The pit's slick sides of orange and red glowed, and in places green swords of pine trees protruded, having tenaciously grown back over the years, clinging to the sheer walls of this man-made scar. A sweetly damp mineral scent carried from the pit's distant depths, and the sound of bats swirling in a void echoed up.

"Who are you tonight? Lucretia . . . or Louise?"

I turned toward the voice. It was Royer, puffing and breathless from the steep uphill climb.

"I am me. Simply that."

He sat beside me and placed at his feet a sack he had been carrying. He squinted in the moonlight. "So good to see you are shapely again. Such nice curves. Not that you weren't sumptuous when you were pregnant. I like stuffed goose, it's delicious. But I'm no snob, I will settle for a lovely summer partridge in wine sauce." His nostrils twitched as he leaned toward me, sniffing my hair. "Did you come because you too are hungry? Are you setting the table for me?"

"I'm here because of the letters."

"No more brave Lucretia of the night?"

I nodded at the black shawl covering my hands in my lap. "I can't do anything for you. My hands are useless."

"Oh, you are not entirely useless."

"What do you mean?"

"Perhaps your hands are no longer the pretty picture they once were, but when the chef prepares the partridge he always cuts off the extremities, the rest of the body is left untouched and succulent. You are no longer Lucretia, but you are Louise. You have one thing left to offer."

"If I had hands to slap you with I would. Give me the letters so that I can leave."

Royer smirked and pressed his shoe against the sack on the ground, pushing it toward the edge of the precipice. "Don't be so sensitive. You should be flattered that I find you have anything at all left to barter with."

"Barter?"

"After I'm gone you must still be able to receive your letters, those precious letters for which you risked so much. I can make certain they will continue to reach you."

"How can you do that if you are transferred?"

"I have my ways, but you must fulfill your part of the bargain. There is still more for you to do, if you wish to keep your secret safe and get what you want." He peered at me closely, judging the effect of his words, waiting out my silence until I replied.

"Yes, there's still more for me to do." I stood and faced him, my back to the pit.

"After all this time you are finally setting the table for me! Why don't you drop that shawl covering your hands and raise your dress to show me what's cooking?"

"I can't undress myself. You have to help."

"Yes-yes, I've brought the spices!" He knelt before me, his fingers at the hem of my dress, pushing the material up my legs. "I want this quick, like a lovely sauce boiling to its essence."

"Like a lovely sauce." I looked down. He was about to press his face between my thighs. I dropped the shawl.

Francisco, in the moonlight I could see your straight razor, its sharp blade glinting, its pearl handle taped tightly around my blunt hand. Your razor was all that I asked you for when we parted. Francisco, I wanted you to end him with me. I wanted him to feel it from both of us. I raised my hand to slash our blade across the back of his neck. I shouted my last words at him before swinging down my arm: "You're the one who betrayed us all!"

He pushed the dress above my hips and glanced up in surprise, seeing the blade. He knocked me back. I fell, not knowing if I was falling into the pit or away from it. I kicked toward him. When I hit the ground I turned and saw that I had knocked him over and he was clinging to the inside of the pit. His hands clawed into soft dirt. One hand reached up and grabbed the sack of letters, hoping for a secure hold, but pulled the sack over the edge. He slid down the slick embankment, falling so far that when he hit bottom his final cry came as a distant whimper, insignificant as a dissipating puff of red dust.

Francisco, the one who collaborated with the new emperor's army was dead. His last act was to try and touch what he could never have in this world. With him went the last person here who knew my true identity, and with him ended my only connection to your letters. I had made my choice, I was alone. I recalled the collaborator's words. "This is war. You must decide which side you are on. You must ask yourself: are you motivated only by love for a man, or will you serve a higher purpose?"

I edged closer to the precipice and stared down into the abyss. I thought I could see a body far below, a black dot in a sea of crimson. A tear dropped on my cheek. I realized fully what my love for you had brought me to.

I gazed at the moon. I clung to the light, followed it like a river of honey, as I had the night before when I searched for the ghost of the Fly after the smoke cleared. I had wandered among the charred remains of burnt hives scattered along the base of the fire-blackened cliff. There was no one alive there, not even the bees. I went into the woods. I knew the bees who survived would ultimately cluster, creating a nucleus for a new beginning. On I walked until I came to a clearing. In its center was a dead oak tree, and in the bare branches were huge clusters of bees, hanging like golden fruit. Beneath them, lying on the ground against the trunk of the tree, was the Fly. I knelt at his side. He smelled of burnt leather, smoke, and blood. His clothes were scorched and punctured with bullet holes. I cradled him in my arms, pulled the leather mask off, and exposed his face. I gently drew his eyelids open and the bright blue of the Bee Keeper's eyes stared up, but they did not see me.

I needed him to see me. I wanted him to know. I broke the buttons of my blouse open with my clawed hands, one of my breasts swung free. I rubbed my nipple against the Bee Keeper's cheek until a drop of milk began to form. I held my nipple over his face and let the fully formed drop of milk fall into the sky of the Bee Keeper's eye. I rocked him in my arms. He could see what I see now, the moon overhead, that perfect sphere shining; he could see it reflected across the sea where I row my boat, dipping oars into water, destroying the moon's perfect image, my boat moving on.

Love,
LOUISE

PART SIX

Road to
Zermano

THE ROAD to Zermano was unlike any I had ever traveled before. It led high into Mallorca's Sierra Tramuntana, the spectacular mountain range that I had seen in the distance the day I climbed to Ramón Llull's cave on Mount Randa. Speeding along in the car with Serena at the wheel seemed more like a surreal ride in an amusement park than the life-threatening journey it was. The road was terrifyingly narrow, only as wide as the Roman chariots it was built for centuries before—stop one chariot and you stopped an army. High stone walls, impossible to see over, lined the road on both sides. Serena drove fast, swerving to hug a stone wall as a bus swung around the corner ahead, bearing down on us. The passengers stared from the bus as it passed, nearly sideswiping us. Serena sped ahead, honking the horn to warn oncoming vehicles of our presence. She was wearing a dress today, not pants and a blouse as she had the day I met her in Palma. As she shifted gears, forcing the car into hairpin turns and around blind curves, I couldn't help but notice the hem of her dress as it rose above her knees. It made me think of Louise and Zermano's drive into Provence on that fateful Day of the Bees. Without taking her eyes from the road Serena, sensing my interest, drew the hem of her dress back over her knees. I wanted to tell her that I hadn't meant to be rude, but I was reminded of another time. "Pardon me," I apologized. She shifted again and spoke loudly above the squeal of tires.

"Let me tell you about my father. He's ninety years old. At least we think he is, there never was a birth certificate, or if there was it's been lost or destroyed. He doesn't function at the level he once did; his brain has been traumatized by all the anesthesia he was given for various operations he's had to keep him going. Because of that, and his age, he sometimes acts very odd. It's not that he's lost his powers of intelligence—I wish I had half of what he has now—it's that sometimes he loses the ability to organize his thoughts. He can be amazingly lucid, other times he makes no sense at all. This is one of the reasons we have protected him from the public. It's also why I didn't want you in particular to see him, to bring up the past. We were afraid it might undo his mind, making him so fragmented that he'll leave the present completely. His mind must be protected, but also his heart. There's the sensitive matter of his . . . hallucinations."

"I'll be very careful with what I say to him. What do you mean by hallucinations?"

Her jaw tightened. "He floats constantly in and out of reality, and then shouts uncontrollably. It's a terrible disjointed outpouring. It's hard to know if what he's saying actually happened in his life, or if it's hallucinations."

"Is he speaking to someone when he does this? I don't mean someone there at the time, but someone who is *not* there."

"Yes. He talks to—or about—a lot of people."

"Any one name you can recall?"

"Not offhand."

"What period of his life do you think he's in when he's doing this?"

"During the war."

"Which war? He was in Spain at the beginning of the Civil War, and France during World War Two."

"I'm not certain. His knees were damaged in a war but we don't know which one. He always refused to talk about it."

"It must be very hard for you not to be able to give him all the comfort he deserves."

"When it rains his knees swell and he howls with pain. He waves his wooden staff at some distant figure that no one else can see. It's sad and horrific, and he's so convinced the figure is there that sometimes I think I can see it too."

"And what do you see?"

"A woman. He's always calling to her. He . . ." She wiped a tear away. "He shouts that he's coming to her."

"It must seem like a nightmare to you."

"A fantastic nightmare." She fell silent.

I gazed through the window. The passing landscape was also fantastic. The road broke free of the Roman walls and the mountainous coast came into view, carved by ancient glaciers and the violent shifting of continents. Everything was so poetically balanced that it seemed to have been drawn rather than created. No wonder the artist Gustave Doré had been inspired to use it in his illustrations for Dante's *Commedia*: it was a mystical moonscape with a startling overlay of the tropical—orange, fig, and lemon trees cascading down mountainsides to the sea. As we drove higher it felt as though we were piercing veiled atmospheres into brilliant Mediterranean light that flooded the sky with violent extremes of color.

My mind raced back to those who had taken this road before, like Jules Verne, seeking a landscape that could spark his prodigious imagination. Or Chopin and George Sand, who spent the winter of 1839 in a fifteenth-century Carthusian monastery we had passed earlier. The consumptive Chopin, coughing blood and tapping out warm notes with cold fingers, composed many of his Preludes here while his lover George Sand, dressed as a man, smoked cigarettes and drank coffee all day, then worked on her novels all night, scandalizing the locals. The light we were passing through must have been the same that Chopin experienced when he described Mallorca as *"the most lovely country in the world."*

Ahead of us, beyond a bridge over a plunging gorge, appeared what seemed to be the last mountain before all land ended, leaving only sky and sea. On the ridge of the mountain was a Moorish fortress, its circular towers still rising defiantly to the clouds, its thick stone walls capable of sheltering a caliph's army. Serena stopped the car. A steel gate blocked our way. Next to the gate was a guardhouse with two soldiers inside.

Serena turned the car engine off. "From here on we have to walk. Ahead it's only a *camino conejo,* a rabbit road."

We got out of the car. The soldiers came out of the guardhouse, rifles slung over their shoulders. One of them saluted and smiled at Serena, "Bon día, Señorita Zermano."

The other soldier looked suspiciously at me, for I was carrying one of Louise's large baskets. He laughed sarcastically and mumbled something; they both laughed.

"What's so funny?" I asked Serena.

"They think you're gay."

"Tell them I've got a bomb in the basket."

"That's not funny. What *do* you have in there that's such a secret? Maybe you think we're going on a picnic?"

The soldiers unlocked the gate and pushed it open. We walked through and followed an old stone path that led down into a valley of ancient olive trees. The massive trunks of the trees twisted up from the plowed red earth and their gnarled branches fingered the breeze with silver leaves. Between the trees goats moved, the bells around their necks tinkling as they skittered away and stood back, their limpid eyes taking us in with haughty disdain. Serena walked ahead. She untied her hair and let it spill down her back, shining and black against her white dress.

Watching her, I recalled something Zermano said in an interview he gave in the nineteen fifties on one of his rare trips to the United States. He was asked about the inspiration for the style of painting he was doing in Mallorca, which was completely different from what he had done in Paris. He said he was not interested in talking about inspiration, because there were only two ways an artist would be perceived if he did so—as a finicky romantic or as a taboo-breaker. Mallorca for him was not about the outer eye, as was Paris, where all the landscape was man-made and man's mind was his religion. In Mallorca everything was below the natural surface, beneath the spread of venerable olive trees where roots sank deep to suck precious moisture. To miss that was to miss life, and he didn't give a damn for those who considered he needed psychoanalyzing for thinking such a thing. The only head-doctor he needed, he said, was his "doctor of poetry," Federico García Lorca, who put the whole idea of making art into its purest context: *Human hands have no more sense than to mimic roots beneath the soil.* "I am a mimic," Zermano declared to the interviewer.

Following Serena beneath the spread of trees formed by centuries of wind made me see it Zermano's way. Everything he said became clear in this context. Cities didn't exist, museums and universities were unheard of, there were no theories of art. I spoke Lorca's words aloud:

"Human hands have no more sense than to mimic roots beneath the soil."

Serena stopped and turned, startled. For the first time her eyes met mine and she spoke directly to me.

"You know Lorca's poem?"

"Not really. Just that line."

She walked back down the trail and stood before me, her brown eyes excited.

"My father lives by that poem. Do you want to hear the first stanza?"

"With pleasure."

"I have often been lost on the sea with my ear full of fresh-cut flowers, my tongue full of agony and love. Often I have been lost on the sea, as I am lost in the heart of certain children."

"Beautiful."

"Yes."

She turned and continued up the trail.

Finally I had broken through. I wanted to keep her talking. I called out a question.

"Why are the soldiers guarding your father? It's as if they have him under house arrest."

"It's more like they are protecting a national treasure."

"We all know how important he is, but he doesn't need to be guarded like the Pope."

"You're so far from the truth. All of this land, my father bought it forty years ago."

"He was planning his hideout that far back?"

"No. He bought it because this is one of the last places in the Mediterranean where there are still giant black vultures. They're almost extinct; fewer than thirty are left. Do you know the bird I'm talking about? It has a wing span of more than six feet."

"We have similar birds in California, called condors."

"Yes, they are like that. My father gave this land to the government with the restriction that it remain protected. The birds nest on the cliffs on the other side of the Moorish fortress."

"So the soldiers guard the condors and the condors guard your father?"

"Something like that. So you see, this was already a private area before my father disappeared. No one thought of searching for him here."

I looked above Serena. We were just below the stone walls of the ninth-century fortress. Only now was it possible to grasp the intimidating monumentality of the architecture; it appeared to have been built by giants who expected to fight other giants. There were hundreds of slots in the soaring towers for archers to aim arrows at anyone approaching from this direction. Walking the final few steps to the forty-foot-high entrance with its solid wooden gate, I had the uneasy sensation of being exposed. At any moment arrows, spears and boiling oil could come raining down.

Serena banged the heavy iron knocker. "It will be a while before he comes." She turned and lifted her hair away from the nape of her neck, letting the air cool the sheen of perspiration there. "Whew, it's hot."

I didn't want to appear to take undue notice of how graceful the curve of her neck was, so I looked back down at the trail we had just climbed. We were so high up that the tinklings of goat bells in the valley below mingled together, sounding like the melodious flow of water rushing over stones.

The timber gate creaked as its enormous weight swung slowly open with a screech of iron hinges. I followed Serena into a huge cobblestone courtyard the size of a football field; an army on horseback could have assembled here. An old man with a shaved head stood before us, clad in sandals and a coarse woven cloak. He beamed at me in greeting with all the fervor of a long-lost relative. He took my hand in both of his and pumped it. I was at a loss for words, so Serena spoke.

"It's all right, Professor, you can speak. He hasn't taken a vow of silence. He's one of the Buddhist monks who live here and watch over my father."

The monk's grin grew broader and he heaved words from his chest in a half-laughing, half-crying voice.

"The . . . maes . . . tro . . . is expecting . . . *you!*"

He turned and set off at a fast trot across the cobblestones. We followed him, racing across the courtyard and under the wide stone columns supporting overhead parapets, then into an immense hall. Its domed ceiling was covered with intricate tiles revealed by shafts of sunlight that played like spotlights through openings in the roof. It was clear we were in the former mosque, large enough to accommodate the faithful of Damascus. The monk opened a door and sped across a walled-in patio, then through another door and down a dark stairway. The air thickened with the musty scent of rancid wine. At the bottom of the stairs the monk struck a match. As it flared, he took down a lantern hung on the wall and lit it, smiling. He raised the lantern, throwing the room into shadowy relief, and illuminating rows of wine barrels unlike any I had ever seen. The oak barrels were thirty feet wide and belted with bands of rusted iron; they contained wine enough to keep an army drunk for a two-year siege. The monk darted off between barrels with us behind. The lantern's light cast our passing shadows on the high walls, tiny as three dwarves in this world of giants. The bald monk turned and grinned back at me: he was enjoying the chase.

The monk stopped before an iron door, took out a key, and slipped it into the lock. He pulled the heavy door open, exposing a tunnel hewn into solid rock. The tunnel was four feet high and wide enough only for a single person. Its serpentine path disappeared into the gloom. This was obviously the secret escape passage if the fortress was about to fall into enemy hands. The monk plunged into the tunnel's gloom, followed by Serena and me. He swung the lantern before him as if sweeping away any lingering spirits with the light. If it weren't for the sight of Serena before me, I could have been a condemned man being led out of the Bastille on his way to the guillotine. I wanted to reach out and touch her, to make certain this was all real, that *she* was real. But I couldn't; I could only watch the shape of her, bent over as she moved forward. Her black hair swung off her shoulders, her breathing was a slight pant, and the scent of her skin filled the tunnel.

I thought back to when Zermano had met Serena's mother. I had pieced the event together from published accounts and the few interviews he gave. It was in the nineteen fifties, during the Lenten carnival. Palma's narrow medieval streets were lit by smoking torches. Pipers, drummers, and fiddlers played music to spur on a prancing menagerie of revelers costumed as Greek fertility goddesses, shepherdesses with sprigs of rosemary in their hair, and demented demons deformed by leprosy. The parade of carousers was led by a blood-red Lucifer with pointed horns and a swishing tail. In their midst, Zermano spotted a devout young woman going up the cathedral steps. He followed her into the incense-scented interior.

She knelt before a bank of votive candles, bending toward the rows of flickering lights. He watched the arc of her body assume the very line he had painted on his last canvas in Paris. Now the line seized upon itself and seemed to form a redemptive point, the closure of a wound. He wanted to reach out and touch her, but instead he waited politely until she finished her prayer, then asked if she would allow him to sketch her one day, just as she was, illuminated before candles. He assured her that no one would recognize her likeness in the sketch, for his art at this time was not representational; it was the idea of her he wanted to capture. He married her two weeks later.

We wound through the tunnel so long that my back ached; I thought I'd never be able to stand straight again. Finally the monk stopped before another iron door. I heard his keys jangling in the semi-darkness, then the door was pushed open. Warm, salty sea air rushed into the cool tunnel. I passed through the doorway behind Serena and entered a vaulted room cut into stone. The only furnishings were a bed, a dresser, and a porcelain wash basin with a pitcher of water next to it. The monk sighed, with his enigmatic half-cry, half-laugh, "The . . . maes . . . tro!" He turned back into the tunnel and locked the iron door behind him, leaving us alone. I set the heavy basket down on the dresser.

"No," Serena said. "Out here."

I picked up the basket and followed her through an arched doorway. Suddenly the world opened—we were on a stone terrace cut into a cliff a thousand feet above the sea. Looking straight out the view was limitless, the sky blurring into ocean on the far horizon. I was so taken by the spectacle of this aerie that I was surprised to hear Serena's voice.

"I have brought the Professor."

I turned. At the end of the terrace a white-haired man in a wheelchair sat with his back to me. I didn't quite know how to make my greeting.

"Sir," I began. "I'm so grateful to—"

The man's large hands grabbed the chair's wheels and spun

around. It was Zermano. He exuded a forcefulness surprising in a man his age. His penetrating eyes were set off by a white beard. His deep voice commanded:

"Tell me quickly, where did you get that piece of writing you sent?"

"In an old book of Ramón Llull's."

"But why that *particular* piece? Who do you think you are, calling me the fool of love!"

"I didn't mean any disrespect. I meant it in the philosophical sense in which Llull—"

"Damn you!" Zermano gripped the wheels and propelled the chair straight into me, knocking me against a stone wall that prevented me from falling over. My legs were pinned by the weight of Zermano in his chair. I struggled to right myself, but he grabbed a wooden staff balanced on his knees and whipped it into the air, bringing its tip under my chin and pressing it into my throat. I could barely breathe. He pressed harder, pushing my head to the side so I could see the jagged rocks pounded by the sea thousands of feet below.

"Tell me why you are here or I'll push you over!"

I tried to get my words out. "In . . . the . . ."

"What!"

". . . basket."

"I don't give a damn about your basket! Serena, pick that basket up! I want you to throw it over the side of the cliff if we don't get the right answer. Professor, *why are you here?*"

"'I embrace you across . . . the sea of memory. Your Columbus of the night . . . sails on.'"

"What the hell!" The staff dug harder into my throat. "Where would you have heard *that?*"

"I didn't . . . I read it."

"Where would a little American bookworm read something like that?"

"In a letter written by . . . *you.*"

"Jesus!"

"To Louise."

"No!"

The pressure on my throat released. I pushed up from the wall.

Zermano's eyes were fixed straight ahead, staring out to sea, seeming to search for something on the far horizon. He raised his staff and swung it with a bang against the stone floor. The force of the blow recoiled through his body. His shoulders hunched forward and his face fell as tears streamed from his eyes.

Serena knelt next to him, taking his hands in hers, rubbing them tenderly, trying to bring him back.

"Papa, forgive me. I never would have brought him here if I had known. I'll send him away."

Zermano said nothing. He sobbed as the waves crashed below. His body began to shake violently as he was pulled away into a sea of memory.

I was afraid to move. Serena was right, this was too much for his mental state, he had suffered enough trauma in a lifetime. I had not intended to spring the idea of Louise on him so suddenly; I had hoped to ease into it. Now I might be the one to have killed him. I turned to leave. My movement alarmed him. His voice was a whisper:

"Do you know how high we are?"

I looked at Serena, not certain I should speak, afraid to say something wrong. She nodded that I should answer.

"No sir, I don't."

"So high there are no flies. Did you know that? No flies. But eagles don't hunt flies."

How astonishing he should say this. It made me think of the line in Louise's letter, and I spoke it:

"Eagles don't hunt flies in a normal world, but this is not a normal world."

He slowly turned his head, his eyes focusing on me as he spoke.

"The high mountains of Mallorca were once filled with monasteries. When I was a boy I went to one of the last of them. Boys of my age then were expected to go and live with the monkeys—that's what we called the crazy old monks who never said a word, the monkeys. I was twelve years old when I was sent to live with the monkeys and I learned how to resist the urge to relieve a sensation new to me, a carnal itch growing between my legs. There were no books to read, only the Bible. There was no one to talk to except the priest in the dark confessional. He asked only one question: 'Have you had any impure thoughts, my son?' At night I was forced to sleep with a rosary wrapped around my left hand and a skull cradled in my right hand. A skull, a *man's* skull! This was their subtle way of warning me that if I scratched my carnal itch I would be condemned to the hell of the temporal world, never to walk through those pearly gates above, where nobody has the itch and all thoughts are pure. What about you, Professor? Are your thoughts pure? Can I trust you?"

I glanced at Serena for a sign. Should I engage him? She nodded that it was all right. I thought I knew where he was going with this talk, what his test was. He was the eagle, he wasn't going to hunt flies. I had to respond to him in kind.

"I desire to be a fool. I will have no art or device in my words."

He nodded in agreement. "You know the sentiments of Ramón Llull quite well. I think you know that I desired the same as Llull: no art or device in my painting, just the thing itself, that famous thing not named."

I knew that for him, that famous thing not named was Louise, but I had to proceed with caution. I spoke carefully.

"Llull said that the way to accomplish this desire for no art or device in the act of communication was with the greatness of love."

Zermano shook his head in agreement. "Yes, but it's an unfashionable idea today. And look what happened to poor Llull! When he tried to get all the religions into one universal boat the Jews ignored him, the Catholics betrayed him, and the Moslems stoned him. Llull dreamed of man himself being *holy.* That was an impure thought for his time. Got the son of bitch killed."

"It's still a deadly notion."

"Let me tell you my religion, Professor. I believe a man and a *woman* can be holy *together.* Do you believe that?"

"Yes, I do."

"The Moors who ruled here centuries ago were right in their philosophy: *First you dream, then you die.* In other words, wake up! Mallorca was their dreamland, but they knew life itself was the paradise—it's how we *act* in paradise that determines our hell or heaven. I stayed alive. I had faith in the holiness. I refused to believe Louise had abandoned our love."

Zermano's head slumped and his chin came to rest on his chest as his eyes closed with weariness. Serena was alarmed; she motioned me not to talk, it was enough. But I couldn't stop, I couldn't leave him like this. He had to know.

"Sir, I'm here because Louise believed too. That's why I brought the basket."

Zermano raised his head slowly, trying to focus. "Basket? I don't remember a basket."

"It's right here. I'll get it." I brought the basket to him.

He looked at the basket blankly. "I've never seen this before."

"No. It belonged to Louise."

"They told me when she died, she left behind the art and jewelry I gave her. They never said anything about a basket."

"It wasn't considered important. They weren't trying to hide anything from you."

"I demanded that they tell me *everything* that was in that little cottage of hers."

"The basket was overlooked. There were several more. But she wanted them to be found, she wanted you to know."

"Know?"

"That she didn't stop believing."

"Then why?" Zermano's voice choked. "Why didn't she ever answer? I kept writing."

"I know."

I untied the cloth cover I had placed over the well of the basket to protect the letters. I pulled out the first bundle of envelopes and placed them in his lap. He stared at them, uncomprehending.

"These are the letters you wrote to Louise."

He seemed to stop breathing. I looked to Serena for help.

She knelt next to him. "Papa, are you all right?"

"I can't . . . can't see."

"Of course, your cataracts." She reached into his coat pocket and pulled out reading glasses with thick lenses. She put the glasses on him.

He peered closely at the top letter of the bundle, recognizing the distinctive handwriting. "This is my writing! This is addressed to Louise in Ville Rouge. How did you get these?"

"Louise left them in her cellar, hidden in the false bottom of her knitting baskets."

"My God!"

"They belong to you. I've come to return them."

"Did you make copies?"

"I did not. No one else knows of their existence."

"So you've come to sell them?"

"They aren't mine to sell. They are yours."

"Maybe I was wrong about you, Professor Bookworm."

"But there's more. I discovered something more."

"Aha!" Zermano's eyes narrowed with suspicion behind the magnifying lenses of his glasses. "I knew it! You've come to make your reputation and your fortune! What are you holding back?"

"Nothing. I've brought Louise's letters to you."

"Impossible!" Zermano raised his staff and swung it angrily. "Louise is dead. How could she write to me?"

Serena's words came quickly. "Leave us, Professor! It's over. Leave us in peace."

I was growing as angry as Zermano. Moving away from his swinging staff, I shouted, "Do you think that all anyone wants is a piece of you? Do you think you have the only truth?"

Serena stepped between us, her own anger matching mine. "Don't you *dare* talk like that! What do you know? My father has been abused, cheated, and vilified!"

"Yes! And he's been stoned by his critics, just like Ramón Llull!"

"Just leave!" she shouted furiously.

"I *will* leave! I don't want anything from either of you! I came here because someone else told the truth!"

I grabbed the basket and turned it over. Louise's letters rained down onto Zermano.

The letters—so anxiously awaited, so long hidden, now finally out in the open—stunned us all into silence.

Zermano looked incredulously at the letters that had fallen into his lap. His hand shaking, he carefully picked up an envelope and peered at the handwriting. It spelled out his name and his old address in Paris. He whispered softly to the letter as if it could hear him: *"Dimidium animae meae . . .* half my soul." He gathered up more letters in his trembling hands. He was holding the weight of his lost world. His tears fell onto the letters. He looked like the most ancient man in the universe. He struggled for speech, his voice weak, his words crushed, almost inaudible. "I *must* know . . . what she has been saying . . . all this time."

I spoke to Zermano as gently as I could. "You can read them in peace. Louise wrote them for you. I promised her in my heart I would deliver them." I walked away.

"You can't go—you love her too."

Zermano's words stopped me. I turned.

"Only a person who selflessly loves her, understands her spirit, would make the sacrifice you've made."

"What sacrifice is that?"

"To bring her back to me before I die, expecting nothing in return."

"She loved you. It was only you. Read the letters, you'll see."

He held out a handful of letters. "Please, my friend, you saved them. Will you do me the honor of reading them to me?"

"I'm not sure I can do that. They are so . . . personal."

Serena took the letters from Zermano's hands and brought them to me. "My father's eyes are too weak to read for long. He would . . . *I* would be grateful if you read them."

I accepted the letters from her. I went through their contents, arranging them in an order that would make some chronological sense. Then I looked at the first line of the first letter: *"I have nothing to hide now except myself."* I found I could not speak the words. Not because I didn't believe in them, but because they needed to be heard in Louise's voice. They needed the voice of a woman. I handed the letters back to Serena. "These can only be read by you. They are a woman's thoughts; they are not for a man to speak."

Serena's eyes widened in surprise. "But I'm his daughter!"

"It makes no difference. He should hear these as a woman's words."

"Daughter," said Zermano softly, "the Professor is right. You should read them. Perhaps it will help us both to understand."

"I'm sorry, but I can't." Terror was in her eyes. "I can't read the letters of your lover."

Zermano reached out and took her hand. "I do not know what is in these letters, nor what truths they will reveal. I do know this—and it is a difficult thing for a man to say to his child—but if things had gone differently, if the war hadn't forced me to make my choice, my agonizing decision, then in another world, Louise would have been your mother. To understand me, to understand my love for you, you must understand the love I have for this woman. It is not a love that betrays your own mother. Professor, tell her it's the right thing to do."

"It is right, but it's her decision."

Serena gazed at the two of us in anguish. She knelt before Zermano as if to ask his forgiveness. She placed one hand on his knee and picked up the sheaf of letters with the other. Boldly then, in a voice filled with emotion and empathy, she began to read.

"'I have nothing to hide now except myself. Our agreement? It wasn't our agreement, it was *your* plan. You seem to think that who you are would put me at risk. Where else should a woman stand in time of risk but next to the one she loves? Could you not see in my eyes the sadness of parting from you? No. You were crazy with protecting me, sending me far from harm's way. If bombs are to fall why shouldn't I be a target as well? Why should I be saved? What life is left after separation from the one you love?'"

As Serena continued to read, letter after letter, I was struck by the sound of Louise's words spoken aloud in a feminine voice. It seemed I was hearing their deepest meaning for the first time—the ache, the tears, the tenderness, the rage, the anger. I watched Zermano leaning forward in his chair, attentive to each syllable. It was clear he was hearing *Louise's* voice. He was shocked at her pain and outraged by her hardships. Out loud he cursed his blindness to her. He laughed with her, argued with her, suffered with her. He clutched Serena's hand, thinking it was Louise's, and shouted:

"Tell me more! I must know it all!"

Serena's voice kept on, changing in tone, assuming colorations not natural to her but matched to the words on the page as if spoken by Louise's lips—the revelations of an open heart.

I went to the terrace edge and looked out to sea. Until today Zermano too had gazed at this view, haunted by horrific visions of what might have happened to Louise. Now he was hearing the truth. I gazed down at the cliff below me. In the darkness of a crevice I glimpsed movement. From the crevice's shadow emerged the curve of a wing. Then there was a flurry of feathers and a giant black vulture appeared, pushing off from the stone escarpment, falling into space before spreading its majestic wings and soaring up into the sky. The sun cut out the prehistoric silhouette and cast it downward onto the water's surface. Where had I seen this before, this shadow moving across a liquid void in a reversal of light, this black flower drifting toward the infinite horizon? I had seen it in Zermano's most mystical painting, but I had not known its source. The painting was entitled *A Torrent of Black Flowers.*

I turned back to Zermano. He was struggling to stand, pushing up on his staff, shaking his fist at the shape of the bird. The agonized expression on his face was a cross between the mystical and the manic, a messianic determination not unlike the look on the statue of Llull in Palma. I was standing between Zermano and the vulture. It was the last place I wanted to be as he swung his staff violently overhead. He began shouting. Did he see me as his tormentor? Did he even *see* me?

Serena stopped reading. Zermano became even more agitated, calling her Louise and urging her to continue. Then I understood. This was what Serena had meant about his going in and out of reality, between the present and the past. As Serena read, Zermano's rush of words flowed over Louise's and I heard him clearly:

"Life is a clever and untamed thing, empty as a desert where it never rains, but the mirage distance is filled with the ocean. Expect what you least expect and you won't be surprised. Look! Do you see Louise? She is a space carved of volatility, attracting calamity, offering a slippery place for a fool to rush in. She condemns me for sending her away. She condemns and forgives. Burning wax! I wake up with the scent of burning wax in my nostrils. A beehive burning. Holy candles burning. The scent of shame and hoped-for atonement in the church where Llull chased his love after pursuing her on horseback. The gargoyles on the steeple above laughed with antic delight, knowing what a fool he was. Knowing that his blunt romantic notions would be destroyed in the confessional when she unwrapped the soiled bandages from her breasts and death's rancid smell of mildewed oranges would explode his illusions. Instead of embracing his suffering love he fled. Llull's shame at running away is my shame. Louise, forgive me. I tried to put our love into one boat but like Llull trying to gather all faiths into one boat, the weight was too much. The boat sank.

"Louise, I see myself looking out the window of the train riding back to Paris after leaving you, my heart breaking over what I knew would seem to you a betrayal. Outside the window, the road running parallel to the track is a river of cars loaded down with the personal effects of those fleeing from the east. Carts and wagons, piled high with household belongings, were being swept along too, pulled by horses, pushed by terrified families. The train stations were filled with boxcars full of people on the side tracks, huddled in blankets against the cold, waiting for a locomotive engine to hook up and pull them south or north, wherever their fate might be. On and on my train went, unimpeded for it carried mostly soldiers. The people outside were on foot now, with their bundles strapped to their bent backs; old men on older bicycles, pale mothers carrying babies and dragging ragged children, ancient women too weak to go further, abandoned and crying on the roadside. Dead young men with ropes around their necks hung from telephone poles, the word TRAITOR painted in white on their black leather jackets. At every village we passed I glimpsed some wretched human catastrophe. All I could think of, selfishly, was that you were safe. Was I a criminal for that? You were safe and I was headed back into the belly of the beast. My reason was clear: the further I went from you, the safer you were. In Paris, cars raced through night streets with their lights off; intersections were not only sandbagged but had been turned into concrete fortresses with machine guns and checkpoint guards. The air during the day was filled with the drifting ash of papers burned in fireplaces, people consuming their past, destroying any evidence that might incriminate them. Paris with coils of barbed wire surrounding every important public building. Paris where black Citroëns now patrolled, packed with men and electronic apparatus, hunting for clandestine radio transmissions. Paris with its underground Métro cars hurtling along, crowded with people in paranoid silence, the sickly yellow overhead light staining their faces. And I am thankful you are not here to be stopped by the innumerable gendarmes, inspectors, guards, militia, all checking identification papers. Suspicious eyes are everywhere. Bombs fall on factories in the suburbs, I hear the distant thud of explosives, like a man clubbing a chained dog. Dirty snow in empty squares. Roof rats sell for fifteen dollars; four dollars for the rat's tail so you can have a little meat in your soup. My greatest fear is that you have died or vanished in Ville Rouge.

"I prowl the whorehouses of Pigalle searching for women to use as models for my painting—women who might resemble you by the look in their eyes, their hair or skin. I find a young gypsy whore, a Communist who fled Barcelona years ago thinking she would be safe here; now she hides by day, hunted even more than she was in her own country. I bought her for the evening so I could paint her. The next night I went back to the streets of Pigalle but she had vanished. Was she swept away in one of the police raids rooting out the 'foreign trash' in the whorehouses? I kept looking for weeks. She was a clever enough survivor to slip through holes in their net. Finally I came upon her on the banks of the Seine; glowing coals from a brazier illuminated her naked skin, pinpricked by foggy cold. I took her to the atelier and warmed her with bean soup and brandy. I bathed her and massaged her breasts with olive oil and lemon juice, I broke sprigs of rosemary in my palms and rubbed its fragrance into her cheeks. I wanted her to smell like you, to carry the scent of Provence. I wanted that fragrance to mix with the scent of my oil paints. But the girl would not hold still for me to paint. She did not want to be a model, she wanted to be a whore and get paid. She brought her naked body to me and offered it. She smelled like you. She grabbed the paintbrush from my hand and swiped its tip across her breasts, leaving a glistening vermilion streak. She smelled like you. I pulled that scent of you to me, but it was the body of a girl, not the woman you are. I pushed her away. She laughed and grabbed me between the legs, forcing her tongue through my lips. When her tongue came into me I felt the tip of her own loss. She opened her legs with a sigh of mourning deeper than my own. I awoke the next day wanting to paint her naked in first light, as I had painted you. But she was gone, and so was all my money. In Spain we say, Never turn your back on a bull—or a gypsy girl with a hunger bigger than your own. The scent of you still lingers in my atelier.

"My Louise, with traces of earth on her palms, holding her open hands to me, pressing her fingers against my face, saying, 'I can't believe *you* are real. That *we* are real!' I miss your touch—not just your beauty and grace, but the caress of your spirit on my daily life. Do you hold me responsible for the Day of the Bees? I couldn't have prevented that. My knees were smashed, I was forced to crawl, forced to bear the humiliation of having you ripped from my side, the rib torn from my body. Louise, I will never surrender you! Absence is to love what wind is to fire: it extinguishes the weak, rekindles the strong.

"Everything is black and white now in my atelier; there is no texture, no saturation. I am still crawling toward you in my painting: streaking, stroking, striving. When you live only in memory your life dies. All day alone I push a brush against canvas trying to get to you, but it is like making love with my hands tied. I need to feel your flesh, slide my body against the grain, tattoo the canvas. I've got this energy to create amidst all this destruction. A painter must *earn* his eyes. How I remember your eyes. . . . Now I am losing mine, for it seems a frivolous act to make art in wartime, to paint a goldfish in a bowl, an arm being blown off by a grenade, flowers in a vase, a field of wheat crushed beneath armored tanks. Your eyes rise from the flattened field, give it shape again. Ironically, only the art will be left after the destruction. What the artist does is actually an act of recovery. I must fight the inertia of despair, force myself to stare into the volcano, see color again, earn my eyes, bear witness to the sulfurous eruption that is war. But how does one see such ancient hate in a new light? I must find a way, create an irreverent invention. No one knows that I am trying to construct from chaos, trying to order the destruction of my heart, the collapse of myself without you. The reality is immediate, for each war is personal, each battle is intimate.

"Forgive me for keeping you away. Both of us should not have been in harm's way. Inevitably the war would end. People would be liberated out of one confusion only to end in another—like us separated as lovers. Our history, so intense, crucial and close, becomes distant and removed. There is no middle ground in the heart. Once cut off from love one lives either in the past or the present; one must choose. You are the mistress of my memories. You had the power to write me, to choose a future after the war. And you *were* writing! All of it locked in a secret vault now exploding into daylight . . . I hear your voice in my ear, I hear your story. Don't stop speaking. I don't want to be without your voice now that it's returned. I can never go back to the solitude that once sheltered me . . .

"Do you remember that day in the cherry orchard? The Officer who surprised us had a gun. I walked away because I had nothing to defend you with. I had to pretend to be a coward. I got the tire iron from the trunk of the Bearcat and came back to confront him. Then, later, I insisted you stay in Provence instead of returning with me to Paris. I could not say then why I did that, but now I can. Like that day in the cherry orchard, my only way to defend you was to appear to leave you. I intended everything to be revealed when you went to the farm of Elouard and found what I had hidden for you in the Bearcat. Then you would *see*, and we would be together. I slept with nightmares for years after losing you. Then I slept without dreams, not out of release but of escape. Memory distorted the physical vision of you; your body became a blur, the blur became a spirit, and that spirit became the foundation of my art. Anyone who claims to create art devoid of the heart is a liar, for they are not making art, they are making only Voltaire's famous sausages—rules of the intellect that fall before the whims of the muse. It's not the danger of painting that attracts me, but using it to reach the corrosion beneath the surface lies of the world. One must not be afraid to confront artifice and crack it open, just as the jackboots of the conquering army marching through this city of conspirators split open the earth. I stared down into the earth and I painted the shivering crowds in the Métro, the one place where true democracy flourished: everyone was forced to be there because no gasoline was available for cars. I captured faces melting with fear, betrayal, and torture in the Métro's putrid yellow light.

"Why do I feel compelled to confess my past to you? I hoped that when the new emperor returned Napoléon's son to Paris, Napoléon's own tomb would break open and he would arise, swear the conqueror's army to allegiance, and send them marching back east.

Then everything would change and I could marry you in public. But it was not to be. We were married the night Napoléon's son returned, but in the most secret of ceremonies. The falling rain of our last summer still bruises my heart, wet droplets striking the dusty grape leaves, gently invading the vineyards. At the end of each row of vines a rosebush blooms. You left the surprise of flowers for me wherever I worked, their fragrance surrounding me as I sketched the curve of your arm, the turn of your cheek. Heaven has no value unless hell exists. Your morning kisses cover my face, raindrops of love; where each drop falls, a scar of memory fades. From the open door of my Villa Trône studio I see bees buzzing in the lemon groves. Through the window of my Mallorca studio I see a black vulture in flight. Above the bird is the vaporous trail of a jet moving toward its destination. Everything moves so fast, my time away from you slips through my fingers. The landscape of Provence has been petrified, tamed to picture-perfection. The savagery of the Spanish countryside has been scraped away, old paint chips blowing in the exhaust of cars. No more rough edges: one currency, one people, no difference.

"Louise, I have so many things to tell you, half a century of changes! The army took over Villa Trône, officers lived there. How could I return after the war and restore it, waiting for you to come? I had questioned every postwar commission for displaced persons in every country, asking for news of you. Nothing. The Villa Trône was damaged from fighting, our dreams scorched by gunfire. How could I go back, knowing that the soldiers who once lived there now drive luxury cars, masturbate to money, and come dreaming of the days when they were paid to kill? I remember the flowers you left the last time you went to my Villa Trône studio—wild petals from the fields, as if God had laid out His loveliest palette of colors and you presented it to me.

"When it rains in the high mountains, the peaks get lost in mist and my arthritic knees ache with remembrance. I recall watching you naked, singing while you cooked at the stove. Sometimes sauces splattered your skin and you licked the flavors off. You don't know I'm watching you. You don't know it, but I rebuilt Villa Trône here in Mallorca—the same kitchen, your stage. No one knows I built the house for you, the house I promised, so that you might enter like a ghost, touching the life we lost amidst the new one I created: the family, the children. Often I would walk through the house at night and discover you there, naked and waiting. I would put my ear to your breast and listen to sea waves and birds' wings beating in your heart. I married you when I pierced you with the gold ring. Since I never found you, we have never been divorced.

"What joy that day we danced in Ville Rouge, so oblivious, like lambs, our animal minds not understanding the language of humans as we were being led to the slaughter. Time is leaping backward and forward. The bells of Paris are ringing in liberation but there is no liberation for us. We're not there. The black vulture flies toward Mont Ventoux, sentiments cut from my heart, carved from the anguish of your years of silence. Your baby, our baby? The bees! My God! I cannot console you. Something's been broken that cannot be made whole again; all my words, all my paint on canvas, useless. I can only offer the key that has hung around my neck for half a century. The key that will unlock it all . . ."

"Papa!" Serena's cry cut through Zermano's voice as she dropped the letter she was reading and leaped up to catch him just as he fell back exhausted into his wheelchair. His breathing was labored, his head slumped on his chest. I knelt beside him on the other side of the chair. I looked across at Serena, her face twisted with worry.

"Forgive me. Maybe I shouldn't have come."

She shook her head. "No, it had to be. He's been waiting all his life for this. I was wrong, thinking that he was losing his mind between disjointed bouts of ranting and lucidity. Now I see everything was part of one life. The sequence of events no longer matters in the end."

"I'll help you carry him to his bed."

"Yes, that would be best."

We lifted him together. His body was surprisingly light. The sun was sinking into the sea and cast golden light across the terrace as we held him between us, walking him into the small bedroom carved into the cliff. We placed him on the bed. Serena tucked a blanket over him. His face was white, as white as his long hair and beard. Serena sat next to him, wiping perspiration from his brow with a damp cloth. I leaned against the wall in the corner, watching them both as the light outside faded.

Slowly the roar of the sea subsided, and the throb of crickets announced the night. Serena lit candles. Hours passed. The torrent of Zermano's words still resonated in my mind. Few spoke like that anymore, few thought like that anymore; fewer still loved with such passionate ferocity and refusal to let go. He was alive because he loved, and because he loved, he did not fear death. Candlelight flickered in the room. Serena had resumed reading the letters in a quiet voice. She squinted, trying to decipher the once exquisite handwriting that had been reduced to a pathetic scrawl when Louise's hands were mangled.

The scent of sea air drifted into the room and mixed with that of burning beeswax. A moth fluttered erratically toward a candle flame. With a subdued hiss, the flame snuffed out its life. The moth dropped to the floor. On the wall next to me a spider was already moving toward the moth, soon to entomb it in its web. More candles were lit. A glow fell on Serena's face and bare arms. I could only imagine what thoughts must be running through her mind as she read. The scent of her skin mixed with that of beeswax and sea air. I wondered why she had never married. Was she married to her father's myth? Or perhaps it was true what they said about Mallorcan women: that like the wild olive trees growing on the island, they bore the most fruit if they weren't pruned.

"Louise!"

Zermano reached out in the night, the flesh of his hand thinned by age, the bones gnarled by time, the fingers grasping at air.

"Louise!"

Serena took his hand and leaned her cheek against it.

"Louise, I can't hear you!"

Serena softly began reading again.

Louise was safe now, she could row her boat across the clouds back to Zermano. I'm certain he heard her words, for long after Serena had finished reading the last of Louise's letters and the sun began to rise, there was peace on his face, even though he had stopped breathing.

Serena did not move, nor did she let go of Zermano's hand. Outside the first birds began to chirp. The morning sun shone through the window and cast its light on the floor where the moth and spider had been. Serena released her father's hand. Her fingers traced his face and ran down his neck, unbuttoning his shirt and pulling it open. Around Zermano's neck was a leather loop with a key knotted to it. The key was not modern and lightweight, but heavy and dulled by age. It rested on his chest above a still-visible scar carved into the skin above his heart: **L**.

Serena slipped her hand under the key and closed her fingers around it. She turned to me:

"I'm going to Elouard's farm. Do you want to come?"

PART SEVEN

The Key

I T W A S no simple matter for Serena and I to find the farm
of Elouard. In his letters Zermano mentioned that his man
Roderigo had driven the Stutz Bearcat to the farm and hidden it
there before he returned to his native Spain. Perhaps a subdivision
of houses or a shopping mall now stood on the site. The only way
to find out if the farm still existed was to trace the ownership of
the painting *Big Blue One*. Zermano had traded this painting to
Elouard in exchange for the car in the early nineteen forties. *Big
Blue One* itself was now embroiled in controversy, for it was the
most important modern work in a London museum's collection, and
its provenance was being contested.

How the museum acquired the painting was clear. *Blue* was pur-
chased from a Japanese insurance company, which had bought it
from a prestigious gallery in Zurich during the speculative run-up
of modern art prices in the nineteen eighties. The gallery had, in
turn, obtained it from a prominent collector in South Africa. The
collector had recently stated in court documents that he had pur-
chased the painting from someone "very high up" in the French

government in the nineteen fifties. The heirs of Elouard brought suit against all parties involved, maintaining that the painting, and others by modern masters, had been illegally appropriated after Elouard was arrested in Paris during the last days of World War II. No records existed as to Elouard's fate after his arrest.

Serena and I decided that I should be the one to make contact with Elouard's heirs, since they would suspect her, as the daughter of Zermano, of intending to lay claim to *Big Blue One.* As a historian who had written about Zermano it was only natural that I should be conducting research on such an important work of art. There were two heirs, brothers. I traced one to Tel Aviv and the other to Brooklyn. The brother in Tel Aviv refused to speak with me, assuming I was actually working for the London museum. The other brother was a high school science teacher and knew, to my astonishment, who I was. He had read my books on Zermano and happened to agree with many of the conclusions. We talked for three hours about Zermano's painting, and I found him a knowledgeable enthusiast. He said that of all the paintings in Elouard's appropriated art collection, the one work he personally wanted most to see returned was *Big Blue One.* As far as he was concerned, his brother could sell everything else if they prevailed in the courts, but he wanted *Blue.* Finally I was able to slip my question in.

"Besides his apartment in Paris, didn't Elouard have a farm somewhere in France?"

"Not one farm, *two* farms. One was sold after the war, and my mother lives at the other one. The farm in the south was the one I loved. I went there every summer until I was forced to leave France as a kid."

"I'm surprised, but delighted, that your mother is still alive. She must be quite old now."

"Old, she's ancient! Why don't you go see her? She complains that no one visits any more . . . which is true, since my brother and I rarely go to France. Too many bad memories mixed in with the good."

"I would like to visit her."

"I'll give you her phone number. Call her and let me know how it goes. She's quite unique."

"What do you mean, 'unique'?"

"She's a real character. You'll see."

THAT SAME DAY Serena and I took a plane to Paris, rented a car, and drove the one hundred and thirty kilometers to the city of Reims. We passed by the gothic cathedral, with its majestic towers and glinting array of stained-glass windows, looking very much as it must have when young Joan of Arc gave her famous impassioned speech that galvanized the French to rally around their Dauphin. Beyond Reims the landscape unfolded into lush champagne vineyards, then hills lazily rolled out, smoothed by fields of wheat. The church steeples of small villages pricked the distant horizon. Suddenly, as we came over a rise, a surreal apparition loomed ahead. It was a concrete spire, taller than the towers of Reims cathedral, and shaped like an artillery shell. The spire marked the center of a World War I battlefield where more than 400,000 men had died. The bodies of 130,000 of those men were so blasted apart that only their shattered bones remained to be entombed beneath the concrete spire.

On the telephone earlier Madame Elouard had instructed me, "Go left at the Big Bullet and right at the first crossroads, then up two kilometers. You'll see the farmhouse across from a potato field."

I followed her directions and we soon pulled up before a tidy little farmhouse and got out of the car.

Madame was waiting at the front door. She leaned on a cane, in more of a jaunty pose than that of an infirm person in need of support. She wore a long beaded dress, the kind that had been fashionable in Parisian nightclubs in the thirties. Her white hair was cut short like a boy's. Her lungs, not as sound as they once were, gave her words a distinct timbre, as if each one were another breathless step up a steep staircase.

"You can't get lost with the Bullet. That's what we call that concrete monstrosity, the Bullet. Why couldn't they just put those poor boys in the ground and grow oak trees over them?"

I tried to look on the bright side. "I guess there are those who consider it a fitting monument."

"God, that's stupid! Bullets killed them, a bullet they buried them in. They'll need a bigger bullet next time," she said with grim satisfaction.

Serena smiled sympathetically. "It's a tragedy."

Madame squinted at her. "Who are you? I talked to an American professor on the phone."

"That's me," I assured her.

"So who is this? One of your students? If you're cheating on your wife I want to know that right now."

Serena offered her hand in greeting. "I'm very pleased to meet you. And no, I'm not his wife."

Madame grabbed Serena's hand and squeezed. "Are *you* married?"

"No, I'm not."

"You don't know much about life, do you? Tragedy, let me tell you about that. The real tragedy of the Bullet is that almost no one comes to visit it any more. People would rather be up the road at the fancy champagne-tasting rooms. They see the Bullet and say, 'That's not for me,' and they keep driving. Well, that bullet *is* for them." She studied Serena's face closely. "Why aren't you married? Won't he marry you?"

Serena tried to gently change the subject. "Thank you so much for letting us visit."

Madame, clearly, would change the subject when she was good and ready. She looked at me. "You should be ashamed of yourself."

"It takes two to want to get married," I answered.

"That's the problem today. Don't get married, live together, have children—what's everybody afraid of? It wasn't that way with my Elouard. 'I'm a fast girl,' I told him. 'If you want to slow me down you'll have to marry me.' People today, they're just selfish and cynical."

"I couldn't concur more," I nodded.

Serena tried to extract her hand from Madame's grip as she gave her opinion. "Maybe people today don't get married because they're afraid."

Madame refused to release Serena's hand. "To live together without being in love, that's not being afraid, that's just pathetic."

Serena pulled her hand free. "I'm not married—and I'm not cynical."

"You're the last one, then." Madame grinned. "They should put you in a wax museum right next to Joan of Arc with a sign saying, 'the unmarried and the naive.'" She peered closely at Serena. "You look a little familiar. Do I know you?"

Serena glanced at me and I shook my head no. We couldn't take the chance of Madame thinking Serena had come to take whatever works of her father's might be here. All we wanted was to find out if the Bearcat still existed.

Serena purred sweetly to Madame, "I can honestly say, you don't know me."

"Well, I do now." Madame opened the door to her house. "Do you like pickled herring?"

We followed Madame inside to a small living room, where she insisted we sit as she served herring and fruit wine, talking the whole time, so pleased to have company. As she spoke I noticed on the wall a small etching in a simple wooden frame.

Madame caught my eye. "You know *his* work?"

Clearly she had forgotten our earlier telephone conversation, that I was an art historian coming to visit her to talk about Zermano. So I reminded her.

"Yes, I admire Zermano's art very much. I'm particularly interested in your thoughts about him."

She walked over to the etching, holding a monocle up to it. "So glorious. It's such a pity."

"Pardon me, what's a pity?"

"He's so out of fashion in some quarters. Such a debate about him. How he used women, how he might have been a collaborator during the war, how he's from the old school that considers beauty something to be prized and painted, 'objectified' as they say now. His work is worth a lot of money though, oh my, so much money! But I'll never sell this, never. It's the last Zermano I have."

"You're lucky to have it."

"Oh, yes. What do I care about fashion? Art is art. The length of women's dresses goes up and down, but the important thing is not the dress, it's the woman. Her worth doesn't change. It's the same with art."

"That's a refreshing notion. You should teach an art history class."

"Oh, they wouldn't like me. They wouldn't like me at all. I'd want to dress up when I taught. I'd want to be *wonderful.*"

Serena laughed. "How did you get this *wonderful* etching?"

Madame touched her fingers gently to the glass protecting it. "I knew him, you know. Many people say they knew him, but really they didn't. He saved me. That's how I got this etching."

Serena went over and stood next to Madame, both of them lovingly examining the etching. Serena asked, "How did he save you?"

Madame braced herself on her cane and took a deep breath, preparing once again to run up the steep incline of her words.

"It was . . . he was . . . *everything* was confused. That's why I moved here, not to be confused any more. The Big Bullet is my reminder; there's no ambiguity. They destroyed my husband. You see this ring on my finger? It's his ring. I never remarried. They can't take your second husband away if you don't have one. They took away everything then, and left me with nothing but this ring. We had a good life before. Elouard was a doctor, he worked hard. One day during the war the militia came to his hospital. Elouard was in the middle of surgery, can you imagine? He had the scalpel in his hand when they told him: 'It's now against the law for you to practice this profession. You must leave at once.' That was it. Elouard immediately went to the bank and found that all his money, our life savings, had been 'impounded for ideological reasons.' All he had left of value was his art collection. So many desperate people were selling their art that there was a panic and the market dropped to nearly zero. He sold everything for a fraction of its value, but he kept Zermano's *Big Blue One*. He was going to take it to the farm in the south and hide it. With the money from the sale of the collection we were able to get our children out of the country by sending them to Nice, where they were put on a Red Cross ship. Elouard and I remained behind, selling what little furniture we had left for travel money. The night before we were to leave for the south everything became horrible. Seven militia men broke down the door of the apartment and swarmed around us on our last piece of furniture, the bed. There was screaming, accusations, they pulled my husband from my arms. I was naked. I had to try something. I jumped out of bed and started to kiss Elouard passionately, rubbing my body against his. The agents were stunned. I cooed to them. 'How can you snatch my little rooster from me just when I was cooking him?' They grabbed my arms and threw me back down on the bed. They handcuffed Elouard. One of them pulled a knife, walked over to me on the bed, and raised the knife above his head. Elouard shouted, struggling to help me. The man stabbed the knife down, striking the mattress around me again and again, until it was completely cut open, its cotton stuffing scattered, exposing a paper packet wedged into one of the underlying spring coils. He pulled the packet out and tore it open; inside were identity papers and travel documents for Elouard and me. The man put the knife to my throat. 'Don't tell me you two Jews didn't know you were fucking on top of fake documents! I'll be back for *you* later. Don't try to run!' They left. I was terrified, more for Elouard than for myself. I called all my close friends, but everyone hung up when they heard my voice. Then I called Zermano. He didn't hang up. I told him what happened. He shouted at me. I'll never forget his words. 'There is something bad happening here! It stinks!' He hung up. Now I knew I was alone. Two days later, right before dawn, the phone rang. I was afraid to pick it up because it might be the militia calling. The phone didn't stop ringing all morning. Then I panicked. Maybe it was Elouard! I picked up the phone. A strange voice said: 'I'm a friend of your husband's. Are there any more forged papers hidden in your house?' I answered no. 'All right then,' he continued. 'I want you to leave your apartment. Do not take anything with you—it must appear that you are only going to the market, not running away. Go to the first Métro stop and get in the first train headed to St.-Cloud. You've got to trust me. I am a friend.' This was so suspicious, but what could I do? Everyone else had abandoned me. I had no choice. I did as I was told and left the apartment. I went down into the Métro station. The Métro for St.-Cloud came. When it stopped I started to get in but someone grabbed my arm from behind and pulled me back, then pushed me along the station platform into the crowd. It was Zermano. He kept moving us quickly through the crowd, down a busy corridor to a different platform. There a Métro stopped, headed for another destination; Zermano pulled me into it with him. We exchanged no words. There were strange men in the car, constantly taking off their hats to peer inside their hat rims where they had pinned photos of those they were hunting. The men looked up from their hats, scanning the faces around them. Several stops later Zermano took my arm and we got off at a railroad station. We boarded a train leaving Paris. Police demanded to see our identity and travel papers. Zermano opened his briefcase and presented the documents for both of us. The police looked at the papers, then looked at us. One of them said, 'Have a pleasant journey, Mr. and Mrs. Zermano.' Finally we stopped and got off at the biggest train station I have ever seen. There were scores of tracks with deportation trains on them, guarded by soldiers. Inside each of the cars were hundreds of people, *hundreds* in each car. They were shouting at the regular passengers standing on the platform. Zermano hurried me along. He spoke under his breath. 'Elouard is here somewhere. Look for him.' I searched frantically as we walked. Locomotive engines were starting, steam hissed, the deportation trains were beginning to move. The people inside became more hysterical, screaming out at those of us on the platform to take what they were tossing from the open windows and deliver it to their loved ones. They were throwing money, watches, rings, letters, photographs with messages written on the back. . . . They were screaming names and addresses. I wanted to help them all. I grabbed the bottom of my dress and held it out to catch what was being thrown. Nothing reached me, everything fell onto the tracks. The trains were rolling. I was crying so hard that if Elouard was there I couldn't have seen him. Zermano whispered, 'It's okay. I promised I'd bring you, so he could see you one last time. I'm sure he saw you.' An hour later, standing before a regular train headed south, Zermano kissed me passionately in front of the soldiers and shouted, 'Hurry back, darling!' He handed me his briefcase and pushed me up into the train and it pulled out. I looked back. That's the last time I saw him, waving and blowing kisses as if I really were his beloved wife."

Madame stopped, out of breath, at the top of the staircase of words she had climbed.

Serena touched her open palm tenderly to the glass protecting the etching. "It's such a treasure."

Madame spoke again, her voice thin now. "It was in the briefcase he gave me, along with my false identification papers and money. No matter what happened after, how hard it got, I didn't part with that etching. I peeled the wallpaper off the walls of the shabby rooms I stayed in and ate the bugs underneath rather than sell it."

I tried to offer some condolence. "I'm sorry about your husband." She didn't respond. I tried, clumsily, to let her know I was moved. "Perhaps it's best if these nightmares are put in a box and buried."

Finally she spoke. "I don't believe in that—in forgetting. People back then didn't ask questions for fear of finding out *everything.*

They were terrified that if the truth were known the consequences would be too horrible to contemplate."

"You are right. The suffering was immeasurable and we shouldn't forget. I even read of a woman who had been crucified."

"Crucifixion." She looked at me dismissively. "That was the least of it. Worse things happened."

I didn't have anything to say to that. Serena broke the silence.

"Thank you for the wonderful pickled herring! The most delicious I've ever eaten in my life!"

Madame's old eyes began to shine. "You liked it? I must give you the recipe. Come right into the kitchen." She led Serena into the kitchen and I heard Madame giving her the recipe. "Now you go home right now and make this."

It was clear the visit was over, and all we had managed to get was a recipe for pickled herring. I was trying to think of a way to remind her why we were there when Serena slipped the recipe into her purse and spoke.

"What a lovely gift. Thank you so much."

Madame took Serena's hand. "You come back and visit, dear. I hope that next time you are married."

"Well, I might be—you never know. And if I do get married I'll honeymoon in the south. Maybe I could visit you there, at your other farm."

"Other farm? Oh! I sold that years ago to have enough money to live on."

"What a pity. I'm so sorry you had to lose something like that."

"I'm lucky. I have this farm, and another barn to keep Zermano's Bear in."

"His Bear?"

"Yes, the Stutz Bearcat he traded us for *Big Blue One.* His man Roderigo drove the Bear to the farm in the south and hid it in the barn. The final thing Zermano shouted to me from the platform of the train station when I last saw him was, 'Keep the Bear safe! It belongs to Louise!'"

"She never came?"

"Never. Too late now, she's dead. But I moved it up here and haven't touched it."

"It's very valuable, a rarity. You're a rich woman."

"I won't sell it. It belongs to Zermano. He's still alive, you know, despite the fact the newspapers say he died. He'll come for it."

"May we see it?"

"Yes, dear, but you'll have to be very careful."

"We won't do anything to damage it."

"It's not the Bear I'm worried about, it's the two of you."

"What do you mean?"

"The barn is in the middle of a killing field. They were all killing fields here, every tree and bush blasted away by the fighting. Just last year thirty farmers died from hitting old bombs and artillery shells while tilling their fields. They don't just harvest wheat and potatoes, but blood turnips too, deadly things that worm their way to the surface and *boom!* It's so dangerous that no one will work this farm. The last man who tried plowed up barbed wire, bayonets, and skulls. He should have stopped, but he kept going and cut through a mustard gas bomb. I came home and found him still sitting in the tractor with the engine running. He was killed before he could make the sign of the cross. Terrible look on his face. Tons of bombs are found each year. The good thing is, it's kept everyone away from the barn. People are afraid to go near it."

Serena looked at me. "Do you want to take the chance, Professor?"

"We'll have to watch our steps," I replied.

Madame saw us to the back door and waved good-bye as we started off, calling out:

"Watch for the blood turnips!"

Serena and I stepped cautiously through a field grown wild from years of neglect. The problem was that we couldn't see what was ahead or underfoot. I broke off a branch and used it as a probing stick. Brambles tore our clothes. I poked through the bushes and the stick hit something that moved. The air exploded—and a hen pheasant flew up from its nest of eggs, her wings whirring loudly.

Serena grabbed the belt of my pants from behind, holding close to me as we carefully inched forward until the barn appeared. The barn's weather-beaten siding was dilapidated and in some places had collapsed completely. It appeared doubtful that anything inside could still be intact beneath the crushing weight of fallen rafters and broken roof slates. We found the one place where it seemed safe to enter. The overhead beams inside appeared ready to crumble from the very sound of our breathing. Rusty farm machinery and bales of mildewed hay were scattered everywhere. The Bearcat was nowhere in sight. We made our way in the gloomy light through the debris, surprising pigeons who flapped up with a great racket and landed on rotting roof rafters. Before us was a jumble of furniture, piled high and forgotten for years. Through a hole in the barn siding sunlight shone on the furniture, and something glinted from under the splintered chairs, ripped sofas, and broken dressers.

I started digging into the pile, tossing aside furniture as if a living person were trapped underneath. Serena joined in, helping to move the heaviest furniture until we could go no further and our hands touched something hard beneath a layer of straw. We pushed the straw away, revealing the Bearcat. The black paint of its long sloping roof was cracked and peeled, exposing metal underneath. We wiped the dirt-encrusted windows and peered inside. The interior, once luxurious, had been destroyed by animals. The elegant wood dashboard was clawed and scratched; the mahogany steering wheel gnawed down to a nub; the mohair headliner hung in tattered strips, and the leather seats were ripped open. I could see rusty floorboards underneath.

We shoved more furniture aside until the automobile was completely visible. It was a marvel of the machine age, with its massive chrome grill, high spoked wheels, and flared fender skirts. It seemed more of a yacht than a car, a treasure to equal Cleopatra's ornate river barge. I ran my hands over it, not quite believing that this wonder existed. This was the car I had read so much about. I felt as if

I had driven it. There were dents and scrapes on the front fender and along the car's side, left from when the tire had blown out, bringing the car to a stop at the cherry orchard in Provence. I could see Louise standing there in her white dress and Zermano, shirtless in the heat, fixing the tire. Serena's voice brought me back from that fateful day, the Day of the Bees.

"I'm going to try the key."

She attempted to get the key in the door's lock, but it wouldn't fit. She tried the lock on the other side. The key refused to go in. She looked at me in despair.

Now there really was only one last chance. I was almost afraid to speak, for if the key didn't fit everything was over and Zermano's secret vanished. "In one of his letters, your father wrote that it was in the trunk."

"Yes!"

We shoved furniture from behind the Bearcat until the downward slope of the trunk was exposed.

Serena put the key to the lock—and it went in. She smiled. We were in luck. She turned the key and metal snapped. The key had broken in the hole. There were tears in her eyes.

"Damn! Damn! Damn!" She pounded her fists on the trunk lid and it sprang open.

We both stared under the lid. Staring back at us were baby rats curled in the nest of the deflated spare tire. Behind the tire, covered in cobwebs and rat droppings, was a long rolled canvas clamped together by wire.

"Would you mind?" Serena gestured toward the rats. "I don't want to hurt them."

"I don't mind." I pushed the squealing rats aside with my hand, grabbed the rolled canvas, and maneuvered it out of the trunk. It was heavy and stiff. I pried off the wire. After being rolled up for more than half a century, the canvas unfurled slowly. I was standing behind it, so I could not see what was on the front, but I could see the astonished expression on Serena's face.

"My God! It's Velázquez's *Las Meninas*!"

"Impossible. That painting's in Madrid."

"Look for yourself." Serena excitedly grabbed the canvas and swung it around.

She was right. It was Velázquez's seventeenth-century masterpiece, *The Maids of Honor*. But how could this be? That painting was the centerpiece of the Prado Museum, where for hundreds of years a brass plaque beneath its baroque frame had borne the inscription: *orbra culminante de la pintura universal*, the culminating work of world art.

The room in the Prado where the painting hangs is always crowded; shocked admiration can be heard in twenty different languages as visitors gape at it, for in its heavenly perversity it is unlike any other painting: it makes the viewer the *subject*, not the observer. Velázquez himself is in the painting, standing at his easel. A regal blond girl is posed before him. She wears an enormous bell-shaped satin dress; in fact, she is the daughter of King Philip IV. The haughty princess is surrounded by her fawning court of maids-in-waiting, all awestruck except one, a dwarf, who grimaces with a queer expression of disdain. In the king's palace dwarves were deemed enchanted fools, allowed to wander the gilded corridors passing out insults and farts with giddy abandon, disputing the glory and vanity of the royal household. The dwarf beckons the viewer to look past the princess, past Velázquez himself, to a wall of framed paintings behind. From one of the frames the blurred image of the old king and his very young wife peer out. The trick is, these two are not painted, but reflected on a mirror within the frame. They are actually beyond the tableau playing out on the canvas. It is they whom Velázquez is actually painting on the easel before him. It is they, standing outside of the painting, who are the true subject. Velázquez had smashed the containing frame between art and life, demanding a dialogue between the artist and the subject.

"Do you think it's real?" Serena asked.

"No. Your father made many copies of *Las Meninas*. He wasn't alone in his fascination. Many important painters in history have made their own variations. This painting's invention forced the artist beyond merely representing his world; it held him accountable for his collaboration with the *subject* of his creation."

"But what was my father accountable for? What was his collaboration?"

"I don't know. We have to find the true subject of the painting." I stood back and tried to look at the painting from every angle. What was it I wasn't seeing?

"You know," Serena offered, "in the Prado there's a mirror positioned across the room from the painting. If you turn your back to the painting and look in the mirror, you see reflected precisely the view that the king and queen had while watching Velázquez at his easel. They were the painting's subject—which means you and I now are."

"It's the mirror. We've got to find a mirror." I rummaged through the pile of furniture, found a battered armoire, and tore its mirrored door off. I leaned the mirror against the barn wall. It caught the entire scale of the painting. All I could see at first was my own agitated face reflected on the painting. I tilted the mirror and suddenly my face was superimposed on that of Velázquez. What deflected truth was I to see in this final bend of illusion? Velázquez was wearing a black vest with a red heraldic cross embroidered across its front. He held his brush poised in one hand and his palette in the other, caught in the act of creating, ready to tip his brush into the paints on the palette.

I peered closely at the palette. Zermano had placed something there that did not exist in Velázquez's original. The dabs of paint on the palette vividly spelled out YHVH.

Zermano had revealed the name of his God, and the reason he had abandoned Louise. I looked again at the artist standing behind the easel. It was Velázquez, but the dark and volatile eyes were Zermano's. Around them the colors had been forced and deepened, carving out a space of hurt for fools to rush in, a space for the spirit to be reborn.

"Professor, what do you see?"

I glanced up. Serena's face peered intently from above the canvas
⸱ was holding.

 You were right," I said. I took the canvas from her. "Go look in
 ̄ror."

 ̄y."

"Do you see the palette Velázquez is holding?"

"Yes."

"Notice how the swirl of paint on the palette forms four letters."

"I can see them."

"Without the mirror the letters spell nothing, but in the mirror
they are reversed; they read right to left, the way Hebrew is read."

"What do they mean?"

"They signify the personal name of God in the Old Testament,
the Name of Four Letters, the creator of the universe. From earliest
times Jews were in awe of the power and magic of these four letters
and wouldn't utter them aloud, fearful of the retribution such disrespect would bring. No one knows today how the name is pronounced—it is the secret of secrets, the greatest mystery of all."

"So why did my father paint them?"

"To tell Louise he was Jewish. That's why he married her with
the secret piercing of the gold ring. No one could know. If the truth
were discovered he would be killed, and if she was his real wife, she
would be killed too."

"How do you know this?"

"When I was researching an article about the religiosity of your
father's work, I traced the family on his mother's side back to the
fourteenth century, when the Jews of Mallorca had to convert or die.
Many converted, but secretly remained faithful to their true religion. Your father revealed his secret in this painting."

Serena fell silent. I continued to hold the painting, not wanting to
disturb her thoughts. The pigeons in the rafters stirred, cooing their
deep-throated song. I watched Serena. Finally she spoke.

"My father didn't give Louise a chance to stand by him. He didn't
give her a choice. He betrayed her to save her."

PART EIGHT

Last Letters

Sevilla, Spain

My Dear Serena,

I am here in Sevilla going through the ecclesiastical archives of the Spanish Inquisition. I have discovered many more documents confirming the truth of your father's ancestry. I do not intend to publish any of this; I simply wanted to follow this profound man back to his origins. I hope, as more than a year has passed since you lost your father, that life is returning to normal.

Thank you for your thoughtful invitation for me to attend your father's funeral in Palma, but I felt that really wasn't the way I wanted to remember him. I must confess, his loss affected me deeply, and I was just not up to being around people. However, I do hope you received the flowers and condolences that I sent on that sad occasion. I did read in the newspapers that many famous people came to pay their respects and filled the Palma Cathedral, and that afterward the streets leading to the cemetery were lined with thousands of mourners. I could not help but think that only you and I knew how inside one truth another was hidden.

May I tell you that yesterday, returning from the archives, I was walking through the old Moorish gardens and passed by the lovely fountain of midnight-blue tiles. The local lore is that the first time one passes the fountain one must stop, make a wish, and toss in a coin. I stopped. I made a wish about you. But I didn't have a coin, so I dropped a peseta bill into the fountain. The paper, of course, did not sink, but floated on the water's surface. Some gypsy children who were playing nearby ran up; they thought this was all very funny and good luck—for them. I suppose it was. I watched as they fished the money out.

I'm here for another several weeks to finish my research. I just wanted to leave you with one final thing, a quote from another American who admired another Spanish artist. It is something written by the painter James Whistler about the muse that inspired Velázquez.

In the book of her life the names inscribed are few—the list of those who have helped write her story of love and beauty. She yielded up the secret of repeated line, as with his hand in hers, together they measured rhyme of lovely limb and draperies flowing in unison, to the day when she dipped the Spaniard's brush in light and air, and made his people live within their frames, that all nobility and sweetness, tenderness and magnificence should be theirs.

Sincerely,
THE PROFESSOR

Palma de Mallorca,
Islas Baleares

My Dear Professor,

Things here have finally returned to normal. You, of all people, can imagine what clamor and chaos there was. I do want to thank you for your thoughtful flowers and note of condolence, which meant so much during that painful time. Your recent letter revealing further discoveries in Sevilla was greatly appreciated.

I was quite touched by your quote concerning the artist and muse. In return I would like to share with you something written by Degas not long before he attained old age and was going blind: *The heart is an instrument that grows rusty if it isn't used.*

It would mean a great deal if you could visit me in Palma after you discover everything you need to know for your research.

Ever so sincerely yours,
SERENA

A Note About the Author

Thomas Sanchez is the author of *Rabbit Boss, Zoot-Suit Murders,* and *Mile Zero.* He lives in San Francisco.

A Note on the Type

The text of this book was set in a typeface called Aldus, designed by the celebrated typographer Hermann Zapf in the early 1950s. Based on the classical proportion of the popular Palatino type family, Aldus was originally adapted for Linotype composition as a slightly lighter version that would read better in smaller sizes.

Composed by Stratford Publishing Services,
Brattleboro, Vermont

Printed and bound by The Haddon Craftsmen,
Scranton, Pennsylvania

Designed by Cassandra J. Pappas